Clade
A Post-Self Anthology

Clade

A Post-Self Anthology

Rob MacWolf ⋆ Nathan "Domus Vocis" Hopp ⋆ Madison Scott-Clary

Michael Miele ⋆ Alexandria Christina Leal ⋆ Thomas "Faux" Steele

Evan Drake ⋆ J.S. Hawthorne ⋆ Kergiby ⋆ Joel Kreissman

Other works in the Post-Self universe

The Post-Self Cycle
Qoheleth
Toledot
Nevi'im
Mitzvot

Post-Self: A Tabletop Roleplaying Game Powered by the Apocalypse

ISBN: 978-1-948743-35-8

CLADE: A POST-SELF ANTHOLOGY

This book uses the fonts Gentium Book Plus, Gotu, and Noto Serif.

Given the chance to live forever in a world not built for death...

What do you do?

★

Given the inability to forget—all your joys and sorrows, all your foundational memories and traumas...

How do you cope?

★

Given the ability to create a full copy of yourself—down to every single one of those memories—to do as they will, to individuate and live out their own forever lives, or merge back down and meld their memories with your own...

What paths do you take?

Sufficiently Advanced

Rob MacWolf

Theodred — 2343

On the one hand, this wasn't really a comfortable garden, with a view of a beautiful valley and several apple trees. It was a simulation, running on servers hurtling through deep space on an unstoppable course to who knows where. But on the other hand, it was plainly obvious this was a garden: there was a valley, those were apple trees, this was his home, it was a lovely day, and he had work to do. It mattered how you decided to look at it.

Theodred, Adjunct Professor of Post-Physical Philosophy, comfortably presenting as a wolf for more than a century after an ill-advised month as what he had thought to be an 'idealized' version of his former human appearance, started with his sim: only a ordinary scholar's private dwelling, but it was still important to get the setting right. Dim the lights—the sun raced across the sky till it ripened through gold and red and hovered just above the horizon. Turn down the temperature, not too much—a gentle but constant breeze freshened through the grainfields on the valley floor below. Put away anything he wasn't going to be using—the contents of the modest home behind him, mostly bookshelves, disappeared, followed by the roof and walls. Though after a moment he changed his mind and called back the brutalist-gothic concrete arches as if his home had become ruins centuries ago, because if you're going to design a home that looks good in ruins then it should get to be them now and again. Get out the things he would be using—a cast iron fire pit emerged from the clover and dandelions his garden had become, a stack of firewood lit itself within it, three chairs—well, two stools and a comfortable armchair—around it, a fully stocked drinks cabinet to one side. He hesitated, then decided against a whiteboard. If it ended up being needful it could always be brought out.

He did pull out a sturdy college-ruled notebook and a mechanical pencil. Yes, he could just let his sensorium take notes for him, he could store every word said in perfect photographic memory. But that would be a distraction, would turn his attention to himself, to the process, not the answers he hoped for. Better to do things the most instinctive way he knew: by hand, in a notebook balanced on his knee, as it had been in lectures billions of kilometers away and what should have been lifetimes ago.

It was hard to be both methodically careful and relaxed at the same time, but he several times resisted the urge to manually— well not manually, but the word was close enough—turn down his frustration. He wanted his mind in as neutral a state, as untampered with even by himself, as possible for what had to be done. Not for the first time he wondered whose decision it had been, back in the days when he'd uploaded, that one of the parts of his mind copied and transcribed into the everlasting him he was now would be distractible-type attention deficit disorder.

But he didn't doubt that it was a structural part of the architecture of his mind and personality. Not any more, not since the last time he'd done this procedure.

Or performed this ritual.

Whichever he was going to decide was the correct way to describe it.

Once he'd made some final adjustments—turn off the ocean smell in the wind, it would only make him maudlin and nostalgic, shoo all the simulated sounds of cicadas further into the distance so nobody need shout over them, dial forward the season a bit till the apples on the trees were ripe and the leaves yellowing—he sat back to work on the next step. Suppose this. Assume that. Such-and-such premises. Such-and-such prejudices. All A is B, Some C is A, therefore some C is B etc. Almost convince himself to deny the answer to his question—as close to it as he could come, at least; if he could have gotten all the way there'd be no need for all this fuss.

Once he actually forked, it'd be too late for adjustments. If he wanted an instance that believed certain things, would argue a certain way, he had to become himself that way first. If only just long enough to...

The instance appeared to Theo's left, and began individuating immediately. It was him, after all, and had the same intentions. He knew the plan, and what his part in it was. Theo paid no attention. He was already focusing on realigning his mind and emotions in the opposite direction. He gave himself permission to believe all the things he didn't have grounds for, to jump to conclusions if that's what it took to reach them. He let himself get lost in pareidolia. To be honest, it felt amazing, and he found himself hoping this side won. Which was good, he could use that, give it that hope too...

The second instance appeared to his right. He settled back in the chair, a little bit spent. But his work in this was done. It was up to them now.

The left hand instance resolved first. Hardly surprising. He looked very much as Theo remembered himself on the physical world—he still refused to say 'phys-side,' which amused all his students to no end—tall, stocky, very precisely trimmed beard. Human, to all appearances, which Theo hadn't expected, he'd have to add the implications of that to his notes. The only concession to the professor's present self-presentation was a tastefully small enamel lapel pin of a running wolf. Pinstripe vest. Tie of stained-glass shades of merlot, lapis lazuli, and fir tree—dressed very much as he would to tackle a seminar on Kripke's 'Naming and Necessity,' Chesterton's 'Manalive,' or May Then My Name Die With Me's 'Expanded Mythology.'

On the other hand, the rightward instance was settling into something much more fanciful. Wolf, fur perhaps more ornately groomed than Theo's. When he first resolved all there was to see was a hooded cloak, but when he swept it off he wore an abundance of talismanic jewelry over a bare chest dyed with arcane symbols, the color of a thundercloud lit with internal sheet lightning. Intricately embossed leather belt and loincloth over breeches. Sword scabbarded at his waist. Small velvet pouch of who-knew-what hanging from his belt. Most striking was the mask, a facsimile of their own face over eyes and upper jaw.

'Why wear a mask of the same thing as is beneath the mask?' Theo committed to the notebook, then spoke. "Gentlemen." They both looked at him, probably expecting this. "You know what we're here to discuss. For the sake of the notes, however, what names will you be using?"

"Theodulfr," said the one on the right. There was just a hint of Shakespearean ceremony to his voice.

"Really?" the left hand instance said.

"Our root instance named himself after a Tolkien character." It was surprisingly difficult to read Theodulfr's tone with only the lower half of his muzzle to go on. "You can endure a little indulgence."

"And you can take this seriously!"

"I am!"

"We can save the disparaging remarks," Theo hadn't expected to need to play moderator so soon, "for the actual debate, surely." He turned to the left instance as they quieted. "Your name, please?"

"Theosophia." The two canine heads tilted at the sole human one. "I'm well aware of the ironies."

"Anything to drink?" Theo pointed with the butt of his pencil at the cabinet. When Theosophia opened it, it proved to contain a bottled water and a gin and tonic with blackcurrant syrup for him, and a flagon of mead for Theodulfr.

At which point there was nothing else to do but begin.

"I say it would be wrong," began Theodulfr, "to refer to what we do, the way we live, all this, using the term 'magic.'"

"And I ask," Theosophia replied smoothly, "what better word could there be?"

Theo froze. When he'd decided to do this again, to let two opposite instances of himself debate the question on which he'd spent months of fruitless frustration, he'd planned they'd each take the other side than they now apparently were.

"When people say magic, what, in all the history of the term, have they used it to mean?" Theosophia was already presenting his case, so Theo hurried to catch up with his notes. "Formulas of power over the universe. The ability to make one's environment, in every element and detail of it, conform to one's will. Well, we have that, don't we? If you went to any madji in ancient Persia, any post-scholastic alchemist in medieval Europe, any ritual master in imperial China, and explained to them the everyday circumstances of our lives, what would they call it, other than magic?"

Theodulfr raised an impatient hand. By reflex, Theo made a checkmark on the edge of his page of notes, to keep the queue, before he reminded himself there were only two in this discussion anyway.

"What were the ultimate goals of magic, in any practice or fantasy story?" Theosophia continued. "For what was the philosopher's stone sought? Immortality and wealth. Well, we no longer age, we no longer die. And we no longer have any scarcity of anything, so wealth is a long-ago-solved problem. The philosopher's stone is real: we live in it. We all know that we all know the saying: any sufficiently advanced technology is indistinguishable from magic."

"Failure to distinguish between two things," Theodulfr said, "does not imply that those things are the same."

Apparently it was his turn now.

"Magic must, by definition, be an overriding of the material universe by some supernatural force. Whatever else magic is," Theodulfr gestured much more than Theosophia, when he talked, "it has to do the impossible. Snapping your fingers to produce a flame is magic, using a lighter is not. Levitating into the air is magic, boarding an airplane is not. Living forever and being able to shape the world around you to your will is magic, having your mind scanned and uploaded into a computer simulation whose controls you can access is not. There's a qualitative difference: magic is numinous, awe-inspiring, wondrous. The mere fact we're even discussing the question of whether the mundane minutiae of our life counts as magic is proof that they don't. Magic is, by definition, mutually exclusive with mundane minutiae."

"That's how a thing is done, how it works," Theo recognized the rhetorical turn Theosophia was about to use, had used it himself often enough, "not what it is."

"And next you're going to say: Just because the sky is blue by different means than a blueberry is blue," Theodulfr snorted the way Theo had learned to use a wolf's snout to snort, "or indeed the way some blue object in the system is blue, does not mean the sky is therefore not blue. That's a question of how blue works, not what blue is. We all know that one."

Theosophia changed lines of attack. "Very well, then instead I'll say: you say magic has to do the impossible. What does impossible mean, here? If none of what we're doing is magic, then magic doesn't exist, cannot exist, because there is no 'the impossible' left for it to do!"

"It could do all the things we do in here," Theodulf parried and riposted, "in the physical world."

Apparently, Theo noted, his forks shared his refusal to say 'physside.' He doubted it would prove relevant.

"I would submit," Theosophia seemed not to be giving any ground though, "that we are doing all the things we do here in the physical world. All this is happening on physical servers, hurtling through the interstellar medium, in physical space!"

"That's not the same as really happening." Theodulfr took a half step forward toward the campfire, as if to get a closer look at a gap in his rival's defenses. "You wouldn't say having a dream about a miracle was magic. Or telling a story about a spell was the same thing as casting it. Both of those can happen in the physical world too!"

Theosophia looked thoughtful. "What if I did?"

"What?" said Theodulfr.

Theosophia bit his lower lip. It was a nervous habit Theo had found he'd abandoned once he'd begun to wear a wolf's face. The shape of the muzzle made the gesture more difficult, feel wrong when accomplished. But he remembered what it meant: the need for quiet, for just a moment, to be able to hear himself in his head, over anyone else talking, to put some thoughts together.

So he cleared his throat. "Calling a few minutes recess," he clipped his plastic pencil to the notebook's black and white mottled cover. "I need a drink myself."

"I suppose you're going to let him go first, when we start up again." Theodulfr had crossed his arms over his chest and leaned back on one of the gnarled apple trees. It made the cloak hang from his shoulders like a tall narrow tent canopy. He held Theodred's stare a while, then sighed, "Fine, only fair, I went first before."

"I'll let him go first, if you want," Theo finished a gulp of the much-needed cider the cabinet had given him, "but I'm not sure he'll care. Look."

They both glanced across the fire, no longer flames, now burned down to incandescent coals. It hadn't occurred to Theo to set the fire to not run out of fuel. Beyond, the human had his head tilted, eyes lidded, hands raised. Every second or so his fingers would move, in syllable-like rhythms, sketching iambs and dactyls and spondees on the air in front of him even though he spoke not a word.

"You must remember," Theo mused as if to himself, which in a sense it was, "when we used to look like that. What it meant to look like that. How it felt."

Theodulfr scoffed. "You think he's putting together some grand epiphany?"

"If he is," Theo took another gulp of cider, "then it's exactly what I hoped the two of you would do."

Soon enough, Theo took his seat again and looked expectantly at Theosophia.

The human raised an eyebrow. "What?"

"He's letting you go first." Theodulfr rolled his eyes, "You were clearly preparing something. We may as well hear it."

"Oh, no that's alright," Theosophia shrugged. "It can wait until we all feel all the loose ends from the previous debate are tied up."

"Implying you think we finished the debate?" Theodulfr growled. When he got no response, the fantastic wolf sighed, "I was going to say that the saying about sufficiently advanced technology and magic needs to be understood relative to the perspective from which the technology is seen. It being 'indistinguishable' means there's someone who is unable to distinguish, implicitly someone whose technology is insufficiently advanced. The saying is about encountering a more advanced technology than you understand. Once you do understand it, once you do use it, once it's yours, it can't be sufficiently advanced anymore. Does that do anything to the big point you're about to make?"

"Not really," Theosophia shook his head. "So. You said what we're doing, the way we're living—whether or not it's magic—is analogous to telling a story?"

"Yyyyes..." Theodulfr allowed, cautiously.

"Then let's actually talk about what those ancient physical world cultures believed about telling stories. How they understood storytelling. In ancient Greece," like most philosophy professors his mind went first to ancient Greece, "they believed composition of fiction was a form of possession by a divinity. The peoples of the pacific northwest practiced something like a form of copyright, where only specific families had the right to tell certain stories, and stories could be sold, traded, and inherited because telling a story was a sacred act and therefore precious. The Akan and Ashanti god of stories, Anansi, so important that he was the only African myth most of our ancestors had even heard of! Ancient germanic peoples believed in a form of magic that involved going into the spirit world and leaving a story there, and if the students call the other world, the world we left to get here," Theosophia grimaced but plowed ahead, " 'physside' then doesn't that imply 'going into the spirit world and telling a story there' is exactly what we've done? Even in English, the language we'll presumably keep speaking forever, the word "spell" used to also mean "story."

"What's your point?" Theodulfr asked, without hostility. "That... stories were considered important?"

"When you said what we're doing is more like living inside a story than doing actual magic, you were right!" Theosophia was getting an excited head of steam behind him now. He was going to start pacing as he talked any moment. "But we didn't define our terms when we started, we just assumed because we'd just forked that all three of us would automatically mean the same thing by the word 'magic,' But we didn't, not clearly! That's why you," he pointed at Theo in the chair, which was the last straw on his composure, and he went on, pacing, "couldn't make up your mind between us in the first place! You didn't know whether to call our existence magic because you weren't sure what you meant by magic! Probably why we started arguing the opposite positions you intended, if I had to guess. But!

But those ancient humans had to define their terms too, they were the ones inventing terms in the first place, so of course they defined 'magic.' And very consistently they used the same method to define it."

Theodred leaned forward in his chair, very slowly.

"Who decides, in a story, whether or not something is magic?" Theosophia was repeating some of the hand and finger gestures from his earlier reverie. "Who decides how the magic works?"

"...the person telling the story." Theodulfr's voice was only a whisper but his face was too lit up for the mask to hide it.

"Who set the scene for the debate we're having right now?"

"I did." Theo said.

"And what are the two kinds of people who can decide things like 'this conversation should happen at sunset, and the weather should be such-and-such, and a campfire and a cabinet of drinks and stools nobody's going to end up sitting on should all just Be There?'"

"A magician..." Theo began.

"...or a storyteller," Theodulfr finished.

"And, and... and further," Theosophia was clearly beginning to get ahead of his own words, "if you heard about people who went and lived inside a story they were all telling together, wouldn't that sound like magic?"

"Who coined the saying about sufficiently advanced technology being indistinguishable from magic?!" Theodulfr's rhetorical question was filled with contagious excitement. His defenses were breached. His surrender was underway.

"A storyteller!" Theosophia crowed, driven higher by the feedback loop of excitement, "you could say the real point was: any sufficiently advanced storytelling can make whatever it likes indistinguishable from magic!"

He finally wound down. All the words, the orgasmically unstoppable epiphany of it, subsided and left him.

He looked up, winded, to find the other two staring at him. "What? Did I get too excited?"

"No," said Theo, and quietly activated his hallway mirror back into the sim, "but look at yourself."

The human was gone. A wolf, still dressed in tie and vest, same rough dusky fur as his other two selves, looked back at Theosophia, who reached up to feel his ears as if that would prove anything about their reality. "When did that happen?"

"While you were shouting about sufficiently advanced storytelling." Theodred said.

"You told yourself a story," Theodulfr ventured. "You got swept up in it, and this is the result, I guess."

"I suppose." Theosophia loosened his tie and undid the top buttons of his shirt. "As root instance you're previous evidence there's a part of our personality that wants to present like this, it doesn't mean it was the story or magic that made me–"

"It was," Theo said, "if we decide it was."

The three of him looked at each other over the remains of the fire. The sun was set. The ritual was concluded.

"Guess I won the debate, huh?" Theosophia said, and quit.

"Keep the memory of his whole epiphany," Theodulfr said, "I want to know if it felt as amazing as it looked like it did."

"I was curious about one thing, before you go," Theo said, "why the mask?"

Theodulfr chuckled, took it off. His face, underneath, looked exactly the same as the mask, as Theo's, as Theosophia's by the end. He handed it to Theo. "You'll figure it out," he said, and quit as well.

Theo sat back in the chair to process the merge and let his house reappear around him. It had, indeed, felt amazing to have that epiphany. And really, the mask he was holding was just another way of expressing it: of looking the way one looked not because one looked like that, but because one chose to look like that. Of telling the story, and making yourself the story you were telling, which was just another way of describing individuation.

It meant something if you decided it meant something.

Was that the same as saying it was magic if you believed in magic?

Theodred, Adjunct Professor of Post-Physical Philosophy, comfortable as a wolf, and—he now supposed—magician, decided to sleep on that question. He was tired. Anyway, should it prove insoluble, he knew a pretty simple ritual to conjure up an answer to questions like that.

He lay waiting for sleep, and wondered what his students would think when he showed up to lecture tomorrow wearing a little lapel pin of a running wolf and a mask of his own face.

Outside, the story he and all the others with magical powers like his had woven into the fabric of a spirit world, written in secret languages known only to learned adepts, with letters made of lightning on pages made of glass and rare metals, in a library hung amidst all the stars of the firmament, continued to tell itself, as it had for centuries, as it would for centuries more.

It mattered how you decided to look at it.

Genre Clade

Nathan "Domus Vocis" Hopp

Dante — 2251

Walking away from my former home felt like a herculean task. However, nothing had felt easier than uploading to the System, even as I looked back on the memory centuries later.

Simply put, my life never really started until after I woke up in a blank simulation, was instructed on how to give myself clothes, how to fork, as well as how to navigate my way through the System and earn currency in the form of reputation. I didn't really begin living until I stumbled through digital realm after digital realm, gaining a sense of my boundless surroundings. The first sim I'd went to was called Infinite Café#06f4c37a, an entire cityscape composed of cafes, bakeries, juice bars, and coffee shops. There, I interacted with friendly, outspoken, and kind users who welcomed me to the System, and who in turn, gave me the opportunity to try many different pastries and baked goods for what seemed like days as I slowly opened myself up to others.

One of the eternal friends I made during my time there was Zion, who appeared as a deathly-pale but lively person with ruby eyes. Identifying as non-binary and dressed clothes that they liked to call 'Neo-Gothpunk aesthetics', Zion spoke like a System denizen who'd seen almost everything but approached it like a new experience. They were also an excellent conversationalist. The moment they offered me a seat in the crowded interior, Zion successfully kept me in an hours-long discussion on what the System offered to creatives.

"I like to generate intricate landscapes made up of historical locations," they boasted without looking away from me or dismissing my intrigue. "Just yesterday, I helped create a sim for these die-hard fans of live-action role-playing games, who wanted me to build a high detailed Gothic castle with hidden chambers, secrets, unknown treasures, and more. Do you like to LARP?" I shook my head, which didn't surprise them. "It's not for everyone, but I'm still curious to ask: now that you're here, what do you want to do with your immortality?"

"I...I'm not sure," came my confession. "I...only wanted to get away."

"Get away?" Zion pondered, "From whom, Dante?"

"My...family," I finally said after a moment.

Ever since I could remember, my choices were made by my parents and grandparents. As the youngest son in a religious family, they did everything to mold me as a perfect believer. I dressed how they wanted me to dress, watched what they wanted me to watch, went where they wanted me to go, said what they wanted me to say, felt how they wanted me to feel.

But not think.

For all their influence into what I would come to recognize as an unhealthy childhood growing up, my relatives couldn't force me to think the way they needed me to think. That was among the few privileges God gave me, plus the downloaded books I managed to sneakily read in the school library during lunchtimes, if I even could find the opportunities in late high school.

"I always thought that the religious types were extinct outside the System." Zion mulled remorsefully over my story, expression remaining calm as distracted users walked or talked around us. "I know a few sims which are heavily closed off and feel more like cults, but that's it."

"My family believed that the world is in an apocalypse because of humanity's past sins," I said, then sipped on another cup of pumpkin spice latte. "By the way, whatever this 'pumpkin' is, it's tasty."

They chuckled. "You must try it with some pumpkin bread, hon."

"Will do." I nodded as I set down my cup. The sensations still felt too real to be zeroes and ones. "As far as I know, my family think I just ran away to the other side of the world. They don't know I uploaded myself, but if they did...they'd consider me dead to them."

"Do you plan to reach out to them?" Zion asked, to which I shrugged. "I understand. For now, you should consider this a new chapter in your life. The first thing I did after uploading a couple decades ago was do everything that I've ever wanted to do on my bucket list. You should too."

★

That I did. With insightful directions from Zion, I set out to explore the rest of the System. Little did I know that it would unravel the last remnant of shy indecisiveness clinging to me since childhood, as I found myself bouncing between virtual worlds that only existed in the imagination. Or even dreams.

After the Infinite Café came other public sims I explored like a happy child visiting its first toy store. There were sims composed entirely of junk food, sims that hosted reenactments of historic events, as well as sims recreating hypothetical alien worlds throughout the Milky Way.

My five senses experienced digital smells, sounds, sights, and tastes I never knew could exist. Besides places that showcased lost nature and impossible architecture, I found sims trapped in various time periods and settings only seen in history lessons; among them my favorite to frequently visit was called Athenaeum#f6f6ff01, a sim which presented accurate replicas of famous libraries throughout history, with the ancient Library of Alexandria and its iconic lighthouse serving as a spawn point for newcomers and a sea of floral gardens connecting every standing library to each other.

After spending hours marveling at the Alexandrian wing, I traveled between the Boston Athenaeum, National Library of China, and the Old American Library of Congress before taking a temporary break inside the Wiblingen Monastery Library. Although I didn't know much of architecture, I recognized the whimsically ornate ceilings, walls, and archways as 'Rococo'. I sat down on a bench beneath a marble statue overlooking one of its extravagant hallways as a tear welled in one of my eyes. Never before did I realize how beautiful the past looked.

What good was going to libraries though if one didn't take the time to read? Unlike the tablets though, almost every single reading material within the libraries were archaic paperbacks, hardbacks, scrolls, magazines, textbooks, and so much more to choose. Just seeing so many lined up along the mahogany shelves overwhelmed me, at first. My childlike wonder didn't know which to take off the shelf.

So, I choose whatever my arms and my several forked instances could carry.

One of the first advantages I discovered after being uploaded was that human limits no longer existed. I could eat and sleep whenever I felt like it. The fact most humans phys-side slept through a third of their lifetime didn't matter anymore. This applied to forks too.

My forked versions and I learned very quickly not to let my digital clones quit directly after finishing a novel, nor while I was reading something at the same time. Otherwise, I developed an absolutely splitting headache with only a blurry recollection of what had just been read. So, over the course of several days, we took turns. For days, I eagerly paced myself to actually enjoy the books on every shelf. No more work hours, awkward family dinners, being interrupted, fighting against sleep as I stayed up way past my bedtime, pretending to be asleep, or skimming quickly to the end. I was allowed to enjoy each page for as long as I wanted.

A million books later, I got bored. As each memory of my forks accumulated more novels into my head, I didn't find them as exciting anymore. Novels I thought would be amazing either were mediocre or shared too heavy of similarities with other books. Plenty followed a similar narrative or held similar dialogue. Most relied on tired tropes and overused cliches that didn't amaze me after seeing them play out over and over and over again. The longer I caught up on these endless books I'd always wanted to read, the more I thought back to when Zion asked me what I wanted to do.

Well, half-way through reading yet another generic pulpy romance novella, I reached a sudden conclusion. I didn't just want to read. Without anyone to hold me back, I wanted to...

"You wanna write books now?" Zion repeated my statement back to me during one of our rendezvouses at the Infinite Café. "That's great, Dante! What do you plan to write?"

"I'm thinking of an autobiography so far." I shrugged between distracted sips on another pumpkin latte (after having dunked my pumpkin bread in and utterly devoured it, much to Zion's giggling amusement). "Nothing too major. If anything, it might help me unpack some things, or at the very least give me some closure of some kind. If not, I'll just write the first thing that pops into my head."

"You'll need your own sim then," Zion said.

"My own sim?"

"Where else are you going to work from? This café?" They chuckled after finishing the rest of their chai latte. "Of course, you're going to need to gain reputation. Sims aren't free."

The reputation market required me to interact with other people. Purchasing and designing a sim required using the reputation market too. Without reputation, I wouldn't really be allowed to make a place for myself to sit down and write. I'd already accumulated some from speaking with Zion and traveling to other sims, but gaining more reputation to afford a private sim was easier said than done, at first. Even so, the work was worth it.

⋆

My very first sim started off crude, like a child's first attempt at a landscape, but over painstaking and devoted time I now possessed, it transformed into my new home. At first, the end result appeared like a painfully rendered imitation of what an artificial intelligence thought a log cabin looked like. After scrapping it, I started again from scratch. Only this time, I didn't rush the construction, but slowly built it brick by brick and tile by tile.

Assistance from Zion during our now-scheduled weekly get-togethers at the Infinite Café helped a long way as well. They gave very useful advice on how to make the simulation feel real to me, and how to be intricate with each aspect in the grand design, from the simplest gusts of wind to the casting shadows of the Sun.

In the end, I felt content with the final rendition; seemingly nothing more than a vast North American timber forest in spring-time, the private sim's only man-made structure resembled a medium-sized rustic log cabin. The unlocked front door led to an open interior with a kitchen and granite counter-top table in one corner, a comfortable living room in the opposite corner, and a circular writing desk between a cozy ergonomic chair and a glass window overlooking a lake. One of my favorite features included an old-style typewriter which came with an endless supply of ink, plus a neighboring chalkboard on wheels to plan out my stories.

I called my finished sim Writer's Retreat#a9f5d4e2.

My first few days spent within the digital sanctuary led to zero results. Aside from a few typing noises and agitated mutterings, I only really stared out the beautiful window. The first thing I initially wanted to focus on was jotting down the biggest accomplishments in my life (uploading being the ultimate achievement) and my favorite memories from growing up. The more I reflected on my life though, the more I chastised myself for past failures and regrets, none of which I bothered writing down. Instead, there was this nagging feeling at the back of my mind, thinking about how much better that one bad romance novel would've been if the main character's love interest had a little more interest in getting to know her.

"I'll work on it after I'm done with this project," I promised myself.

Another few days passed. I broke away from my isolation in order to join Zion again at the Infinite Café, only for my melancholy to disappear when they mentioned how busy they were with a sim commission and had sent a fork in their place. Seeing the duplication of my friend sitting before me, relaxed and completely invested in our conversation about backlogged projects, caused a great idea to pop into my head.

"That's it!" I suddenly shot up from our table with the widest of smiles. A few heads turned but didn't remain focused on me. "Zion, you're a genius! A brilliant, brilliant genius!"

"No need to heap praises on me," their fork replied after laughing. "By the way, why am I a genius?"

I demonstrated it by suddenly creating a forked version of myself, who promptly returned to the Writer's Retreat.

They immediately understood, sharing my grin. "You're right, I'm a genius, sweetie. Just don't push yourselves too hard, okay?"

Not at first, we didn't. After renovating my one-room cabin for dual capacity, my days were spent at that desk, either jotting down vague notes or thinking back to repressed memories I'd been trying to erase. When I couldn't bear just staying in the cabin as my forked instance eagerly typed away on his own typewriter, I decided to venture outside and explore the sim. Within a couple of days, my fork asked if I'd be interested in reading the novella's rough draft. I eagerly accepted it, much to his delight, and mine.

"Not bad, actually," I said after skimming through the first chapter. "It'll need some work."

"We've got all the time in the world, right?" He sat across from me in the living room, now communal. "If this'll need to be edited and reworked, I'll want to stay for longer. I've got some other ideas I want to work on too." My fork began to snicker.

"What?" I asked.

"From now on," he explained, "you can call me 'Romance Genre'."

I stared blankly at him. "Really?"

"Yes!" He nodded vigorously, wearing a glint in his eyes I never thought was possible to see on my own face. "If I ever feel like making any forks to write other book ideas, let's name them after genres! I'll be Romance Genre, and if you ever want to start working on a political thriller, but won't get away from this slump you're in, you'll fork out Political Thriller."

I shook my head and laughed. "Whatever."

Romance Genre was the first fork, soon joined by Horror Genre after a particularly vivid nightmare, which then gave me an idea for a setting full of existential dread. The next Genres to join our quasi-family were Fantasy, Adventure, Slice-of-Life, Humor, Drama, Science Fiction, Young Adult, Horror Genre's twin 'sisters' named Paranormal and Lovecraftian Fiction, Romance Genre's close collaborative brother Historical Fiction, the latter of whom also liked to collaborate with Alternate History, and who in turn forked out Steampunk, who had a begrudging respect towards Historical Fiction despite their antithetical differences and close similarities. Even Zion became an extended member of the clade after forming a relationship with Steampunk Genre. I remembered voicing my sheer confusion, similar to when Horror Genre introduced me to his younger sisters, but a long discussion with Steampunk and Zion together helped me realized how much he'd become a different person from me. Steampunk described to me how he didn't view someone's gender (or lack thereof) as a reason not to form a romance with someone. He sincerely loved them, regardless.

Genre Clade

Well, not that either of them needed it from me, but I approved of their relationship.

Over the years, Writer's Retreat#a9f5d4e2 expanded from a small writing cabin into a massive woodland mansion the size of a city. Every 'house' within the mansion catered to the needs, wants, and aesthetic desires of each 'Genre' in my growing clade. We talked, exchanged stories, ideas, drafts, and manuscripts before publishing them, supporting each other in our separate but connected endeavors to be the best writers in all of the System.

Our most recent addition was Anthropomorphic Fiction, who came into existence after I'd joined Zion at a sim gathering hosted by a lively, awkwardly charming skunk author from the Ode clade named Dear The Wheat And Rye Under The Stars.

Though she preferred to be called 'Rye', I liked calling her 'Catcher in the Rye', much to her chagrin and my utter amusement, even decades after our friendship formed.

"Anthropomorphism is more than just a subgenre," she explained to me—or rather a forked instance of me—as we discussed literature inside the Old American Library of Congress within Athenaeum#f6f6ff01. "It is more akin to a meta-genre, Dante. A book about archaeologists going after a lost treasure in the jungle is just an average adventure, but if your protagonist is, say, a handsome lion and his foil a sultry vixen, you can have more fun displaying personalities that cannot be done with humans, yes?"

"Not unless the writer's being lazy and just makes them animals with no reason," I argued.

Rye frowned.

"What? If a main character's a furry, but it's only brought up in the description once or twice, are they really a furry?"

Rye's black-and-white-furred frown softened. "Fair point," she admitted. "But you are not really thinking about the storytelling possibilities, are you? Instead, you spend your days holed up in that cabin mulling over that autobiography."

"Is Anthro worried about me again?" I groaned.

"He thinks that you are obsessed with the past. You came here for a better future, yes?" When I didn't answer, Rye said, "If there is one thing that I have learned in my century and a half, it is that the past is very complicated, but fiction need not be. Not all stories must be told. Otherwise, that is all that you are going to do until the end of the universe."

I still didn't say anything, but instead nodded meekly as she leaned over to give a hug.

"Anyway, my apologies, but I must cut this short. I have another meetup in a few minutes and would like to keep conflicts to a minimum." She grinned with perked ears as I'd been temporarily distracted by her swishing tail. "You take care of yourself, okay?"

"No promises," I shot back, my earlier snark returning.

She waved at me and said, "See you later, Memoir!"

My forked instance rolled his eyes before quitting, promptly sending those memories to me. As the root instance and our quasi-family's patriarch, everybody else either called me by my real name Dante, or if they wanted to be a little humorous, 'Memoir'.

Before uploading, my lifelong objective had been to be never seen or heard unless required. My tall, lanky frame prevented me from being invisible, and despite having a deep voice, I kept it at a lowered volume until the day I had enough. Over time though, my old self dissipated with the previous life I'd had outside the System. I expressed myself more fully. I joked with friends, with my clade, and they joked with me. Laughter bubbled freely out of my lungs like oxygen, and I smiled without feeling forced whenever I walked into a conversation by accident. The scars lingered like ink blotches though, leaving stains.

Rye's words stuck with me for some time. They remained at the back of my mind especially during one of my outings with Zion to the Infinite Cafe, who didn't fully notice my slow, contemplative sips as they described an ongoing project needing to be canceled after having it 99% completed. The client cited trivial things and ballooned each one into seemingly unfixable things until Zion had enough of it.

According to them, "It brought me back to dealing with my father. He supported me following in his footsteps as an architect, but...well, I guess he grew jealous, and when he did bother to keep in touch with me, Dad liked to nitpick my public sims that were shown back on the 'net"

"Glad to know I'm not the only one with...family complications." I shrugged.

"Heh, I'll drink to that!" They tapped their latte to mine, and we sipped together.

One day, before attending Steampunk and Alternate History's collaborative book cover reveal in another sim called Grand Gala#e39b94ee, I found myself staring at the comprehensive notes I'd collected for the autobiography. They started off gradual, over time brimming the entirety of my writing desk, the chalkboard, and the walls, until each paper harshly mimicked the whites of my parents' judgmental eyes.

To this day, I don't know what came over me. Hours before, I'd been fervently detailing the days building up to my running away. I'd finally scribbled down the fury in my father and mother's faces when they'd discovered my...disinterest in getting married—specifically, not to women. As punishment, they'd donated what little possessions I owned to the church charity. My own personal tablet didn't survive the purge either, especially as they felt reading 'lurid romances' involving men and women contradicted the beliefs I'd confessed.

One note on the chalkboard read, "I had nothing left to lose after that night. Mom and Dad's religion killed me years ago, but after that day, the System resurrected me."

I understood now what Rye had been trying to tell me.

Without thinking further on the matter, I collected every paper, note, or sketch, then sent them into the trash bin. Within seconds, the weight of twenty years disappeared from my shoulders, and I walked out of the cabin a freer man. Thinking about my new family, an amusing thought came to me at the same time I blinked away to the Gala sim.

"I wonder what those goofballs are going to call me now that I'm no longer 'Memoir'?"

Après un rêve

Madison Scott-Clary

Sylvie — 2196

Echoes of Grace singing, memories and emotions, clashed with the doctor's words.

> *Dans un sommeil que charmait ton image*
> *Je rêvais le bonheur, ardent mirage...*

"I know you've signed the waivers, but I need a verbal confirmation," she was saying. "Do you understand the procedure?"

> *Tes yeux étaient plus doux, ta voix pure et sonore,*
> *Tu rayonnais comme un ciel éclairé par l'aurore;*

Sylvie nodded. It was strange not to feel her hair, always so frizzy and buoyant, following the motion a scant second too late.

"I'm sorry, Sylvie, it needs to be a verbal confirmation. The uploading process will be fatal and irreversible. There is some risk, about one and a half percent, that it won't work." The doctor paused and picked up a pen. She added, "Won't work after the point where your body will have died, that is. Do you understand?"

A swallow, dry, and another nod. "What will happen in that case?"

"Your family will receive a payout of ten million francs CFA. Your body will not be available for a burial, unfortunately." The doctor looked strangely abashed. "The results of the process are… ah, not pretty."

"I understand."

"One last thing, then. After the uploading process, successful or not, your blood, organs and tissue will be donated—or, ah… sold—to a tissue bank in central Africa. Your family will receive ten percent of this, and the Centre the other ninety. This is to help defray the cost of the process."

Sylvie thought for a moment, rubbed her hand over her smooth-shaven head. "About how much will that be?"

"The cut to your family?" The doctor fiddled with her pen, twirling it across delicate dark fingers. "Lately, we've been getting about a hundred million francs, so again, about ten million. Not a bad payout, hmm?"

Not bad indeed. Sylvie had little love for her family, minus her brother, so the payout wasn't a huge incentive, as it was for others. She just hoped Moussa wound up with a chunk of it. Unlikely, given her mother. She nodded. "Uh, I agree. Confirm. Whatever."

"So then. Your surgery is scheduled in one hour. You have fifteen minutes before prep, which means fifteen more minutes to back out if you should choose. I'm going to head back to the team and leave you be to think this over." The doctor gestured to her right: a phone huddled, mute, on the table next to the coffee machine, the creamer and sugar. "Dial zero on the phone on the desk if you wish to cancel. There will be no repercussions if you do."

The doctor stood and leaned forward, offering her hand. Sylvie lifted herself out of her chair and accepted the handshake, marveling at such an antiquated gesture, feeling the need, however real or not, to be careful of those delicate fingers. The grip was firm.

As the doctor stepped out of the room, Sylvie settled back into the chair. She closed her eyes against the sight of all the posters advertising the procedure.

"Upload today!" they shouted.

"Experience a life beyond need!" they hollered.

"Work without pressure!" they howled.

Everything was so loud, so loud.

She had them all memorized, anyway. All those overbright promises that hat circled her head like a halo yearning for the System somewhere above the sky had grown wearisome.

Right now, she just wanted quiet. She just wanted peace and stillness. She just wanted to *think*.

She just wanted to think of Grace.

Grace with her silvering hair.

Grace with her fair and smooth skin.

Grace with her liquid laughter and lovely voice.

They'd fallen in love within weeks. A chance meeting at a work party—Grace someone's plus-one, someone in accounting—had led to an hour and a half talking about music. The chat had led to a concert. Then another. Then coffee. They'd shared only a scant few years together after that—one of them married—before being separated again. An impenetrable boundary of distance, of the immiscibility of emulated sensorium and embodied flesh.

Grace's decision hadn't been Sylvie's. Uploading, the very thought of it, made her skin itch and eyes ache. To be removed from this world and sent to another, to the System, didn't appeal to her. What greater life could the System offer? What did "a life beyond need" mean? That one could eat to one's delight? But she'd heard that hunger wasn't a thing, so what mattered satiation? That one could sleep as long as one wanted? But of what use were dreams up there? That one could live forever?

It did appeal to Grace.

Grace with her failing voice.

Grace with her deteriorating coordination.

Grace with her pain, her depression.

For Grace, it was a way to escape her body. That body that Sylvie loved so much, and which was such a prison to Grace. A voluntary procedure—"Help combat overpopulation!" the posters screamed, eugenics veiled thinly, and even then only with a wink and a nudge; the population had been dropping for a decade at least—but also a way to neatly sidestep the multiple sclerosis slowly claiming her body and mind.

After the upload, Sylvie had heard from Grace through text, through mails sent to her terminal which she'd pore over at work, reading top to bottom, top to bottom, a daily *lectio divina*. She asked Sylvie. She begged her. *Come join me, come upload,* she said. *The posters, they're all true, they're all right. We can be together as if nothing had changed. At least, nothing for the worse.*

The thought *still* made her skin itch and her eyes ache, but all the same, she kept dreaming of Grace. Dreaming of softer eyes, of a voice more sonorous. Her Grace shining like the dawn.

So she'd relented.

> *Tu m'appelais et je quittais la terre*
> *Pour m'enfuir avec toi vers la lumière,*
> *Les cieux pour nous entr'ouvraient leurs nues,*
> *Splendeurs inconnues, lueurs divines entrevues...*

Sylvie's mind was filled to overflowing with Fauré, with that rolling, lilting theme, with Grace's voice at the piano. Even as she was put in a hospital gown, even as she was wheeled back to the operating room on a tired gurney, it played in her head. Maybe she hummed, she didn't know.

"We're going to keep you awake, okay? We need to as part of the process, you have to be conscious but you'll be under local anesthesia. It'll make you feel a little dreamy. You may have visual disturbances." The doctor's smile was kind. "Some report it to be enjoyable."

"Okay. How long will it take?"

"An hour and a half, plus about thirty minutes to prep you for upload. The upload will happen in two stages," she said. "You'll be uploaded to a local node at our center, which will give you access to a waiting room of sorts for the System proper. The upload to the L5 point will take several hours via Ansible—it's a lot of data going a long way, you understand—so the waiting room will usually have you stick around."

Sylvie thought for a moment, "What about the copy that remains?"

"It's free to quit, like a program on your terminal quitting. But they—the... ah, sysadmins—usually request that it stay around in case the upload to the system gets interrupted for some reason. Cosmic rays or whatever technobabble fits that day."

"And I just... wait?"

"Wait until the upload's completed, then you'll either quit or the sim is halted.

"And what will I feel if things go wrong?"

The doctor hesitated, looked to her team. It was another team member, a man with a thick French accent, who responded. "We don't really know. The local node will pick up on it and alert us. Death just looks like death to us."

Sylvie nodded. Tried to nod, at least. She was firmly strapped down. "Alright."

There was a pinprick at the crook of her elbow. A feeling of coolness spread up her arm, into her chest. A tightness, there, and then a tightness along her neck. A brief moment of panic as she tried to flex her fingers.

"We are starting the neuromuscular blocker. This will paralyze your voluntary muscles, so don't panic about the feeling," the anesthesiologist mumbled, distracted. He tapped her forearm, sending a pins-and-needles flash through the right half of her body. "But it doesn't numb you. That will be the next one, the anesthetic."

Sylvie attempted to speak, but only managed a grunt of assent.

The anesthesiologist nodded, "Good. Here it comes, then."

The chill ache was replaced with a comfortable warmth.

Not warmth, she thought. *Nothingness. Floatingness. Leaving-the-Earth-ness. Gone-ness.* Some part of her giggled. Dreamy indeed.

"Sylvie, can you hear me? You won't be able to speak or blink or nod, but can you try and take two quick breaths? It may be difficult. We'll intubate if necessary."

Sylvie obeyed. Or thought she did, at least. She couldn't tell if the breaths were actually happening. It seemed to be enough for the anesthesiologist, whose shadow across her vision bowed and stepped out of sight.

Time wandered.

Voices rang with the timbre of bells. Sometimes they formed words, sometimes they were broken down into their component tones and she could only here formants, fundamentals. Surgeons talking to technicians.

A dull, basso organ note of something grinding, her vision vibrating, blurring the sight of the light above the bed.

A light? *The* light? *Are my eyes even open?*

The light took the form of Grace, and Sylvie more readily gave in to the effects of the drug.

Grace with her angelic smile. Grace lifting her up, away from the earth. Grace running, running into the ring of that surgeon's lamp. Into and through, up and up. Clouds, clouds parting.

The organ note screamed up through several octaves.

Calm, ringing voices.

That yearning song tinkling pacidly through her mind, stretched and elongated. She was unable to tell whether it came from herself or from one of the techs. Or maybe from Grace. *Dans un sommeil que charmait ton image...* Tinkling and flowing. Rocking. Drunken. Drunken on dreams.

Minutes fled by. Hours. Days, perhaps. Always, in front of her, her angel. Bright, soft skin that contrasted beautifully against her own, cream spilled in coffee. Always lifting her up. How far did they have to go?

Grace was drifting away from her, receding.

The light flared in intensity. Somehow became black. A shining, blinding blackness amid a field of more blackness, matte and plain.

Tugging, pulling.

Prying.

A snap.

Après un rêve

A sense of wrongness, of gravity.

Falling away. Layers of self peeling back, each successive shedding revealing something more raw, more primal. Molting. The boundary between her Self and the blackness complicating, fraying, fading.

Grace was gone, too, faded to nothing.

Come back! Sylvie shouted into the nothingness. Her fists, raw and exposed to their very core, to the concept of Fist *sans* physical representation, pounded at the blackness. Pounded at herself.

Come back! Come back! Grace! She wailed. Screamed. Sobbed. *Grace...*

A whisper against building chords, Grace's sweet voice.

And then the wave receded.

> *Hélas! Hélas! triste réveil des songes*
> *Je t'appelle, ô nuit, rends moi tes mensonges,*
> *Reviens, reviens radieuse,*
> *Reviens ô nuit mystérieuse!*

★

The team stood still. There was no written protocol as to what one should do while the local node processed the upload, but they always remained silent. The doctor held her breath every time.

A small pinging noise. The local readout flashed red.

Shoulders sagged around the room. The nurse's lips began to move in silent prayer.

"Error in processing upload." The tinny speaker sounded impersonal. Perhaps it was designed that way to play down the loss. "Irrecoverable data corruption. Please check all contacts before continuing or contact a System support technician for a full rig inspection."

"Well." The anesthesiologist's voice, so human, contrasted with the words from the speaker. "That's that, then."

"That's that," the doctor echoed. She sighed and backed away from Sylvie's body. It was empty, now. A husk. A vessel poured out into nothing. "I'll start the paperwork and call her family and the insurance company. Get the payout processed as soon as possible. Third one this month, too."

The other team members nodded. None looked happy.

"Go on, get her cleaned up and sent to the handlers." She trudged from the room, her feet dragging. Pulling off her gloves one by one she added half to herself, "At least someone will get something out of this. Alas."

Support Group for Anomalies in Forking

Michael Miele

Ernie — 2328

Ernie felt a gentle sensorium ping wake him from the deep sleep he found himself in. He blinked his eyes blearily and reached for an alarm clock. When his hand didn't find anything to latch onto, he was awake enough to remember he was on the System, and could just think about the current time to check it. Old habits die hard. It was systime 204+1400, about 2PM or so. He didn't think he had set an alarm ping for himself before taking a nap, but he must have wanted to make sure he was up and ready for this afternoon. Maybe he was just being cautious. Ever since he uploaded, it felt like he was making up for lost time when it came to sleep.

He groaned, stood up slowly, and rubbed the sleep out of the corners of his eyes. He concentrated on the outfit he had planned to wear, a plaid flannel that was comfortable and a pair of blue jeans with a ratchet belt, and his pajamas shifted seamlessly into the outfit he had envisioned. With years of practice, he'd figured out the art of changing clothes on the fly. Though, with the scale and breadth of his usual wardrobe, it was surprising it took that long. He was thankful that he wouldn't have to worry about showing up to a diner with his top half wearing his sleeping shirt anymore.

He walked over to his bedroom closet and opened the doors to pick out the final piece to his outfit. After carefully considering four of his best mesh hats, he decided on the one with a black brim and a logo from a football team that hadn't existed phys-side for at least fifty years. Hard to go wrong with the classics. He could have willed the hat onto his head but this was one part of his ritual to leave the house that he stubbornly clung onto. The act of choosing was one that needed to be tactile for him to feel like he was ready to step out. And with one last check on the time and his reputation balance, he stepped from his home sim.

He arrived at SGAF Forum#4da206f6 a scant few milliseconds later. He could have gotten there a bit faster, had this been a sim he frequented often, but today was a day of new experiences for Ernie. He was just a tad bit nervous, as he hadn't tried breaking into a new social group for a good couple decades now. His current circle was mostly former truck drivers, though there was some occasional overlap with the folks who worked at the various diners that he would visit.

In fact, it was a chance meeting at a diner that had gotten him this invitation.

Everybody's got a hobby, and in the case of functionally immortal folks, they tend to have several. More time to diversify and whatnot. One of Ernie's hobbies was trying to find the best reuben sandwich that he could eat in the wide expanse of the System. This was no small feat either. He'd been diligently eating at just about every diner he could get into for the past seventy or so years and had quite the list going. It was a great way to get him out of the house and he found that over time he was able to home in on the aspects of a great reuben for him. The rye bread needed to be at least a certain thickness with a little bit of give, the dressing shouldn't be too runny, the coleslaw had to have a decent bite to it, the swiss shouldn't be sharp or bitter, and the corned beef needed to provide just the right amount of tension and snap when taking a bite. With new restaurants opening and closing every day across however many millions of sims, he had no shortage of places to visit.

During one of these trips, he had gotten into a conversation with a woman who was sitting at the diner's bar next to him. Her name was Melanie and they had quickly hit it off after Ernie impressed on her that the diner had a really terrible reuben. They had talked a bit more about current events with Melanie catching Ernie up on how the Castor and Pollux probes were doing a few years after the big Launch. He wasn't sure he could wrap his head around a good chunk of the more technical stuff she was telling him, but she seemed to be fine with him nodding his head as though he understood. That had led her to talk about how a few of her friends had left forks on each of the probes. Ernie wasn't a big fan of forking and when Melanie asked why, he had said he didn't feel comfortable going into it. Noticing his distress, she had told him that she had trouble with forking as well. And before he could say anything more, she had slipped a small metallic card under his sandwich plate. She then settled her tab and had told Ernie to keep in touch, before stepping from the sim. When he looked at the card later, he found the address coordinates to a sim underneath an embossed title that read "Support Group for Anomalies in Forking" along with a meeting time. Curiosity had won out and so now he stood outside of a massive glass-paneled building that looked closer to a corporate high-rise suite than a place for group therapy.

He was surprised that he didn't materialize right within the meeting room. There must have been a reason that the entry point for the sim would be outside of the building, but most designers prioritized an instance's ease of experience over realism. While there were doubtless sim architects who would disagree, function often trumped form. Out of the corner of his eye, he could see a small sign crudely printed on notebook paper and taped up to the glass with masking tape. The sign read, "Due to renovations, SGAF meeting moved to the auxiliary room for the time being. Please be patient as a group member will come to assist you in getting into the temporary room."

Ernie thought about leaving and coming back next week, but he had already gone to the trouble of getting dressed in his good flannel. So, he waited for someone to come answer the door and let him in. When he checked the time for the fourth time in a row, he had just about run out of patience.

"Welp," he said while hiking up the front of his jeans, "nothin' for it." He walked over to the door of the building and reached forward to open it. Surely someone inside would be able to tell him where he needed to go?

But before he could put his hand on the handle, the door on his left swung open and a familiar face poked her head out.

"Oh good! You did decide to come after all," Melanie said. Her smile was infectious. She was a middle-aged woman with an olive complexion and thick bouncy curls of hair that came to her shoulder. She was wearing a t-shirt that was a mix of pinks and whites underneath a dark blue satin jacket that had a metallic sheen with pants of a similar color but different material on her legs.

"Yep, figured I should see what this is all about," Ernie replied.

"Well don't just stand there, come on inside. I'm excited for you to meet everyone." She gestured with her hand for Ernie to follow her inside. He grabbed the door and shut it behind him as he walked through.

It was a long walk and by the time they had reached a rather imposing solid oak door, Ernie was having second thoughts about coming. He leaned against the wall as Melanie fished around in her pockets for a set of keys. But instead of going to open the door, she carefully removed a single key from the keyring and pressed it into Ernie's hand.

"While this is more symbolic than practical, I've just given you very limited ACLs to access the auxiliary meeting room. You should be able to open the door and step through now. We can go in once you're ready."

Ernie smiled slightly and said, "Thanks. Don't suppose I can get ya to explain what it's gonna be like in there before we walk in?"

"Oh, you'll be fine. You're encouraged to talk through how you feel about forking but no one is obligated to share if they don't feel like it. And the others will understand since they've been in your shoes before."

Ernie felt relieved at that. He wasn't sure how comfortable he was going to be with all of this, so it was nice that Melanie had given him an out at the start. She must have gone through this a fair number of times with other people if she knew to address that fear right from the jump. He pushed himself off of the nearby wall with a grunt and placed his key into the lock of the massive door. There was a slight resistance as he felt the tumblers in the door click into place. He looked over at Melanie expectantly and she gave a small nod of her head as if to say "go ahead". He twisted the doorknob in his hand and pulled back towards him hard. He was surprised to find that the door was much lighter than he anticipated as it swung open quickly.

Melanie laughed and walked through the door into the auxiliary room. Ernie followed her in, making sure to shut the door behind him.

The room was huge and could hardly be called 'auxiliary'. If this was what they considered a spare room, he would have been blown away by the main room. The walls were covered in a dark brown wood paneling and had framed pictures of people from what looked like previous SGAF events or meetings. The pictures themselves were taken within this room, which Ernie felt was odd. They must get more use out of the spare room than he expected. Along the edges of the rooms were a collection of sofas, couches, and wooden chairs, presumably for the members to use to sit down on. The center of the room looked like it was designed to hold a large circular table, but that space was currently empty. There were a couple plants in the corners of the room to break up the space with a few splashes of green and yellow. No flowering plants though, only ferns and fronds. More colors than that would be too distracting. The room felt like it was designed to give the impression of a psychiatrist's office, even to Ernie who had never been in one back phys-side.

Around the circle sat three other people in chairs that were as unique as them. Ernie did his best not to stare, but his eyes were drawn to the chair that looked absolutely uncomfortable to sit in. Thin seat suspended in the air over a base of interlocking segments of white polished marble with hovering armrests that moved along with their body. He knew of furries, but he had never seen a furry like this one before.

Ernie tried to recall the last time he had interacted with furries and realized that it had been back when he was phys-side. His truck's GPS had crashed on him and he was in a part of the country that was entirely unfamiliar. When he pulled into the nearest gas station looking for directions, a group of furries helped him out by opening up his GPS and fixing the offending part.

This furry in particular was an amalgam of many different animal features that Ernie could only really guess at. Their head was long and canine, but the ears were small and close to the head. On top of their head was a set of deer antlers. Their body was covered in a light brown fur that poked out of a shiny black suit coat complete with coat-tails. Behind them was a long and lizard-like tail that swayed hypnotically. They exuded a kind of confidence in how they carried themself that was intimidating to Ernie. None of their disparate parts seemed to be causing them discomfort and even the places on them that transitioned to a new animal seemed to fade and give way to the next without hesitation.

They leaned forward in their chair and gestured to Ernie saying, "I didn't expect you to bring someone new today Melanie! What kind of morsel do we have here?" As they talked Ernie could see a flash of their fangs and the many rows of teeth inside of their mouth.

"Settle down Devonian, we don't want to scare him off before he's even had a chance to get to know us," said a man sitting backwards in a combined school desk and chair much smaller than him. He was wearing a blue turtleneck and khaki pants and fiddled with a wooden ruler at his desk.

"Do you think so little of me David? I was just implying I would have gotten dressed better had I known ahead of time we'd be having company."

"You're already sufficiently fancy. What would be the next step up? A regency era ball gown with a full train?" asked a woman sitting on a polished wooden bench that was just wide enough for her.

Ernie felt uneasy looking over at her because she looked like she was actively melting. Not in a painful way, but in the sort of way where her facial features were closer to a painting done in Picasso's style of noses, eyes, and mouth off center and rearranged on the canvas of her head.

"My dearest Samantha, you should know that I don't much care for wearing regency gowns. Too many puffy shoulders for my taste. But you do have a point. Perhaps next month I'll wear a dress that matches my sensibilities."

"Oh, that does sound fun. Maybe we could color coordinate the whole group. Young man, would you say that warm tones match better for you? Or are you more of a fan of colder colors?"

It took Ernie a second to realize that Samantha was addressing him. He fidgeted with the back of his mesh cap and said, "I don't exactly know what you're talking about ma'am, sorry."

Samantha laughed out of the corner of her face and said, "Don't worry about it, Ernie. I'm sure we'll be able to find something that would look good on you."

At this Ernie crossed his arms over his chest saying, "Well, I think I look pretty good in flannel."

"It does suit you well, there's no question in that. Melanie, can you help him get a chair?" David asked.

Melanie nodded and scanned around the room until she found the chairs stacked in the corner. A few seconds later she walked toward the group with two wooden chairs plucked from the edge of the room. She set one down in front of Ernie closer to the rest of the group's circle and then took a seat on her own. She looked up at the ceiling and waved her left hand's fingers through the air in subtle gestures. When she was done, she brought her head back down to eye level.

"Sorry about that, old habits from navigating cards in ancient sims back phys-side. I just granted you limited ACLs to make a chair that is comfortable for you to sit in. Unless the wooden one works for you, but as you can see most folks decide to personalize it a bit."

Ernie sat down tentatively and let himself lean back into the back of the chair. He wasn't the best at conjuring things from his mind's eye without a fair bit of practice so he was worried that he'd be stuck in this decidedly uncomfortable chair for the whole time. However, as he leaned back, he could feel the chair shift and morph around him. The wood underneath him reshaped and filled with stuffing, the supporting structure hardening into a lightweight black metal frame. As he reached the limit for leaning backwards, a padded footrest extended out from the base of the chair and cradled his legs and feet. He reached down over the edge of the chair's rapidly manifesting puffy armrests and curled his fingers around the wooden lever he knew would be there. With a grunt and a swing of his legs downward, he pulled on the lever and catapulted himself back to an upright sitting position. It even squeaked with the same loose spring that had been there back phys-side. There was a singular piece of furniture that Ernie knew better than his own body: his trusty periwinkle blue rocking chair recliner.

Melanie asked, "Is that better then?"

"Much better."

She clapped her hands together and cleared her throat slightly. "Alright, we're just about ready to start with our session today then. Since Ernie is new, I want to reiterate that while this could be considered therapy, I'm not a practicing therapist. I'm a retired therapist and as such I want to encourage you to seek out professional therapy services in addition to this group. If you're interested in scheduling one on one sessions, I have a great list of therapists on the System that would love to work with you."

David leaned over his desk and whispered to Ernie, "Just make sure you don't schedule an appointment with Ms. Genet."

Melanie narrowed her eyes and shot a nasty look over at David before saying, "Just because Sarah and you weren't a good fit doesn't mean she's not a good therapist."

He leaned back in his desk looking sufficiently embarrassed for getting caught. For a split second, Ernie could picture him as a student getting called out by the teacher during class.

She continued, "I'm going to go first and introduce myself and talk a little bit about my relationship with forking. I would encourage you all to do the same if you feel comfortable so that Ernie can get an idea of what we're about here at the SGAF. Don't feel shy about asking questions either, as that will help us to loosen up and discuss our problems. You do not need to answer any questions you do not feel like answering. If someone does not want to answer, you must drop it. End of discussion, no exceptions. This process relies on us trusting each other and part of building that trust is respecting our boundaries."

She rocketed up from her chair, knocking it over in the process and placed a hand over her heart. Her eyes scanned back and forth across the circle to make sure that she had everyone's attention. When she was satisfied that they were all focused on her she said, "My name is Melanie Marquetta and whenever I go to fork, *this* happens..."

She then stepped out of her body and Ernie could see the original Melanie along with an almost perfect facsimile of her sculpted entirely out of dark blue metal forks. Hundreds of thousands of interlocking pieces of metal, all very clearly tableware, were woven together into her body shape. Even her hair was made of delicately curled and coiled metal strands. She was the magnum opus of a master metalworker who looked to Melanie as their muse.

Both instances stood still as a statue for a moment and Ernie was concerned that the process of forking had harmed her. Melanie smiled and in unison her and her metal copy moved their arms from off of their chests outward in a flourish. This caught Ernie off-guard and he shouted out, "What the hell!"

The Melanie made of flesh said, "That's the usual reaction I get whenever I do this, so I won't take it personally. What do you think, Metalanie?" She turned her head towards her metal doppelganger and Metalanie said, "I expected him to jump a little more if I'm being honest."

Whenever Metalanie spoke, she sounded like Melanie's voice was being passed through a long metal tunnel. It had an echo to it that made it hard for Ernie to parse out what she had said until a few moments after she had stopped speaking. He also noticed that while Metalanie could move like Melanie, the movements were slower and less graceful. As though she was fighting the metal she was made of to be able to move around. Ernie had so many questions.

"So does this mean you're an instance artist then?" he asked. Ernie had heard of instance artists in passing but didn't know a lot about them. He had heard that people had found a way to use forking as an art medium but that was the breadth of his experience with them as a group. It certainly seemed like it would apply to Melanie.

Melanie bent down to pick up her chair off the floor and sat down. Metalanie moved behind her and draped her arms over the top of the chair. Melanie said, "No, I'm not an instance artist. That honor goes to Samantha."

Samantha piped up and said, "Guilty as charged! One of these days I'll get you to come to one of my shows, darling."

"I swear I'll get out to one eventually. You know how busy I get," Melanie said.

Ernie furrowed his brows together as he tried to formulate his next question.

"So then, what's yer deal? You just like making really fancy copies of yourself in metal?"

"No, it's actually a fair bit less complicated. My 'deal' is that whenever I go to fork, it winds up as a metal copy of myself made out of forks. Every. Time."

And to prove her point she forked four more times until there were four more Metalanie's standing around her chair. Each one was a different color of metal from burnished bronze to gleaming gold, but all of them were made of metal.

"I can influence the color of the metal and even change some aspects of how I'm dressed but other than that, I can't affect my forks."

She crossed her right leg over her left and let all instances of Metalanie quit and merge back down into her. For a moment she was half flesh and half metal, but as she resolved merge conflicts her flesh won out little by little. She opened her eyes and said, "And then merging down brings its own unique set of challenges with just having experienced life as a being completely made of metal. I've gotten really good at experiential merging and that's helped a lot."

"So, when you fork, you're forced to be made of metal? Wouldn't that have come up when you did that initial forking test thingy, they make you do right as ya upload? I would think the System would have caught something as big as that."

"It's actually funny you mention that initial check. But hold that thought a second."

Melanie scrunched her face up and Ernie could tell she was straining against some invisible force. Her right arm wrenched upwards and she strained to pull her pinky and ring fingers down to her palm. She moved her other fingers into position so that she made a kind of gun with her middle and pointer fingers with the thumb as the trigger. She swung the faux gun around and Ernie instinctively ducked. She wasn't pointing it at him, but rather at the inner elbow joint of her left arm. She moved her thumb up and down and Ernie wondered why she was shooting her arm in this way. Melanie didn't say anything and after a few motions, she began to flex her left arm out and in, out and in. She then moved to another joint and repeated the process.

"It's silly if I'm being honest with myself, but visualizing the oil helps to lubricate my joints after a lot of quick merges."

Now it made sense to Ernie. Not a gun, but an oil can. It only took her a couple more seconds until she was fully mobile again at which point, she said, "That's a relief. Now where was I again?"

Devonian spoke up and said, "You were going to explain to Ernie about your upload."

"That's right, thank you." She turned to face Ernie and said, "I may not act like it, but I was one of the first batch of people to upload once they started opening up the process to the public. Now that was back around 2126 and they were still working out how to automate the process of onboarding new users to the System. I didn't know this prior to uploading, but I doubt that it would have changed my mind at the time. The reason that I had the money to upload and why I'm a retired therapist are closely linked. And before you ask, that is something I will not budge on speaking more about."

Ernie nodded in agreement. He could tell from the conviction of her last sentence that prying anymore would get him a one-way boot from the sim.

"So, I get myself uploaded to the System and I hear this automated voice go over some of the basics with me. They get me familiar with how to make clothes and before it can tell me about forking it glitches out. Next thing I know the gray box I was standing in opens up and when I step through the door, I'm in some random city sim."

She took a moment to brush the hair out of her face before continuing. "I wasn't in the best state of mind when I first uploaded. Before I knew it, I had found a bar and proceeded to drink myself extremely drunk. I'm talking completely wasted. Toasty to the max. Knackered and shit-to-face and round the bend. From what people have told me, I was a sight to behold. This was also before I was told you could affect your sensorium and sober yourself up. So here I was at the bar, getting drunker by the minute, and I overheard someone talking about forking. And to me, this is the funniest thing in the world. Some yahoo is talking about making a copy of himself and it's made of forks. What a wild concept. But I'm just drunk enough to give it a try. I go to fork and sure enough, when I step out of my body, there's a copy of me made out of forks. Which just gets me laughing even harder. So, I make another copy, and another copy, and another copy. By the time I got bounced from the sim, I had spent a good chunk of my reputation making copies of myself. It wasn't until a few weeks later, after I had some time to process living on the System, that I tried to fork again and found that metal-me had stuck."

Ernie whistled through his teeth and said, "Geez Melanie! That sure is quite the story. How'd you figure that your metal-you was stuck though?"

"A lot of trial and error, mostly. After I had a chance to meet and talk with other people on the System, I realized that my experience of forking was very different to others. They would talk about forking with intention to change their appearance and at the time I couldn't even affect how my forks would look. That only came with years of patience and practice. Meanwhile, Joe Schmoe over here can fork himself some new eyebrows just as easy as he pleases. It was incredibly frustrating and isolating for years. And then, one particularly bad day, I resolved to find others on the System that I could properly relate to. Build a community, as it were. That project has kept me nice and busy for the last few decades and I don't plan on stopping anytime soon."

She smiled and looked back over to Ernie. Not with expectation, but with understanding. And Ernie could tell that Melanie had been in his shoes before. There was something in the way she looked past him and into all of the arguments he had over the years about his forking habits. He was just about to share, when Samantha cut him off.

"I actually want to talk about the ease of changing your appearance as that struck a chord with me as you were sharing."

Melanie nodded and said, "Go ahead Samantha. Why don't you introduce yourself first?"

Samantha got up from her chair slowly and addressed the room. "Hello everyone, my name is Samantha. Every time I fork, a portion of my face goes slightly off center."

Ernie was waiting for her to fork like Melanie did, but Samantha just sat back down and continued talking.

"There's a reason I can't show you what forking for me looks like. It ties directly into why I can't fork right now at all. You see, I've got a gallery showing coming up and with me as the central piece in the show I need to keep my face exactly as it is for the intended audience I'm seeking out. If I fork even one more time, there's a chance that my canvas will get smudged as it were."

Devonian leaned forward in their chair and said, "That's got to be dreadfully limiting. How do you manage that while working in instance artistry?"

Samantha's smile was nervous and tired. "I do my best, but it is difficult. When most of your friends or colleagues are dispersion-istas, there is a social pressure to fork and fork often. I don't think they're doing it intentionally or maliciously, but subconsciously there is an expectation that while working in instance artistry you will be able to fork often. I was lucky to carve out a niche for myself doing the kind of art that my difficulties in forking allows me to do, but that doesn't help when I am invited to art shows for networking and I can't go. I used to use the cost to my reputation as an excuse for not being able to fork, but as that cost went down, less and less people would accept it."

David leaned back in his chair and said, "I think we all can relate to not having the same freedom of movement that others that can fork normally have. I know that I've had a rough time trying to juggle my schedule when there is an expectation that I can be in multiple places at once. As nice as living on the System is, that is definitely a part I could stand to live without."

The group mumbled a few affirmations of agreement and Devonian chimed in. "I can't say that I have the same problem, but I do sympathize with the sentiment."

"Oh, you don't count. Not with how you fork," David said.

Devonian's snout creased up and they showed a flash of their many rows of teeth. "I suppose not, considering I don't have an issue with forking as often as I please. Yet, I am still affected by this process differently. Hence, why I am here at all."

He sighed, "I know, I know. I didn't mean to come at you so strongly. I had a bad week and I don't want to take it out on you."

Devonian let their lips fall over their teeth once more and made a show of smoothing out their suit jacket. Melanie stepped in and said, "Do you want to talk about your week?"

He looked like he was thinking intently before he answered. "Let Samantha finish first, I want a little time to sort through my feelings before sharing."

Ernie raised his hand sheepishly causing Melanie to laugh a little bit. "Yes Ernie? You wanted to say something?"

He put his hand down and said, "Well, Samantha was talking about how she found instance art she could still do and I wanted to hear more about that. I've not been to a lot of art shows but it sounds interestin'."

Samantha brightened at this, smiling her off-center smile the widest Ernie had seen yet. "But of course, Ernie darling! I've worked a lot with time-lapse photography in the past and that's one of my more popular mediums. I take a picture every day after forking exactly once and combine them into a short video that shows the path my features take as they move across my face. I try to keep the back-drop of the images the same throughout, but when I got bored of that I realized I could incorporate stop motion animation on the desk of the table I would take my photos in front of. That was an incredibly grueling but rewarding period of my work as an instance artist. I had to practice quite a bit before I could make the animation smooth. Not to mention what to use as a subject that would complement the trajectory of my face before I knew where it would end up."

"My bread and butter for my exhibitions has always been displaying my face in new and novel ways. For one exhibit I made hundreds of ornate painting frames and ran between them all while looking at the guests with funny faces. That was incredibly fun. The guests all got into it. I must admit that some of my recent work has been inspired by Melanie in part, as I pose still like a statue in gaudy primary color clothes while a stage light of the same color shines on a section of my face. I invite the guests to walk around me in a circle and as they reach a new part of my face, I change my outfit, pose, and lighting to evoke a new emotion."

She folded her hands on her lap looking extremely pleased with herself. "Thank you for indulging me, dear. I get on a roll about my artistic process and I don't shut up for anything. Are you ready to share David?"

"Yeah, I think I pinned down what was bugging me."

He sat up in his chair and planted his feet firmly underneath the desk. He closed his eyes and took a deep breath, rubbing his fingers over his eyelids. When he had collected himself, he opened his eyes back up and spoke.

"I'm angry and upset because a good friend of mine got miffed that I sent a fork to spend some time with him instead of sending my root instance. The complicated part of this is that he's someone who should know better since he knows how forking affects me."

"Well, that does explain why you've been so combative today. I dare say I'd be a mite bit more growly if that had happened to me. Do you think you're more upset because you didn't expect this kind of behavior from him?" Devonian asked.

"Maybe? I felt like since I've explained this to him before he wouldn't hold it over me if I had to send a fork, but it seems to have had the opposite effect. Now that he knows, he ends up stewing on where my root instance is and that causes a lot of friction between us."

Melanie sighed and said, "I've unfortunately had to deal with this before. It's part of the reason that I keep the people who know about how my forking works to a minimum. Once folks can definitively tell that you've sent a fork, they can get squirrely about why it wasn't important enough for you to show up in person. Never mind that forks are so ubiquitous with everyone else that it's not a problem. It suddenly becomes an issue since you don't fork as often. They start to think that you value them or that relationship less because you're not there 'in person'."

"That does feel like what's going on, I hate to admit it. What makes this worse is that it's difficult to explain this kind of social pressure to fork to those outside of the System. I keep in touch with a few teachers phys-side, but they don't have a great frame of reference for it to compare to."

Ernie raised his hand again and David's training as a teacher kicked in. He pointed to him and called him by name.

"Yeah, I feel like I'm a bit out of the loop here. Why would your friend even be able to tell that you sent a fork? Not meaning to offend none, but you look like the most unassumin' of the lot of ya."

"I suppose I should give you some more context. I don't need to worry about the concept of a body anymore. Ideally, this should have been good for me. I was in a lot of pain before uploading and the retirement plan for a teacher was not promising. But seeing as I was a biology teacher for twenty some odd years at a high school, talking about bodies and their various functions were a daily occurrence for me. So, to exist as this concept of thought and data made it harder for me to fork. I would get caught up in the minutiae of how the human body works whenever I tried. There was a diagram I had hung up as a poster for the class and in this poster was a detailed layout of the different sections of the human body layered on top of each other. That poster burned deeply into my brain after looking at it through class after class. The result is that when I step out of my body, I do so in stages."

David slid out of his desk chair feet first, tumbling forward and springing up on the balls of his heels. He looked back over to Ernie and asked, "You don't get squeamish, do you?"

Ernie wasn't sure how to answer that question. He felt like if David was asking him that now, it was quite the loaded question. He settled for a less than confident "No?"

David must have felt like that was enough for him as he stepped to the right and began to fork. His first fork stepped out of his skin and his underlying muscles were his new outer layer. Another fork and all that was left was a collection of organs free-floating on a transparent frame. The next fork was just the thin wiry nerve endings that made up David's nervous system. When he forked for the last time, Ernie was incredibly relieved to see that it was just David's skeleton.

The original David coordinated his other forks to line up in a straight line with the skeleton at the back and then asked, "Now stand in front of us all and look through." Ernie got up from his recliner and reluctantly did as he was asked. He could see what David had been saying earlier. Each fork when layered on top of each other created a very detailed look at the inside of his body.

Ernie squinted and leaned in closer to the muscle fork and asked, "So which of these were ya when you visited your friend? I could imagine him getting upset if you showed up as a big blob of muscle."

The Skeleton-David walked up to Ernie from the back of the line and put his bony hand on his shoulder. Ernie suppressed a shudder that rocketed through him at the contact with the cold and calcium-rich touch.

His words chattered and echoed through the skull's mouth, but they were still decipherable. "That would've been me. I was sent to spend time with him since the other forks are more unsettling. It's not a great solution, but it beats sending a living collection of loose organs."

"So then, you had to fork at least four times to get to the body that you knew wouldn't upset your friend. And you're upset that he doesn't seem to be understanding the effort you're putting in for him?" Samantha had been thinking quietly, but as she finished speaking the original David started jumping up and down.

"Yes! Yes! This is it exactly! You've hit the nail on the head. I know that he knows that it's a lot of forking for me to get to my skeleton and he doesn't seem to care. And what's worse is that he had to tell me about why he was upset this week, months afterward, because I didn't let that fork merge down."

Ernie gently reached up and took Skeleton-David's hand from his shoulder and let it drop to his side. He walked slowly over to the original David and crossed his arms over his chest.

"Now you let me know if I'm talkin' out of turn, but I think I've got a notion why yer friend was so upset with you."

David shrugged and said, "Shoot."

"You said that you don't merge in your forks. Well, what if he was upset that you wouldn't remember the time you both spent together because he knew that you wouldn't merge? Wouldn't that feel a little bit like he had his time wasted?"

David put his fingers on his chin as he thought about what Ernie had said. He gave the command for his other forks to quit and his eyes lit up. "Shit. I think you might be right. I, uh, might owe him an apology. Thanks Ernie."

"Wasn't any trouble at all. Glad I could help." Ernie uncrossed his arms and pat David gently on his back. They made their way back to their respective chairs and sat down. Devonian clapped from their awkward chair.

"Well done, you're already a natural."

Ernie had to agree with Devonian, yet it was a little strange that the others were so comfortable with him. He had just met them a little bit ago, but the way they talked to him, it felt like they knew him already. Maybe they were just more in touch with their feelings than he was. They've got that practice from coming and sharing that he isn't used to after all. But then why did it feel second nature already? His train of thought was interrupted by Melanie and he put it out of his mind for now.

She tilted her head towards Devonian and asked, "Are you up to sharing this week Devonian?"

They licked the corner of their snout with a forked tongue that was longer than Ernie felt could comfortably fit within their face and nodded.

"But I'm not going to get up. I've just gotten comfortable and if I stand up, I guarantee I'll end up having to reposition my tail for the next half hour."

"Suit yourself," Melanie said.

"I do, every morning."

There was a collective groan from around the circle and Devonian chuckled to themself.

"Alright, enough tomfoolery." They turned their head and spoke directly to Ernie. "When I uploaded, I was human in appearance. That may be hard to visualize, but it's the truth."

They paused for a minute and then said, "I just realized that you may need some crucial context or else this next part of my story will be lost on you. So, do you by chance know what a furry is Ernie?"

"Yeah, I know of 'em. Fine folks helped me out in a pinch once."

"Oh good, that makes this easier. I was a furry back before uploading and had quite a few fursonas to my name. Most furries have one fursona that they pick and stick with for many years. Some will switch it up occasionally and others have a group of about two to three they'll rotate between. I say all this because I was firmly outside of the norm."

"I had a whole menagerie of fursonas that I would swap between whenever the mood struck me. One day I'd be a lion and the next I'd be a deer. Fridays felt like a goat kind of day for a while and then I had my snake period. What I'm trying to get at is that I had a lot of feelings about how to represent myself as a furry and those feelings shifted and changed daily."

"Fast-forward to my upload day and I'm genuinely shocked when I get my bearings that I'm human. I had heard stories of other furries who uploaded who had a similar experience. Their sense of self was more aligned with their human body rather than their animal counterpart. But would I be spared this fate? Surely, I, with my cavalcade of creatures, would have one that would stick. Alas, it was not meant to be. That is, until I went to fork for the first time."

Devonian forked and next to them on their right side stood a bipedal anthropomorphic lion dressed in the same suit that they were wearing. They forked again and on their left was a svelte black bird whose feathers shimmered with blue, brown, and black iridescence when the light caught them at just the right angle.

"Some of my fursonas are more masculine," said the Devonian-Lion in a rumbling bass voice.

"While others are a way for me to explore my femininity," said the Devonian-Bird in a lilting sing-song cadence.

"And so, after a fashion, I realized that my fursonas were still a part of me. They would only manifest when I forked however. Curiouser still, I do not have the ability to affect which one of them pops out of me. I've theorized over the decades that it's related to my emotional state at the time I fork, but how do I pinpoint the emotional cues that will get me 'goat' or 'snake'? A rhetorical question, I assure you. I wasn't that interested in finding out honestly. As I forked and merged back down, I noticed that my physical appearance would slowly shift to accommodate more and more of the appearance of the fursona that had most recently merged."

The bird and lion forks of Devonian quit and merged back into Devonian. "Now come over here, if you please, and observe."

Ernie got out of his recliner and made his way over to Devonian. They motioned for Ernie to look at the intersection of fur along their arm. Ernie had to squint to see it, but sure enough, the pattern of fur along their arm was slowly changing and shifting to match the light yellow of the lion's fur. Devonian shifted around in their seat and ran their claws along the ends of their coat tails. Ernie could see that they were now longer than they were previously. Not only that, but the material they were made of wasn't fabric at all, but was instead hundreds of finely layered black feathers. Devonian's coat tails were actually wings. They had a slight shimmer of iridescence to them that matched Devonian's bird fork. They rustled their wings gently and Ernie took that as a hint to stop staring and back off.

"While it did take a while to adjust, I'm fortunate that uploading really did help me to achieve my transition goals."

"And what were those?" Ernie asked without thinking. He cringed slightly and hoped that Devonian did not take the question personally.

Devonian did their best to grin without showing teeth. "To be utterly incomprehensible and unable to be discreetly defined. My existence as a chimera is a blessing for me, but I understand why it would be difficult for others to experience the same. The reason I come to the meetings is less about venting my own frustrations and more about giving other people an example of a way to live with constant change as a positive aspect. I could scarcely count the number of late-into-the-night conversations that Samantha and I have had over living with a constantly changing appearance on the System."

"In a way, it is a closer approximation to phys-side life that we've lost in uploading. As we age, our appearance is always gradually changing, but that process stops after uploading. It's actually one of the things that helps the System to feel more realistic to me. That's a comfort," Samantha said.

"Thank you everyone for sharing your experiences with Ernie today. I really do appreciate that you are willing to open up like that. Now, there's no pressure to share if you don't want to. It is your first meeting after all. Do you want to tell us about yourself Ernie?"

Ernie became acutely aware of the fact that he was standing in the middle of the circle and everyone's attention was squarely on him. He was less nervous than he expected. After seeing all of the support the group gave each other, he felt less awkward talking about his issues. If anything, he felt like his weren't enough in comparison.

"Well, I'm Ernie. Just 'Ernie' if you please. I don't think my problems quite stack up to y'all, but I'll tell my story."

He took his mesh cap off his head and fiddled with it in his hands.

"I worked as a trucker for my whole life. Driving was in my blood and it was something I was pretty damn good at, if you don't mind me braggin' a tad. Even with my love of the open road, I was having trouble keeping up. The kinds of shifts I had to pull were getting more and more dangerous and I wasn't getting any younger. So, I hatched myself a little retirement plan of uploadin'. But y'see the trouble was that it was still too expensive for me. I had to try and save towards it, but that meant I would have to pick up more work. It was incredibly stupid of me, but I would drive for sixteen to twenty hours a day trying to get that little extra money. As you can imagine, I didn't get any sleep and it took its toll on me. I was tired and listless always, but I held onto that hope of gettin' to the System. I had heard so many stories of what was possible here that I felt like killing myself was worth the chance. And I just about did. My tiredness caught up with me and I got into a hell of an accident. No one but me and my truck were hurt, but I was in a bad way. I was told I wouldn't be able to drive my truck, or what was left of her, even after I recovered. I don't know who in Heaven took pity on me, but shortly after I got the news in the hospital, I heard about the new initiative of paying folks to upload. I didn't have a lot of family I kept up with, so I wasn't sure I even qualified. Thankfully, they were nice enough to swing a deal where they'd use the money to pay off my medical debt and set me up with a little reputation in the System with what was left over."

He took a moment to collect himself and put his hat back on his head.

"I don't want to disappoint you folks, but I'm not going to be forking as a demonstration. You'll just have to trust me when I tell you that whenever I fork my body decides that it's gonna try and catch up on all that sleep I missed phys-side. It's not a big obstacle, but it is annoying to have to deal with. My fork ends up sleeping for about an hour or two and then wakes back up groggy as all hell. I can't tell you the number of times my fork has shown up after me when I go someplace."

Ernie stopped talking as he noticed the rest of the group were trying their best to keep smiles off their faces. He felt as if he might have missed a joke, but he wasn't sure what would be funny. Then it hit him like a semi.

"Wait a minute, don't tell me..."

Melanie called out to an adjacent door in the room and said, "Alright Ernie, you can come back in now."

Ernie's jaw hit the floor as he saw himself walk through that enormous wood door and stand next to Melanie. He looked pleased as punch that their little plan worked so well. Ernie pointed a finger at his original instance and started cussing him out.

"You know damn well how hard it is for me to open up to new folks and you go and do a cockamamie stunt like this? How long have you been standing back there?"

The Ernie by Melanie laughed and said, "Calm down now, I wasn't trying to be mean. I actually warned the group straight away in case you showed up later so they wouldn't have cause to fuss. If it makes you feel any better, you were a lot better at listening to these fine folks than I was."

"Well, this is grand! This is *grand!* I'm glad you all had a laugh at ol' Ernie's expense." He hiked up his pants, pulled up his sleeves, and marched over to the original Ernie.

"And as for you, smartass. Have a little treat for yer trouble."

He wound up for a punch and before it could connect, he quit and merged down. The impact traveled to the original Ernie as he was knocked back a few steps from the force of the merge. Melanie rushed over to him and he waved her away.

"I'll be fine. Just a little shook up. He was mad with a capital M. I've got it on good authority he'll get over it."

Melanie gave a nervous half-smile and said, "I think there's one last thing we need to take care of before we end our session today. Devonian, could you grant Ernie that final ACL privilege?"

Devonian waved one of their clawed hands in a flourish and Ernie felt a gentle sensorium ping. He laughed and said, "Well shucks. I guess you got me back for him after all." Then turned to Melanie and asked, "The whole time?"

She nodded and said, "We've found it's better to meet a smaller group first beforehand. Less chance at getting overwhelmed that way."

Ernie walked over to the corner of the office. He placed his hand on the intersection of the walls and gently pushed with his fingers. The walls of the office teetered backwards and fell down around them with a tremendous crash. The support group were standing within the interior of an office room placed smack dab in the middle of an enormous botanical garden that stretched as far as his eyes could see. In the distance, he could see people talking in small groups like theirs, and Ernie felt a little less lonely here on the System.

"We're not exactly a typical clade, by the definitions of the System, but you'll have a place here if you want it," Melanie said.

"Thank you, Melanie. It's a lot to take in, but I think I'm willing to try."

"Does that mean I can count on you coming to next week's meeting then?" Samantha asked.

"Yeah, I'll be here."

"Splendid! Melanie, make sure to get Ernie's measurements before he leaves so that I can check my closet for his outfit for next week. I've got to catch up with Sharon and Jennie before they leave. Ta-Ta for now!" She walked briskly away towards another group of people.

David cleared his throat and said, "I'm gonna take off myself. I'm feeling pretty lousy about what I did and I wanna apologize while it's fresh on my mind. Catch ya later!"

Without another word David stepped from the sim and was gone in a shimmering flash.

"Don't worry, I'm not leaving yet. But I do want to stretch out my wings a little bit. Having more grackle in me has given me an itch to perch. I'll be over at the massive arch covered in purple and blue flowers across from the miniature weeping willow tree."

They quickly unbuttoned their suit jacket and let their wings expand out behind them in a massive *floomph* of feathers. A flap and a wave later and they were high into the sky.

"Are you up for meeting more people today? I'd understand if you're burnt out," Melanie asked.

"Y'know I think I could. But let's take it slow. I'd love to just walk around a while. It's a real pretty sim you've got here."

"I forget how nice it is until I bring in new folks. The plants are top-notch. I heard a rumor that the person who designed this sim studied under Serene; Sustained And Sustaining."

Ernie shook his head and said, "I'm sorry Melanie, but I don't know who you're talking about. Whoever they are, they must have been a good teacher."

Melanie elbowed Ernie playfully in his side and said, "You've gotta get out more Ernie. Speaking of, I'm feeling a bit peckish myself. There's a cafe a little ways down that I bet we could persuade into serving you a reuben."

Ernie chuckled and said, "I could eat. Worked up quite the appetite talking yer ears off."

She offered her arm to him and he hooked his arm into hers and they walked leisurely towards a cafe filled with folks who understood how it felt to be different.

Michael Miele

Cowboy

Alexandria Christina Leal

Peace System — 2200

"Be honest with yourself. Ideally always, but especially when it's the harder road to take."

— Eleanor Fenix

I: Evi

Therapist's Note: Evi Pirth is a 38 year old female of Chinese-Irish descent with a complex psychiatric and psychosocial history. She is gainfully employed as a principal researcher at Better Worlds Incorporated, and is seeking therapy in order to "expand my cognitive toolkit, after a marked increase in Apygmaliophobiac anxiety." (patient's words). In our first session, she detailed to me her background in brief, and gave me both permission and proper paperwork in order to follow up with all providers involved in her mental health care for the past ten years. She also gave me permission to share details of her case with other practitioners undergoing a residency with me prior to accreditation. As such, I have inserted several footnotes for further clarification.

Evi stared at her therapist, an older balding man with spectacles so large on his narrow face that she half wondered if he wore them for show instead of medical necessity.

"You don't seriously expect me to answer his fucking question, do you?" She asked.

He gave his usual *"You've all asked me not to intervene in these things, so as long as nobody stops anyone from speaking to me, do whatever you want—although, I reserve the right to comment as I choose"* shrug.

There was no one else besides the two of them physically present in the room.

> TN: Evi listed DID, Post Traumatic Stress Disorder, Depression, and Specific Anxiety Disorder (eco-anxiety, System-based) under current mental health conditions; though she stated that she is not explicitly seeking therapy for these conditions, it is important to understand how these impact her life. Let's start with a refresher, as some of you may be unfamiliar with the first one.

She glared at her therapist, sighed, and then addressed the person not physically present in the room.

> TN: Dissociative Identity Disorder, as the name of the condition illustrates—and despite its common association for much of the 20th and 21st centuries with multiple personalities (due in no small part to the original name)—is a disorder primarily characterized by disassociation.

> What is common sense today, that plurality (the existence of multiple personalities within a single brain)

is a naturally occurring neurodivergence, would have been radical to practitioners as recently as the early 21st century. Hindsight as they say, is 20/20. However, even without the modern knowledge of the brain that would have seemed unimaginable two centuries ago, some practitioners at that time were already putting together much of the pieces of our modern knowledge of the condition. Whether this factored into the rename has been sadly lost to time, but the new name is an uncanny prediction of the following two centuries of hard data.

How can DID be so overwhelmingly (but not exclusively or uniformly!) caused by early childhood trauma? How can it be present in both covert and overt forms, or go undiagnosed for decades at a time? How does it manifest in everything from a few years of missing memory around a single traumatic event to persistent, daily blackout? And, of course, how can someone suffering from it be unaware that they have the condition? Because it is not a factor of multiple personalities, but of a failure to form either a single or multiple identities in a non-dissociative fashion.

"No, Eliah[1], my reticence towards uploading is not motivated by what I experienced when I integrated with Felina. Nice theory, cowboy. But you're wrong about it, just like you're wrong about uploading."

---

[1] Eliah. The cowboy. In teletherapy he is an older man with spurs and a cowboy hat to match. His clothing and attitude are what they used to call "salt of the Earth".

> TN: Felina is a common source of contention, and some-
> one I've unfortunately never had the opportunity to
> meet. Shortly before I met Peace, a large portion of the
> system integrated[2], and Felina became a part of Evi[3].

"Oh yeah, okay. Sure Evi. I believe that. You're just doing your job, protecting the system[4]. Nothing to do with your and Felina's integration. Well, thank you kindly for your protection, I don't know what any of us would do without you. You're an absolute saint! Hey, speaking of being a saint, have, uh... you told Dr. Woodward here–" Their physical body leaned back in the chair, and Eliah crossed his legs as he gestured lazily at the therapist "–about those prophetic dreams you keep having, the ones that keep predicting my day?"

> TN: Eliah has a southern drawl, or seems to. I'm not en-
> tirely unconvinced that some of the mannerisms unique
> to each personality aren't played up in front of me just

---

[2] In its original use, this term referred exclusively to all personalities becoming one. Sys-side and phys-side breakthroughs over the years in both general psychology and treatment of dissociative disorders have led to the suite of techniques used today to treat dissociative disorders, and the re-popularization of this term amongst those who treat DID in order to refer to the breaking down of dissociative barriers and the retraining of the brain to use other adaptation mechanisms as a first line of defense.

[3] Prior to this, her and Evi had been at odds with each other for most of their lives. Another personality, Zia, speaks quite fondly of her. Which is more than a tad sad given for much of her existence she seemed to occupy the classical archetype of Persecutor.

[4] Although for the past ten years, Evi has filled the role of the "host", she was originally slotted into the binary of protector personality. In her own words, Evi came into existence to protect Peace from "the internecine conflict that erupted between my father's and mother's sides of the family shortly before her death, as well as the large swaths of time I was left alone in the care of my... unwell... paternal grandmother."

a bit in order to keep me from confusing folks for each other.

"What the fuck are you talking about, Eliah?" She turned toward Dr. Woodward. "Do you have any idea what he's talking about?"

Their therapist shook his head.

"Right okay, let me jog your memory, Felina, Evi, whichever you are now. You have large leathery wings, two pointy horns, and you're *fucking riding my ass every goddamn day!*"

> TN: Personal insults between these two are common, as you've likely noticed. In this case, it's a dig at her integration with Felina, who Zia (another personality, who I rarely get the chance to meet) informed me took the form of some sort of bat creature in both their head and in sims on the 'net. She believes this form stemmed from the system's origin[5] as well as Felina's original role as a persecutor. Both Eliah and Evi have different opinions.

Evi's face filled with instant offense as she took the front. "Oh *fuck you, cowboy.*"

"I have a name!"

"Yeah, Asshole McWestern."

"Doctor Jackass!"

Dr. Woodward sighed and set down his tablet. None of what would happen next would be noteworthy. He was used to this.

---

[5] Zia's words: "When I was about seven, my mother and I were in a car accident. She died shortly after impact, and I was suspended upside down in the car staring at her body for several hours until the rescue workers located us. That's where Felina comes from. Also, there's probably some influence there from the 'fucking vampire, bleeding us dry' speech that grandpa always gave dad. Can we just... not talk about that shit today?"

Evi clutched her face in her hands and moaned in frustration. "Why are you doing this on a Friday? Why are you pushing so hard on this? Why do you *always do this?* Why do you always pick some fucking hill to die on every single Friday? Why uploading, why now, why with me?"

"Oh my god, I've told you a thousand times why! And you never listen! I don't understand it one bit. You used to love the System, found uploading romantic. And now you act like you don't understand why anyone would want to. You're smart Evi—you've got a Ph.D for God's sake—So why won't you even listen to anyone about uploading? Is it because you think it's my idea? You're going to drive me to drink. I just don't get it!"

"Oh please. You've already driven me to drink and you know it."

"I know how smashed you're going to get tonight, yeah, and I'm concerned."

"It's a Friday, Eliah."

"You're dodging my question!"

Dr. Woodward coughed awkwardly. Evi shot him a look of mild embarrassment and apology. Before they could continue the argument, he cleared his throat and interrupted. "I'd like to hear from Zia." Their eyes blinked, and he felt like both of them were looking at him as if he had said *"I would like the moon to be made of cheese."*

"Why?" Evi said, pursing her lips.

"I think Zia would've told me, if that was the case." Eliah followed up, cocking his head slightly to the side.

Dr. Woodward sighed. He could feel the suspicion in the air. It was like being surrounded by a pack of wild dogs. He wasn't keen on dealing with this today, either. "Then perhaps each of you can summarize your thoughts on the other's motivations. You've both been doing a lot of talking past each other today, and not a lot of listening. I'm not sure that is the wisest use of your time. Perhaps thinking about how the other views the world might lead to more, productive outcomes?" It was a long shot...

"Alright."

... but somehow, it seemed to be working.

"Yeah, sure."

"I'll start." Evi responded far too quickly, which was when Dr. Woodward suspected that he had in fact, hit on something rather deep. Hopefully, they were finally getting to the root of the issue. He picked his tablet back up. "Eliah, thinking about your motivations from your perspective, I am forced to come to the conclusion that you don't *have* any deeper motivations, which is why none of your actions make sense to me. Sure, you think you have deeper motivations. But at the end of the day, you've never moved past being the good guy in your own story, literally and metaphorically—by the way, you're not even the good guy in your own story[6]. Opinions of losers on the 'net be damned. You've never moved past being Zia's personal protector. Past the system integrating, past there only being three of us now. You need to move forward, move on past being a cowboy. Your girl's all grown up."

Dr. Woodward beat the cowboy to the draw. "Eliah. Do you need time to–"

"Nah. I've had enough time doc. I've got this all prepared." He cleared his throat. "Evi, you need to get over our ex[7], and admit that you blame the existence of the rest of us for your breakup. You resent

---

[6]Eliah is based off of a fictional character. Isn't DID a fascinating condition? However, his origins are often yet another point of contention.

[7]A woman named Eleanor who had a fairly complicated relationship with Evi. Multiple members of the system credit her with saving their lives. The relationship

us all for it, but especially me. This is why, since you integrated with Felina and the others but got broken up with anyway, you lost the plot. You did the work, but you still lost the girl. This makes you feel awful, and is why you have ignored Zia, your job, and your own health. It's also why when I picked up the slack, you decided to blame me most of all, because I accomplish what you can't. Please move on, from both your ex and your irrational hatred of me. Yours truly, Eliah."

Well shoot. That hadn't gone how he had hoped. But maybe, just maybe.

"Thank you, Eliah. Now, I would like you both to take a few minutes to think about what the other person said before respo–"

"You motherfucker how dare you bring her up–"

"How have you managed to make it feel like you're on an entirely different continent when we share the same brain? Do enlighten me, Evi."

"I wish you could feel what it was like to be me for even one day."

"If you'd open up to me for a single fucking minute, then maybe I would–"

"Maybe I would if you were actually a good person instead of just someone who dressed up like one."

"I don't need this. Go spend your night getting drunk off your ass."

"It's called coping, and it's the only way I can stand living in the same head as you."

Dr. Woodward sighed. "I was going to ask if either of you felt that the other accurately understood the other, but I can already tell–"

---

did not work out, and seems to be a source of guilt for all of them, but particularly for Evi.

"Nope."

"Yeah, no."

"At least there's one thing we agree on." Evi shot back.

Woodward sighed and glanced at the clock. "Well. I believe our time is up. I'll see you all next week. Oh, and one last thing." They were already halfway to his office door. "I trust you'll *both* drink responsibly."

False affirmations followed.

"Of course we will."

"Evi prefers self-destructing in her own home, so it's not like we're going to ruin anything besides a public sim. The 'net is where she spends most of her time these days anyways."

"Eliah stays up until God only knows, and I don't know what trouble we could even get ourselves into at that time of night. It's not like anyone is awake."

Woodward frowned. "Just don't make any permanent decisions that either of you may regret later. I know the last few months have been hard, but you've both come so far, and there are some things in life that are quite irreversible."

"Oh come on. What do you think I am going to do, get so drunk I don't notice him walking into an Ansible clinic?"

"You see how paranoid she is about me?"

Woodward's frown deepened, and he sighed. "I'll see you both next week. Please do try to treat each other nicely and don't die of alcohol poisoning."

> TN: The Peace system falls into an odd grey area here
> that illustrates just how complex this condition can be
> to treat. Although the Peace system is obviously able to

cooperate to an extensive degree and does not suffer working memory blackouts that impede the feat of carrying on a conversation with each other out loud; Peace lacks anything that could be describe as a shared coherency, a shared sense of consciousness or purpose, or an absence of all dissociative barriers. The presence of one or more of these states of existence is regarded as a key treatment milestone.

I worry about them.

*

Eliah grumbled as he walked down the hallway. Another wasted session, more wasted time. Evi had promptly told him to "fuck right off" and squirreled herself up somewhere in their head. Of *course* she was going to force him to make the trip back. He had half a nerve to–

And that's when he heard Zia's voice. "Eliah."

Instantly, he softened, just a bit. "Mm?" He grumbled, not quite feeling like responding. He still felt burned after being denied even the semblance of personhood once again.

"Eliah."

"Yeah. I hear you." He muttered.

"I have an idea."

"I'm all... ears, kiddo." He paused, looking at a picture of a really fucked up cat. Or fox. He couldn't tell. It was definitely all ears though. Where did these types of paintings even come from anyway? Was there a therapist's office décor supplier?

"Okay so, please don't hate me for this."

"I couldn't hate you if I tried, you know that."

"Yeah I do. I just. Okay..." He could hear her taking deep breaths.

"Spit it out."

"Hypothetically, like, in a video game hypothetically. What if, when Evi got really drunk... We just walked into an Ansible clinic and uploaded anyway?"

He stopped in his tracks. "Well *shit*. Zia. That's..."

He paused, adrenaline racing up his spine. "That's not half a bad idea..."

II: Eliah

Like most things in his life lately, Eliah's memories of the most important decision in any of their lives was clouded by alcohol. Had they been arguing about Eleanor? He'd definitely been drinking, he knew that. But the other details he didn't remember in whole. It was like a shard of fractured glass. The main thing that pierced through was Zia's voice.

"Eliah. Think about what you're doing. Please. Like, I'm as shocked as you are that this is working but..."

"I know what I'm doing," he slurred under his breath; his voice unsteady. He was half panting in exhaustion from hauling himself up the steps to the clinic. He leaned against a rail. "I'm doing what you want, right?"

She sighed. "Yeah. But... I wish it didn't have to fucking be like this."

"I do too, but it is what it is. It's now or never."

"Yeah. I know."

He stumbled up to the door, paused, turned around, and looked around at the dirty grey and black of the city, the ugly concrete and black sleet of the numerous office buildings flecked at every point by red dust. Overhead, the moon hung low in the sky. He wished that he had a hat, so he could tip it goodbye. They stood there silently, for a few seconds, taking it all in, before turning around, walking up to the automated doors of the clinic, and entering.

"Rest. I'll take care of it."

"Thank you."

He gave the mental equivalent of a nod, then realized he had said both parts of the conversation out loud. His heart rate spiked as he looked around. He would have rather assumed no one had noticed, but long dulled instinct prompted him to glance at the front desk clerk out of the corner of his eyes. His heart rate slowed. Just as he suspected, either no one noticed, or no one cared. Why was no wonder. They were hooked up to a rig. Eliah shook his head. *What was even the point of having a flesh and blood person in this place if they were going to be hooked up to the net anyway?*

"*Are you of sound mind to undergo this procedure?*" a voice buzzed in his ear.

Turning his attention back to his goal, he placed his hand back onto the panel.

"Yes."

There was a brief pause as every inch of his vitals were measured up to some baseline.

Somehow, he very much doubted that being within that baseline actually mattered.

"*Are you undergoing this procedure consensually?*"

"Yes."

Another brief pause, another scan. More nonsense.

"*...based on these criteria and your CIN, your family may qualify for Uploading Benefits as per–*"

He chuckled. If there was one thing that they could all agree on, it was fuck those people. "Next question."

"Are you sure that you don't wish to-"

He let it finish, just in case it took hastily answering into account. But mentally, he had already checked out.

"Next question."

"Would you like to upload?"

"Yes."

"Do you understand that this is an irreversible procedure, carrying with it a risk of mortality?"

"Yes."

"Would you still like to upload?"

"Yes."

"Understanding that this is an irreversible procedure that carries with it a risk of mortality, do you want to upload?"

"Yes."

He could 'see' Zia next to him. Her lip was curled, she was looking away. He wanted to put his hand on her shoulders, reassure her, but there wasn't a way to do so without being noticed; the clerk was disconnecting from their rig, blinking as their eyes readjusted to the 'real' world. Outside, the city's emergency sirens roared as a dust storm tumbled over buildings. The clinic doors automatically closed in response; the filtration system went from a slight din to a howl.

"Alright, Miss... Pirth? Right this way, please."

Mentally, he checked in again with Zia.

"This is what you want, right kid?"

The mental equivalent of a nod.

"Good, let's get out of this shithole."

Cowboy

He turned to the clerk, doing his best imitation of Evi's sickeningly sweet smile. "After you, please."

The clerk chuckled and shook their head, evidently their mind was elsewhere. "Yeah, one of these days."

The sirens grew louder, and the protective metal screens unfolded slowly from the building, creaking as they extended to cover the windows. Eliah and the attendant watched as they locked into place just in time; a loud *thunk* echoing throughout the building as bits and pieces of rock and concrete crashed into the side of it.

The clerk shook their head, looking on with eyes dulled with false hope and endless determination "First chance I get, I'm getting out of here too."

III: Evi

An irreversible decision, in an instant.

Later, she would mull over everything that led to this point.

On some level, she should have seen this coming. On some level she wondered if she *had* seen this coming.

After all, it wasn't like during the lowest points in their dying relationship, she hadn't leveraged the omnipresent threat of uploading over Eleanor...

Control over the system—the DID system—wasn't a perfect thing, especially not when it came to Eliah. But, as she was fond of reminding herself, she did—or at least *should*—have control. And usually, when it came down to the really important things, she *was* in control. Eliah might be able to wrestle it away for a short time to make an impromptu decision, but he could only grab it for longer time periods or more important decisions if she was either particularly triggered or particularly inebriated. When it came down to brass tacks, she had spent *years,* not to mention the better part of a half a decade long failed relationship, strengthening her control over the others who lived in her brain into an iron fist.

So why had she failed? Why, at the most pivotal moment, with the rest of the system depending on her, with Zia depending on her, with all of her preparation, and her power, and every tool at her disposal, why had she failed?

A part of her worried very much that the reason she failed was simple: because she never really wanted to succeed.

At first, it felt like she was waking up. She had the half-formed memory of a distant trauma in her mouth. But it was blurred, like something viewed through a film grain. She tried to remember what had happened before, and bumped into a couple of realizations that demanded greater attention.

1. She was naked.
2. She was not in her bedroom.
3. Something felt *wrong* in her brain.

I'm dead. She thought. *I'm dead. I've died. That's the only possible explanation for what is happening.*

"We will now go through some assorted questions that you might be asking yourself:

- 'Am I dead?' No, you are not dead. You are inside of the System.
- 'What happened to my body?' As you did not specify post upload handling of your physical form prior to your upload; your ashes will be–"

Evi blinked. She did not know how much time had passed. The twin snakes of disassociation and derealization were overwhelming, but this time their poison tasted subtly different.

Something was so, so wrong.

She did not know how long it lasted, but she let out a scream. Nondescript faces, indistinct jumpsuited figures turned to stare at her.

At the front of the non-room, a very nonplussed anthropomorphic, suit wearing... *skunk*—certainly a furry of some sort—with her longer headfur tied back in a conservative fashion paused, frowning, pulling her gaze away from a gold pocket watch to glance down at her. The very face of efficient bureaucracy, upset at the inefficiency of being interrupted.

She stared down at her skin, so unfamiliar after years of seeing another person's form, another person's skin. Every mole, every freckle. Every blemish and imperfection was there. Just like she remembered it to be.

She cried out into the night, gone, gone, it was all *gone*–

"*Miss Pirth.*"

She blinked. She was sitting in a grey room, across from the skunk. She was still naked.

The skunk sighed. She was looking away. "Miss Pirth, *please* clothe yourself."

She could barely speak, she tried to take in the room, and found she couldn't.

"The room is nondescript on purpose to get you to focus on the here and now," the skunk said, as if reading her thoughts. "Now please, picture yourself wearing the clothes that you wish, and want it. You *do* want to be clothed, yes?" The skunk peered over the rim of what could only be described as librarian glasses.

She thought of how she had been dressed all those years ago, her comfortable orange athleisure shirt, her cargo jeans, sports bra, undergarments, the combat boots she had gotten so used to wearing, her hair in its usual bun. She added the more recent addition, the lab coat, for some extra flair.

She opened her eyes; and saw that it was so.

The skunk nodded her head. Pleased was the wrong word, but she at least looked significantly more *neutral* than she had before. "Very good. Now, are you ready to rejoin the rest of the class?" She tapped on her pocket watch, as if to emphasize the invisible schedule that Evi had interrupted.

She tilted her head. "Where– how... *I don't belong here.*" She whined. "Please, please, please tell me this is a dream please oh god no I can't– I can't be here I shouldn't be here I–"

The skunk waited while Evi talked herself down from hyperventilating. Sat there, patiently as Evi went through three or five panic attacks. As she came up from the last one, the ashes of her hopes and dreams fading into nothingness around her, the skunk cleared her throat. She looked up.

The skunk's frown returned, deeper this time. Followed by a loud sigh. Her clipboard was gently shaking. Presumably, she was resisting the urge to snap her pen in half. And then the neutral expression returned, and an identical skunk appeared next to her; clipboard and all.

"What– I don't... Huh?" Evi was dumbstruck. The skunk in the chair nodded to her counterpart, who promptly vanished. "Fuck! What was that?!"

The remaining skunk frowned deeper. "Well, this illustrates how much you were paying attention. Unfortunately for you, you *need* to have been paying attention; because *this,* miracle though it may be–" She gestured to the space around them. "–will not pay attention for you. Nor will it prevent you from becoming so panicked that you cannot act on knowledge that you have. However, on the low probability that you were listening to what I said, you should be able to remember everything I carefully enunciated prior to your..." the skunk waved a paw dismissively and lowered her glasses, doing air quotes that seemed to take on a life of their own, "little freakout... *s.*"

Somehow, the pluralization took up accusatory space.

Evi blinked. The skunk stared at her. This went on for a few minutes. The pocket watch ticked the time by, omnipresent.

"If you are going to just sit there and do nothing, then it logically follows that this will take all day. And unfortunately for us both, we *have* all day. Luckily, we have all of eternity, though I do rather doubt this will take that long." The skunk lowered her glasses again, and Evi unintentionally scooted her chair back. Prompting a rather unfortunate screeching sound and a wince from both of them.

The uncomfortable silence went on for a few moments longer.

"Eternity?"

The skunk sighed. "You are in the System now, surely you have *some* idea of how it works. There is–"

This too, continued.

After a while, Evi shook her head and the skunk sighed.

"Well–" Evi opened her mouth, interrupting. "There, were two of you."

The skunk frowned. "One: do not interrupt me. Two: correct. There were two of me. And that is called...?"

"Forking," she answered instantly, and with a start, everything she had gathered about forking before the skunk had pulled her away from class into this private room flooded her mind.

"Correct." The skunk nodded, but Evi wasn't listening.

She had turned away and clasped her hands over her mouth, as if to block some invisible knowledge from exiting, but to no avail. While some of the memories around what the skunk dismissively called her "little freakout" were rather hazy, everything — including the panic attack itself—was in pitch-perfect detail. "Oh, no. Oh no no no no," she stammered. "Oh no– This can't be happening. This *cannot* be happening." She could feel herself starting to hyperventilate again.

The skunk huffed, and a cup of tea on a saucer appeared out of thin air. She stirred it twice, then tapped the spoon on the rim of the cup. "It is normally considered rude to hand to someone you have only recently met tea laced with pharmacologically calming substances, even if you inform them of it beforehand." The skunk continued to mutter to herself with such speed that Evi didn't catch a bit of what was said. "And even if, unlike your down-tree, you actually have studied dispensing neurologically altering substances *in virtu*, not to mention actually doing coursework in therapy and psychiatry instead of just *LARPing*..." She trailed off into grumbling for a few seconds before catching herself. She cleared her throat and peered over her glasses at Evi.

"But, in light of the circumstances of how much of my time you have taken up, I feel that I have earned a *bit* of rudeness." She thrust the tea into Evi's hands. "Drink up."

Evi blinked. "I don't understand."

The skunk furrowed her brow and lowered her glasses. She stretched back her muzzle (lips? Did skunks have lips?) in what Evi guessed was an attempt at restraining a growl—or perhaps she was getting ready to growl. One of the two.

"Drink. This. And. Take. Deep. Breaths. *Now.*"

She couldn't tell skunk emotions well, but *fucking pissed off* was universal, and one she knew too well. So, she drank the tea, and under the skunk's watchful eye breathed in and out. It was hard, but with the skunk's encouragement/chastisement ("Acknowledge it, set it aside for later, focus on your breathing...") she managed to get to the point where she could calmly open her mouth and-

"No." The skunk held up a finger to her halfway open mouth. "No, no, no. No, *no.*" The skunk pointed a claw at herself. "I am talking. You are listening."

She blinked, and the skunk clutched at her clipboard all the tighter. "I am not..." There was a pause that felt about five seconds longer than it should. "... unsympathetic to what you have described yourself as going through. But it is critical that you learn how to safely navigate the System, and-" She frowned at her timepiece. "-that we do it before you have another panic attack. I am not chasing a bunch of panicked, half naked forks through most of the public sims on the server. I do not pay myself enough for that."

Before she could ask about... well, any of that, the skunk tapped the teacup into the ether, and then gently grasped Evi's empty hands and pulled her into a standing position before quickly letting go. The skunk paused to flatten some creases on her dress, clear her throat, and center herself. It was the quickest 'I am ready' that Evi had ever seen. If she blinked, she would have missed it. That was, assuming she even still blin-

"We have gone over articles of clothing, so let us go over everything else. Starting with, our location. Where are we?"

Evi paused, unsure if she was supposed to answer.

The skunk began to speak, and as she did, something...*happened* out of Evi's mouth. "Aetherbox#00000053" Evi said, *knowing* instantly that that was where they were. It was as though her mouth was on autocomplete.

The skunk smiled, nodding. "The System does not witness things for you, but it *does* remember things for you, and for anything stored in the perisystem architecture, it does so on demand."

Before she could ask questions, the skunk continued. "Aetherbox#00000052 is currently empty, let us try heading there."

Once again, the skunk split, and then there were two. One of the skunks curtsied and vanished, but at this point Evi knew what was expected of her. If there was one thing that she was good at it, it was reading other people. She closed her eyes; and was immediately reprimanded. "You do not need to do that."

Ignoring the skunk, she thought "*I want to go to Aetherbox#00000052.*" There was a moment of *something and nothing*, and then she was there. It was identical to the first location, and the skunk gave a little golf clap as she arrived, followed by a bit of a frown.

"You really do not need to close your eyes. It is not necessary."

Evi smirked, "Well it worke–"

"The last lesson is forking." The skunk interrupted, as if Evi's response was simply unimportant in the grand scheme of things. Irrelevant. It made her feel like shit. For every bit of praise the skunk doled out, there was a corresponding something that she had done wrong.

She knew this pattern well. And if she wasn't going to take it in the physical world...

So, she said nothing. She sat there, staring the skunk down.

"Well, I am waiting. Do you require a hint?" The skunk said, tapping a foot.

"I don't want to fork," Evi stated.

"Perhaps not, but you want the reputation bonus that comes with completing this, though, as well as the lack of a very distinguishing 'Refused to complete orientation' box next to your profile."

The skunk clicked open her timepiece again.

Evi had just about had it. "I'm not going to fork."

The skunk slammed the timepiece closed. "This is ridiculous, and you are being very rude. What is your objection? Name it. Teleporter paradox? Worried about losing the coin flip? Read some scary 'net story about the System? Name your objection, we will settle it right here, right now, rather than having you unable to enter the majority of public sims. Surely this is the better outcome–"

"No. I am not going to fork, and I'm not going to explain why. I don't owe this place–" She gestured around. "–jack shit." In a rather uncharacteristic gesture, she held up both middle fingers to the anthropomorphic skunk, whose frown was rapidly deepening into a snarl.

Before she could figure out what part of her speech was the most offensive, the skunk fucking *lost it*. She whipped off her glasses. "*Fuck it.* I have devoted far more individual time to you than any other struggling upload today and you do not show a single care in the world for my efforts. I have tried being nice. I have tried being kind. I have tried being considerate and you have deliberately delayed and interrupted me, and now you dare disrespect the sanctity of this 'place', as you so brazenly call it." She made jazz hands—or jazz paws. "*'This place'? You* do not owe this 'place' *anything,* you claim? You selfish child." The skunk advanced on her, teeth bared. "You have no idea of the sacrifices that were made for this 'place' to harbor you, to hold you, to *protect* you. You are like a dying lamp, scorning the one who refills your oil, thankless and ignorant of the cold darkness that would subsume you if they were but for a moment to falter."

The skunk stopped, and for a brief second, Evi could swear that she saw her form flicker. But in that second, the skunk regained her composure, and just stood there, looking at her. Something about it was terrifying, like she was having her entire soul peered into like some specimen under a powerful microscope. It felt like a violation, an observation she had explicitly not wanted. A demonstration of the power of the person in front of her to see her at every level. "Or perhaps," the skunk said, putting her glasses back on and staring Evi down as she began tearing up. "You desire to be an outcast *here* too. Well, I for one am happy to oblige that utterly nihilistic–"

IV: Zia

At first, Zia assumed that she had simply switched into the front. She assumed that things still worked the same way they did phys-side, and that she was now in control of Evi's body. Although frustrating to her, the lack of her own physical form worked hella well as an ambush tactic when she could lead someone to the conclusion that they were no longer talking to the same individual without openly stating it.

"What the *fuck* is wrong with you?!" she roared. "Like what the fuck is your problem? You're, what, an orientation instructor?

Aren't you supposed to be, I don't know, anything but actively hostile? She kept giving you chance after chance, and you kept doing this passive aggressive bullshit. What the actual fuck is your deal? Leave us the fuck *alone*."

The skunk was shaking, but Zia was so furious she didn't notice it immediately, attributing it to her sudden swap into the front and the subsequent change in the body's mannerisms.

She was ticked. Seeing red. It was bad enough when she had to put up with this from seemingly almost everyone else in her life, but to have it thrust on her by this... stranger? "Like, holy fuck! How can you be so... so– Did you really expect her to, what, fall in love with this place given the reception *you're* giving her?"

Evi's voice was shaky and soft. "Zia."

Again, there was something off, but Zia assumed that whatever mechanism was allowing them to still have internal dialogue was responsible for the offness.

"It's okay. I'm putting this bitch in her place," she said out loud, thinking that she was speaking internally.

"Zia–" A little louder.

The skunk was backing away from her—or, in Zia's stale perception, away from Evi—arms trembling. Gesticulating wildly at Zia, at something else.

"Yeah, you thought you were picking on one person, right? You saw this," she gestured to herself, "and figured, 'Oh, she's not going to fight back.' Figured you could just, what, be a fucking asshole with no consequences?" She advanced towards the skunk, whose hackles were raised in alarm, her teeth chattering.

"Zia–" Evi whined, even louder.

"Not now."

"Well guess what, motherfucker." She did her best Eliah impression, "Actions have consequences."

The skunk *was* flickering now. She could see it. Ghostly apparitions of a human form eerily matched in many an aspect faded in and out, layering the skunk like a hologram. With her shaking hands/paws, she dropped the timepiece.

"Zia!" Evi yelled.

"Shut *up*, Evi!" She yelled back. "I'm in front! Let me do this! Let me do *something* for once."

The skunk was making strange, half-garbled noises, switching her gaze rapidly between the timepiece and Zia.

"Zia *listen to me!*" Evi yelled, grabbing her arm.

Zia stopped in her tracks, and the skunk seized the opportunity to grab the timepiece between her shifting paws/hands and scuttled backwards. Blinking, Zia tried to comprehend what was happening to her. She could *feel* Evi's hands on her. Her stomach dropped, and she looked down.

Instead of their physical body—their *shared* physical body—she saw her *own* body, her *own* arms with every detail exactly how she recalled, and Evi's hand, Evi's actual physical hand, gripping onto her arm. She swallowed and looked over to where the skunk had been pointing only to see Evi—actual, real, *embodied* Evi—standing next to her.

They both had their own body. She hadn't switched in front. There *was* no more front, as far as she could feel. She was alone in her own head, in her own body. Her mouth dropped open, "Holy shit..."

The look on Evi's face cut her off. She was holding a single finger up to her mouth, in a gesture universally understood. When she was sure that Zia would stay still, she took her arm off of hers. Zia marveled at the weight of it. She could *feel* the weight of Evi's hold releasing. She could actually feel it.

As she watched, Evi retracted her now free arm, and held her hand up to her ear in a cupped gesture, still making the *shh* gesture with her free hand. She nodded silently in the direction of the skunk, and that's when Zia realized that the expression on Evi's face was one of horror.

In the corner, the skunk had stopped flickering. She was instead, curled up, clutching the timepiece to her chest and reciting vaguely familiar scripture that made Zia's heart sink and Evi's hands tremble.

Tick!

"*Eili, Eili, lamah azavtani...*"

Zia realized that she had, in fact, fucked up. And, looking over at Evi, the fact that they were *separate* and all its ramifications hitting home, she felt her own panic start to rise. Although the skunk's creepy, pitiful behavior elicited some sympathy from her, she was also an asshole and a potential threat. She would analyze whether she had gone too far later. (Or, she would hear about it from Eliah). But what, exactly, *had* she just done? And where, she wondered, *was* Eliah? If she couldn't feel him, and she couldn't, then that would mean that. She stared at Evi, who was frozen in place, staring at the skunk. Oh fuck no. Oh *fuck* no. And so of course, that was when she noticed the timepiece started ticking louder.

Tock!

My God, my God,
why have You abandoned me;

why so far from delivering me
and from my anguished roaring?

And in the meanwhile...

Tick!

...two skunks forked into being, reciting the same poem...

My God,
I cry by day—You answer not;
by night, and have no respite.

Tock!

...four additional skunks. Evi began to walk forward...

But You are the Holy One,
enthroned,
the Praise of Israel.

Tick!

...there were *sixteen* skunks.

"Fascinating." Evi said, pausing to look at the row of chanting, curled up skunks, before moving towards them. Zia had never been the best at math, but she *knew* what was happening here. And with a start, she realized she knew the name for it too: exponential growth.

Cowboy

In You our fathers trusted;
   they trusted, and You rescued them.

                                                        Tock!

The chanting was deafening. The skunks were *piling on top of each other*. She could no longer even see the original one. Evi held up her hands protectively, as if the sudden instantiation of tens of who knows how many skunks had suddenly displaced the air (did this place even *have* air?) previously occupying the now fluff covered space.

"Evi, wait! I just want to talk!"

The newly straight-laced protector paused with military precision, further tightened the bun she had pulled her black hair into, then turned and shot a glance full of daggers at Zia.

It was if a fire had been lit under Evi's ass, although quite why the change was this dramatic, Zia couldn't begin to comprehend. Was this simply what it looked like from the outside when the other members of the system jumped into action to protect her? She didn't have time to think about it further, because three identical Evis forked into being, rushing towards Zia. She tried to dodge, but one of the them circled right and grabbed her. Together with the other two, they held her against the non-wall.

"Hello Zia," one of them said. "I'm listening." The System helpfully informed her that the Evi talking to her had two tags, Evi#1 (canonically Evi#00000001), and that the other two were Evi#2 and Evi#3.

Zia struggled. "Not to you, to her!"

To You they cried out
and they escaped;

in You they trusted
and were not disappointed

Tick!

The skunks extended a third of a way across the room. Like a great black-and-white-furred jungle. Evi stood tall before it, looking up and down as if sizing up a tree to cut down. Zia tried her best to yell, but the chanting of the increasingly numerous skunks was starting to drown her out.

"Evi! We can't do this alone! You know we can't do this alone."

The Evis holding her down frowned in near unison.

"Oh?" one of them asked.

"And who would you suggest?" Another finished.

"Eliah?" the third sneered with disdain and sarcasm.

Zia struggled with all her might, biting and thrashing against the combined hold of the Evis, but to no avail. "I don't know! Maybe! Do you have a better idea?"

But I am a worm, less than human;
scorned by men, despised by people.

Tock!

She could see the skunks in the background, looming larger and louder. Evi#3 turned to glance back at the skunks, though she and Evi#2 still held onto her.

Evi#1 laughed bitterly. Her face was a portrait of anger, though it was hard to take seriously with the ever-looming sea of skunks in the background. "Do you understand at all what is going on here?"

All who see me mock me;
they curl their lips,
they shake their heads.

Tick!

The skunks had passed the midpoint of the room, they towered overhead, devouring the table. Zia realized that she had been yelling.

Evi#3 let go and looked around. "Holy mother of–" She turned back around to her compatriots. "We need to move! They'll crush us!"

They both nodded, and together, Evi#1 and Evi#2 painfully twisted her arms behind her back and hastily started to march her towards the far wall. Evi#3 fell in behind them all, walking backwards and staring at the skunks.

"Yes! I get what's going on here! We're going to be crushed by fucking skunks! Evi please! We need him! I need him!" Zia pleaded.

Evi#1 snorted and shook her head, Evi#2 frowned, and Evi#3 muttered, "If I could frown backwards, my hair bun would be frowning at you. I want you to know that. I also want you to stop wasting my precious time."

The other Evis nodded in agreement.

Let him commit himself to the LORD;
let Him rescue him,

let Him save him,
for He is pleased with him.

Tock!

"Wrong, the skunks aren't fucking. Try again, Miss Williams," Evi#1 calmly stated.

Zia burst out a rephrased version in panic, "We're going to be *fucking* crushed by exponentially increasing skunks!"

Evi#3 turned around from her skunkwatch. "Since when did you know the word exponential?"

Evi#1 waved dismissively at her. "Technically accurate, but also wrong. No, let me tell you what's happened. Let me tell you what's *going* to happen."

Zia gulped. Evi had been angry at her before, but never like this. She could read every crease of stress in the woman's face, see her lips settling into a sort of upside down snake of a frown. The anger in her oak-colored eyes was like a fire. For just a moment, the skunks faded into the background.

You drew me from the womb,
made me secure at my mother's breast.

Tick!

"Eliah *uploaded* us. Do you know what that means? What that entails? Remember our friends, like Mateus? We'll never see him again, any of them. Period. Any chance of reconciling with the family? Dead. Gone. Zilch. We might as well not exist. We're in the digital world now, and it means jack shit. You remember, right? The place where people go when they fucking abandon us? Paradise in a bramble of thorns. Limbo is more like it. That's where we are. *That* System. *That* is what that opportunistic, ruthless, double-crossing son of a bitch did for–"

"How can you fucking talk about him like that?!" She bit Evi#1, *hard.*

"You little shit! I'm trying to protect you!" Evi#1 yelled back, stepping away from Zia and clutching her wrist in pain.

I became Your charge at birth;
from my mother's womb You have been my God

Tock!

"Hey, no, we don't talk about each other like that!" Evi#2 glared at her compatriot. "You're better than him."

Evi#1 screwed up her face in disgust, "You're really gonna try to defend him *and* her? Really? She just bit me! And *he* got us uploaded! I don't need this from myself a few minutes before I die or get deleted or whatever."

Internally, Zia winced. What would Evi say if she knew who had *actually* gotten them uploaded? The thought made her even angrier at Evi's presumption of Eliah's guilt. She didn't regret biting her.

Evi#2 let go of Zia and turned to face Evi#1. Meanwhile, Evi#3 was off somewhere in the distance, trying to... well, she had no idea what she was trying to do, but it certainly wasn't holding back the tide of skunks. It looked like she was trying to duplicate the tables, form some sort of barricade against the living wall of skunks. It wasn't working.

Do not be far from me,
for trouble is near,
and there is none to help.

Tick!

"I'm not defending anybody, so you can take your rhetoric and shove it up your ass. Also, how did you take that personally? I *am* you. I'm *checking* you. Think logically. What does what we do, what does protecting this system matter–" Evi#2 began.

"–If we fail." Evi#1 spat at her counterpart.

Evi #2's face twisted into loathing. "Wow. I can't believe I'm saying this to myself. Alright, big guns then. Did you really learn so little from Eleanor? 'If we fail?' And to think I thought I knew myself. I guess the only thing you learned from our therapy sessions was how to gaslight yourself. Seriously what is going on in your head? How am I– ugh, how are *you* coming to these conclusions?"

Many bulls surround me,
mighty ones of Bashan encircle me.

Tock!

Evi#1 made a disgusted sound, it looked like the two instances were a second from going head-to-head.

"It's never been about failure, it's been about doing what's right for *her*. Right for the system," Evi#2 said. "That's what matters."

"Oh, don't give me that self-righteous–" Evi#1 began.

Zia looked up. The multiplying skunks were looming over them like a living tide. There was no sun in Aetherbox#00000052, but if there had been, they would have blotted it out. The Evis continued their war of words, oblivious to it.

This is how I die, Zia thought. *Drowned in a sea of fur. Sunken underneath countless skunks. Suffocating in black and white tails.*

The two Evis were still shouting back and forth at each other, though how much of it was in anger and how much of it was to be heard over the increasing chanting of the skunks; she was unsure of. Evi#2 appeared to be winning.

"That's what separates us, from him!" Evi#2 hollered at Evi#1. "We do what's *right for her.* Even when it costs us. Even when it results in us not getting our way. Even when we go through a break up with someone we wanted to *marry,* even when we suffer that much, we're not tyrants, we're not our predecessor, we're not Eliah, we're not our father. We do right by her, by the system, by ourselves, even when it would be so much easier to just subsume the whole damn system and her in the process. We are honest with ourselves; we don't cut out pieces of our heart and bury them six feet under. That's what you spent years teaching me, Evi! What you learned from Eleanor! How to fucking love ourselves!" Evi#2 shouted at her counterpart."

Evi#1 and Zia shared a glance, they were both equally confused. Evi#2 *also* looked confused.

She froze, her mouth half open, then forked. The person who came out looked *very* different to Evi's 'why yes, I *do* have a Ph.D, thank you very much for noticing!' aesthetic. Her short hair was a greyish brown, her eyes blue and yellow, a long pair of black wings grew from her back, and her skin was a shade or two darker than Evi's. Black ears and a tail the same color as her hair (headfur?) completed the look.

Her original instance quit before any reputation cost could be incurred.

Zia recognized her instantly. "The fuck?"

By the look on Evi's face, she recognized her too.

They open their mouths at me
like tearing, roaring lions.

Tick!

Evi#1's jaw dropped. "Felina?" she asked unbelievably. "But you dissolved! You were gone! You became a part of me!"

"In the fur," the bat said, crossing her arms impatiently. Her tail flit back and forth and she was tapping her claws on her left elbow impatiently. "If you don't believe me, check."

And true to what she said, the perisystem architecture indeed identified her as Felina. Not for the first time, Zia wondered if the System really was that intuitive, or if the members of Peace had a leg up. If, as she'd heard it described, the System was closer to a dream or hallucination, the shared mental space that Peace constructed and inhabited may not be that far off.

If Felina was surprised at who she ended up being, she didn't show it. "By the way, about that 'becoming a part of you'?" She walked over to Evi#1 and tapped her on the nose.

"Don't!"

"Yeah, that was a mistake. Honestly, an even bigger one than that time you tried the carrot with Eliah, and the stick with me. You obviously didn't learn from that, because it looks like the first thing you did after we integrated was ignore everything I brought to the table, and when you couldn't ignore it, you just took a q-tip and shoved it in between your ears!"

Evi#1 was livid, face red with anger, "How fucking *dare* you, comparing all the shit I had to deal with after you and I integrated to Eliah *fucking uploading us.* Do you not have any shame?"

"Oh, I have plenty of shame—guilt too—but unlike you; I can deal with it." Felina looked down, examining her nails for a few seconds, before resuming her pacing around Evi—who looked like she was about to explode. "Evi, I call it like I see it. You know this! It takes a pretty big fuckup to outrank one of the biggest ones we ever made. I regret it. Somehow, me plus you equals your bad side." She snapped some finger-guns Eviwards. "And that's weird, because I used to be the persecutor alter in the system, so I figured newly minted Paladin plus Defender equals Good. But nah. Don't get me wrong, Eliah fucking uploaded us. That shit is *evil.* But you are better than that. So, what's your excuse?"

And there it was again; he was always the villain in their eyes. In *everyone's* eyes but hers.

She couldn't fucking stand it.

My life ebbs away:
all my bones are disjointed;
my heart is like wax,
melting within me;

Tock!

Skunkmageddon. While Evi#1 and Felina kept bickering, the room exploded into Skunkmageddon. Any minute, it would all be over in a sea of black and white fluff. The skunks would rain down from the aether, and all life in Aetherbox#52 not part of the Mephitidae family would end.

And Zia seemed to be the only one who cared. Evi#1 and Felina were too busy glaring at each other and trading insults to pay attention to the end of the world. *And,* she realized. *To me.* It hit her like a lightbulb. She rushed the two of them, and shoved them forward, then she jumped in front of them and pointed at the avalanche of skunks.

"Goddammit look at them!" Zia shouted. "Just fucking bring Eliah out! Fucking let the whole 'Eliah is the worst person in the system' thing go. You both think you're so much better than him, but if I'm going to drown in skunks, I'd rather do it with him than you two!"

Felina looked like she had been slapped. Evi#1 looked on the verge of tears. They both stared at her as the furry end of the world loomed in the background.

"Yeah, Felina, that means you too!" she emphasized before she could falter. Felina looked genuinely hurt. But she had to keep going, she had to get through to both of them. "At least *he* doesn't pretend to be a selfless protector! If I call him on hurting me, he owns up to it! He tries to make up for it! And he expects me to do the same when I hurt him. He makes me feel like a person. That's more than I can say for either of you! You both still act like I'm some fucking traumatized kid!" Zia screamed.

Evi#1 looked absolutely devastated. Like her world had ended. Between the sparring with Felina, skunkmaggedon, and the angry tears yelling up in Zia's eyes, she seemed to be crumbling to pieces. All the fight had gone out of her. She collapsed onto the floor, muttering something about 'what have I done'.

"Zia." Felina said gently, but firmly. "Eliah is a dangerous person. I know. I used to be one. I don't know what he's told, but he went behind everyone's backs, and he uploa–"

"*I got us uploaded!*" Zia shouted. "I can't believe you're still blaming him when I'm the one who got us uploaded and *you two know that!*"

There. It was out. She had said it. She hastily looked between the two of them, searching for signs that they hated her. They didn't look as surprised as she thought they would, though Felina looked like she was desperately trying to refuse reality. The lack of anger concerned her.

"Right? You two know that. You're just denying it. Because I can remember *everything.* I can remember being you, and you, I can remember being him. And now that I have it all in perspective, you two are still wrong about him. So wrong. Yeah, sometimes he's selfish, sometimes he's an asshole, and sure, he's made a lot of mistakes, but you know what? Whatever the reason, when it comes down to it, he *tries* to put me first. He cares about me as more than just a responsibility, even if he fucks up more often than you two do. I *know* that. I can admit that. He can admit it. So, why the fuck can't you two? Why can't you admit that I was the one who fucked up this time? Why does it need to be him?"

The pair exchanged a glance. Evi sighed. "It's not the same. He has a power differential over you–"

"Bullshit. I'm an adult." She spat back.

"Your history means that he–"

"Goddamnit, Evi, you are *choosing* to believe that."

Felina spoke up, having finally resolved whatever internal conflict was gnawing at her. "She's choosing to believe it because if she doesn't, she'll hate you."

Zia shot Felina a quick, grateful look. She had to focus on making Evi understand.

"I'm choosing to care about you." Evi added, very much looking past Zia, not even acknowledging Felina.

"You do, but if you both actually care about me, then you have to at least take a chance to care about him, because that's what I am asking you to do."

Evi reached out a hand, "Zia, I do care about you, you know that–"

Zia closed her eyes, tried to hold back more angry tears, and lashed out; batting away the hand. "No, I don't, because you're not showing it right now. You're not listening to me. I'm asking you to show that by giving him a chance." She met Evi's tear-soaked gaze, there was so much *guilt* in that look. She had never seen Evi like this before.

Felina's gently maneuvered herself next to Evi, ready to envelop her in a hug.

Zia continued. "You haven't been showing it since you broke up with Eleanor, Evi. I get that you resent everyone in here for that. I get it. Okay. I loved her too. I miss her. But that doesn't give you the right to treat someone who is making just as much a genuine effort to care about me as you used to—I say used to because you stopped trying after the breakup—like *shit*. I'm not asking you to forgive him. I'm not asking you not to hate him. But is it too much to ask for you to treat him like a *person*?"

She looked over at the black hole of black fur. "God, we're fucked." She turned back to them and lowered her voice, pleading "Can we just... Can we die together in a sea of skunks in Peace? Like, you know, the thing we named the system after? Can we at least do that?"

Evi was full-on crying. Felina extended her wings, and Evi fell into them, she put her arms around Evi's shoulders and held her, then turned towards Zia, and patted the spot next to the other side of her. Zia walked over, and Felina embraced her with a squeeze of a winghug. It felt just as safe and warm as Zia remembered, and she shoved back some happy tears as she leaned in and attempted to encompass both Felina and Evi in a hug of her own. They sat there for a minute, crying and being awkward and sniffling, until finally Evi looked up at Zia and spoke. Her eyes were full of tears but she seemed slightly more composed.

"I'm sorry." Evi#1 said.

"I am too. And," Felina added, "If I could fork Eliah for you..."

"... I would," Evi#1 finished her sentence. The conviction in her eyes was genuine.

"...I would too." Felina nodded.

Zia looked away. She didn't want to forgive them, and she wasn't going to. Eliah should have been here too, and he wasn't.

But at least they were willing to try. At least they were willing to give him a chance. And that had to count for something.

> *my vigor dries up like a shard;*
> *my tongue cleaves to my palate;*
> *You commit me to the dust of death.*

Dogs surround me;
a pack of evil ones closes in on me,
like lions they maul my hands and feet.

I take the count of all my bones
while they look on and gloat.

They divide my clothes among themselves,
casting lots for my garments.

Tick!

"Thanks," she said, meeting their gazes.

"She's telling the truth, I would know," Felina added, which earned a glare from Evi.

"I know. And I know why neither of you can fork him. Not enough reputation." She sighed.

Evi#1 began to explain anyway. "Neither of us have enough reputation to fork– Wait. How did you know that?"

"Because I pay attention to things." Zia said, nonplussed.

"It's one of your strong suits," Evi responded, smiling slightly. It was the first time she had complimented her since the breakup with Eleanor. Felina clapped Zia on the back and gave her a thumbs up and a grin. Zia grinned back.

"But where did it all go anyway? Did you not give yourself any?" Zia asked.

"No, I'm not that stingy. I got a big chunk of it from Evi, but I gave it all to Evi#3 to try to build... well something that obviously failed." Evi#1 stated.

"Yeah, no shit." Zia responded. It was like they were in the eye of the storm. If the storm was made of skunks. She sighed. "It's okay. You both tried. You listened to me. That's enough." She didn't feel like it was, but...

"We both know it's not. And, I'm sorry. To both of you." Evi#1 said, "I should have done better by you two. I just, I miss her. I miss Eleanor."

Felina wrapped her even tighter in the winged hug, and Zia returned the squeeze. They stayed there for a few moments as Evi#1 cried, and they comforted her.

Wiping the tears off her face, Evi#1 turned to both of them with a sad smile, "Right then. Let's go down with the ship."

Felina dropped her wings, and the chanting was once again overwhelming. The skunks were overwhelming. They had to shout to hear each other.

Together, they all looked up at the skunkpocalypse.

"Last words?" someone shouted

"I can't fucking believe this is how I'm going to die!" Felina yelled.

"For the record, if I had to choose between being crushed by skunks or dying with my bio family, *I would choose the skunks every day of the week and twice on Tuesday!*" Evi#1 said, which got a chuckle out of everyone.

Zia thought about hers for what she felt was way too long, but she was having a hard time coming up with something. It had to be a quote from one of those old movies Eliah loved so much, but *which quote?* There were so many good ones! She couldn't choose. She habitually scratched at her arm, and marveled when she realized she was scratching at the scar she had remembered growing up with, the one that was decidedly absent from their shared physical body. Ughhhh. So many quotes. How could she pick betwe– *lightbulb moment.*

"Fuck! I have a stupid question!"

"*That's* your quote?" Felina asked, tilting her head.

"There are no stupid questions. You've never asked a one, but you better ask it quick because we're all about to die," Evi#1 said.

"If you don't have the reputation, why not just merge back into Evi? Why not have her fork off Eliah? She's closer to the source of this than we are. Oh, wait shit, did she choke to death on fur? When a fork dies can you feel it?"

Evi#1 and Felina exchanged wide-eyed glances at each other.

"I can still merge in," Evi#1 said. "I can still merge down! She's alive! Evi– Uh, Evi Prime is alive!"

"Holy shit, go already!" Felina yelled. Evi#1 gave her and Zia a hug and then vanished. At that moment, a massive wave of skunks rose up, ready to bury them both. "Get behind me!"

Felina attempted to shove her back. Zia shook herself free, a maniac grin on her face. "You don't get to treat me like a kid either no matter how good your hugs are, and this is just way too ridiculous a death to pass up seeing firsthand," she shouted, grabbing Felina's hand tightly in hers.

Felina squeezed back, holding her hand even tighter, then grinned back at her, a wild glint in her eyes.

"Alright then, bring it!" she shouted at the wave of skunks.

"*Fucking bring it!*" Zia hollered.

The skunks continued to chant, as the wave of black and white fur reached higher, higher, and higher.

Cowboy

> *But You, O LORD, be not far off;*
> *my strength, hasten to my aid.*

Tock!

> *Save my life from the sword,*
> *my precious life from the clutches of a dog.*

VI: Evi Prime

So, this was how she died.

Uploaded against her will by Eliah, getting triggered as fuck, and then triggering the fuck out of the orientation mephit.

Dr. Woodward was going to have a *field day* with that.

Evi felt that she was, all things considered, pretty low on the nightmare reaction scale when she got triggered—with some exceptions. Even considering those exceptions, the rare nine or ten, she could never imagine somehow getting anyone but herself killed. And while she knew some folks' nines and tens were way worse than hers, this was something else. As she struggled to move out from under the pile of fluffy, chanting skunks, she decided that exponentially splitting off equally panicked copies of oneself until either the panic ended or the room had no more space for skunks took the fucking cake.

The only bright light to this whole thing is that she could not have been reasonably expected to have predicted and guarded against such a ridiculous circumstance, and thus; she was content.

Did she want to go out another way? For sure. Dying peacefully in her sleep at a ripe old age would most definitely be preferable. But, all in all, since she couldn't change things her only wish was that the skunk would spare her dignity and cover up the accidental manslaughter.

She could imagine it easily. The skunk coming out of her panic attack several hours later to find herself in a room full of herself. She would merge her forks, clean up her appearance, and realize there were several bodies lying on the floor. Perhaps they would have 'X's in their eyes, like in some sort of comic strip. "Oh dear," she would say, frowning slightly. Perhaps she would click and drag them to a trash can. Maybe she would simply delete the sim. Whoever was in charge of these things would poke her about it later, and she would pretend to look it up, before going, "Oh, transfer #812453? A failure. Irrecoverable. I know. So sad. The technicians are already looking into it. I will forward you the details." On the technician's side, the ticket would already be closed. Or perhaps simply never generated.

Really, having her death covered up would be far preferable. Anything besides "Here lies Evi Pirth, crushed to death by panicked forks of a deranged skunk."

Honestly though, she couldn't really blame her. When she really thought about it, the whole chain of causality linked back to Eliah anyway, and he could go fuck himself.

And then the merge happened.

Instinctively, she accepted it. She might have been able to figure out how not to, but she wanted to know what had happened, after all. Why was one of the copies of her that she had sent to protect Zia and keep her out of her way requesting to merge back in? Why was it coming with a feeling Evi could only describe as 'uncomfortably high priority'? It made no sense. The only data point she could go off of was the urgency. And that? *That* made her worried.

So, she accepted, then let out a gasp, gritted her teeth, and gradually softened her expression as she reconciled what she had just thought was true with the conclusions that Evi#1 had reached. None of their experiences were conflicting *per se*, the inherent strangeness of being one person—then two people—then one person but also two people aside, of course. She hadn't expected to tear up, and quickly choked it back, but this was one hard pill to swallow. She suspected that the primary reason she was able to was because that was all she had to do. There were a few new revelations, but deep down she had known most it all along.

She would need to tackle all those feelings later, because as she had accepted the new/familiar data, she had come to a conclusion about the logical course of action that needed to be taken.

And while she was happy from the respite from her own feelings the necessary course of action offered her, she was also gritting her teeth. Because god*dammit* she was salty as fuck about what she needed to do next. She was also surprised, proud, sad, and about twenty other emotions all at once. But as the merge finished and she set things aside, everything devolved into the emotion she'd always known as 'eating crow'.

"*Fuck*," she spat out loud, involuntarily smacking her fist against the ground with leverage she hadn't known she had. She would have been pissed, but as the skunk that had been on top of her shoulder toppled onto her hand and ended its moment of freedom she was once again forced to confront that she was not getting out from under the pile of panicked mephits on her own.

She sighed loudly and deeply, and took advantage of the very brief moment in time before the skunk horde recoalesced. Some of the copies had scattered, just a few feet in front of her. Maybe it was the sudden swearing, the fist, or the pile shifting when she moved her arm. Maybe it was luck. But it was a chance. She fucking despised the idea that forking Eliah off would quite possibly be the last thing she ever did, but it was a way to move forward, a way to not give up.

And, it was the right thing to do for Zia.

She focused on the gap a few feet away, concentrated on forking, and *prayed* that Eliah would end up instantiated flat on his ass, and that it would *hurt.*

And just maybe, if for no reason other than not being crushed by the System's most densely packed pile of skunks, she prayed for him to succeed where she had failed.

VII: Eliah#Fennec

Eliah#Fennec landed flat on his tail, prompting three reactions.

1. Ow! Son of a bitch!

2. Thank you, Evi. (He turned around to thank her, but only an outstretched hand giving a thumbs up was visible. The rest of her was buried under skunks. What a way to go.)

3. Wait, tail? And fennec? Why fennec?

He scrunched his face together and rubbed his sore backside. His brain felt like a hornet's nest. Everything was happening everywhere, all at once. His back hurt, his butt hurt, his tail hurt, and his pride hurt. Was this what it felt like to be born? If so, no wonder babies came out crying.

But he would deal with all of that later. He could *only* deal with all of that later, because right now, he had a mission to accomplish; something to do.

He shoved the entire hornet's nest to the side, did his best imitation of a linebacker, sent a prayer out for Zia's safety, took a few steps back, and roared like an animal as he charged the pile of skunk copies between him, aiming for the original, catatonic skunk in the corner.

For a fennec, he packed a punch. Fur went flying, inway was made, but not enough. He resorted to grabbing individual skunks, maneuvering them as much as he could to create openings he could crawl through. The world was a mountain of skunks he was climbing over, under, and through. System be damned, he felt he would be finding black and white furs in his hat for years even if he instantiated a new one. (Where *had* his hat come from anyway? He didn't know, but he was glad for it.)

He had no idea how much time had passed or how much ground he had covered, but at some point, the desire to give up began to grow. He was so tired. Every muscle in his body ached. His aching tail was the least of his worries.

But he couldn't. He was right near the summit. She was *right there.* He couldn't quit now. He was so close and had gone through *so many skunks.* A pang of fear and determination struck him through the heart.

Zia.

He had to do it.

He mustered everything he could, gave another yell, and, before he blindly pressed on noticed a small gap in front of him, closing quickly; impossibly small.

He was too late. He was too large, he would never–

A lightbulb lit up in his head. *He* didn't need to make it.

Closing his eyes, he used the last of his reputation and forked himself, but smaller. Fennec sized. Still anthropomorphic, still clothed, but far smaller. At least this new instance also had his own, smaller hat. Actually, come to think of it, that made sense. He couldn't blame himself for that, his hat was far too big, after all, and covered in skunk fur besides.

As the skunks fell on top of him, black and white fur blotted out his entire vision; the end of the world.

The last thing he saw was exactly what he needed to see. His fennec sized doppelganger, flying through the rapidly closing gap in the pile. It was almost like a scene out of one of his favorite old movies, complete with a slow-motion camera pan, and one final thumbs-up and silent nod between the pair as Eliah#It'sNotImpossible made it through the gap. Mission accomplished. What a thing to go out to.

And then, there were only skunks.

VIII: Eliah#It'sNotImpossible

He blinked and took in his surroundings. Then he chuckled as he recognized the quote his tag referenced. Photon torpedo indeed. You couldn't beat Star Wars. Absolute classic. *Focus, Zia needs you.*

Right. Focus. He took stock of his surroundings. Getting used to being this short was going to be... a process. He looked down at his paws, and then around at the position he found himself in. He hoped he had at least gotten the hat the right size; it still felt too large.

The wall of skunks was to his rear, and the opening he had barreled through had already closed. He quickly doffed his hat in respect to his predecessor. Buried alive by skunks. What a way to go. Surprisingly though, in *front* of him was a rather large amount of empty space. If Eliah#Fennec—he started to make a mental note to remind his down-tree to change that tag later, only to discover such a note already existed. Not being capable of forgetting continued to be the strangest thing—had been able to make it here, he could have stood up comfortably.

The eye of the storm, he thought.

And at the center: the storm in question, personified in the form of a very, *very* distressed skunk.

She was shaking, chanting those words, and clinging to her timepiece. *Is she having a panic attack?* he wondered. If so, it would definitely take the cake for the weirdest panic attack he had ever seen, even without the innumerable forking. But he knew from experience that when folks got hurt, their hurt shone through the cracks in different ways. Maybe this was just her way.

But what hurt her? What did *this?*

He walked cautiously over to her, taking his time to observe. Her clothes were disheveled, her hair mussed up. She was curled up against the wall, clutching the timepiece. And there were those words again... He recognized the Psalm, but not the other ones. One thing was clear, unlike the praying, none of the aspects of her disheveled appearance suited her typical formal look.

Another thing: he had no idea what he could do. But he had to try. Zia was depending on him, and he was the only one in a position to do something. Not for the first time, it all came down to him.

He padded carefully over to the skunk, shoving down how strange it felt to be this small. She was lying on her side now, which meant he was a little taller than her head at its widest. He was *not* even entertaining going on four legs.

This also meant that he was dead on with her face, and this close, he could see every expression of distress in it. At first, her eyes were screwed shut. Then, with no external cue he could sense, she opened them. She looked past him, not at him, then she screwed them shut again. He paused for as long as he could to study her gaze.

It was like she was looking into some great horrific beyond that existed even when her eyes were closed.

Was that why she was panic forking? To outrun that horrific eternity? An eternity of what?

The question scratched at the back of his mind, he wanted to know so badly. It was right there.

All of a sudden, he felt the fur on the back of his neck stand up. It was, perhaps, better not to know. The question was an answer to itself.

He could live with that.

And, he realized with a pang of guilt, in the worst-case scenario, knowing wouldn't help with what would he would have to do, it would just make it harder. While her eyes were closed, he patted his side to make sure his knife was still on him and that it hadn't shrunk too much. It was still there, and still usable.

He watched her for a few more minutes, but eventually he just couldn't observe her anymore. It would have felt voyeuristic, with how absolutely miserable she looked, how clearly she wanted to be anywhere else. So, he stepped forward, and cleared his throat.

"Uh, Ma'am..." he began, and then forced himself not to stumble backwards when her eyes snapped open. They were filled with wildness and frenzy. For a few seconds, her stare was everywhere at once, rapidly moving back and forth before finally settling on him.

Then, there was a noise.

A pained wail that made something inside him curl in sympathy and, if he was being honest, fear. He held up his paws "Whoa whoa whoa. I'm not here to hurt you. You just, uh, look like you're in a bit of trouble and I... Well, I wanted to see if I could do anything to help." He kept both of his hands up, resisting the urge to rub his headfur with one, and move the other nearer to his knife.

He did not understand what happened next, but he did his damnedest to roll with it anyway.

She laughed. A painful, bitter laugh. Held her paws over her eyes and let out a whimper, and that awful blood curdling cry again. After a while, she took them away.

"Is this what happens when I fail to be what I then must? In all ways, earnest? When I am not true to myself, always? Do I drown in dreams and memory?" She started sobbing. Again, that awful howling cry. For a brief second, he thought he could see the image of a woman flicker over her like some sort of projection; but then it was gone.

She stared at him for a few seconds. Taking him in. And before he could formulate what to say next, with a voice filled with centuries of calm sorrow, she said quite abruptly "I appreciate you showing up in that outfit. But our last Sadie Hawkins dance was a century ago."

He had no clue what a Sadie Hawkins dance was. But he was 150% sure that he had not taken this girl to any dance at any point, and neither had Evi. It wasn't in either Evi's memories or his own, 'fictional' though the latter may have been.

But there was something in there that he *did* know.

There was something unmistakable, because whether his memories were real or not, his loss was. Reflection of Evi's many losses or not, the way he felt it, the way it affected him, all of that mattered.

Sure, he had never experienced the events in the memories. That was important; he could never lose sight of that. But the feelings they produced, the things he felt... Were they not important too? Was that not the whole point? The reason why memories were important in the first place?

The hole in his heart that would never quite close up was one he didn't *want* to close up.

That *was* real.

Eleanor had taught him that, had taught the entire system that. Memories, regardless of their 'realness', mattered. And how they made one feel, how one felt about them. That mattered too. It made them who they were.

And as the skunk began to speak, the summer conversations on the patio with Eleanor once again came back to him.

The feeling of loss he carried around every single day was real. Not real in the same way as whatever had happened to the skunk, but it was still real. The experiences differed; the feeling remained.

And he had been right. The skunk knew the feeling too.

She knew loss.

But it took an entire musical number to get to that realization and to put it into action. Long after this point, he would reflect on how things might have gone differently had he made the wrong decision.

Sometimes, he still did not know why, in the end, he made the right one. "Oh... I wish– I wish Debarre was here... to see you. I wish– I wish–" The words poured from her mouth like ink overflowing. "*My vigor dries up like a shard.*"

He jumped back a bit. It was like she was speaking in italics. Or rather, like the italics were speaking *through* her.

"My tongue cleaves to my palate."

She jumped forward, and he jumped back. He put thoughts about mutual loss aside as his adrenaline slammed into gear. He considered forking his old self back, , but there was no way in hell he had the reputation and an equally dismal chance any of the rest of them had quit. They would all be fighting to the bitter end. The more he thought about it, the more he wished he *did* have the reputation. If he didn't think too hard about it, the whole 'quitting' aspect didn't bother him, it was like restoring from an instant backup. And, of course, who better to have at your back than yourself–

He realized that one of his hands was reaching for the empty spot where his holster would be. He cut that shit out, and resisted the urge to reach for the knife. He didn't know why. She was clearly gone. Off the deep end. Out to a lunch. A picnic on some green grassy hills that would last forever. And Zia was in danger, so why didn't he pull the knife on her then? It was the safest option. He didn't know. Maybe it was a fear of what Zia (and Eleanor) would think. Or, most worryingly, maybe it was that he just couldn't do it.

The skunk was pulled up like a Marionette by her own words. Each of her limbs rose in a haphazard sequence. He felt that if he squinted, he would probably be able to *see* bits of wire sticking out of her joints and trailing up into the ether; held by a creature he very much did not *want* to meet. For a brief moment, their gazes met. Her eyes were on fire. He had no clue what to make of it. Then, she *shook*, becoming hazy and indistinct.

At first, he thought he had gone mad. Because it looked like there actually *was* something overlayed on top of her.

This was where it would happen, then. She would be unsheathed, her appearance flying off of her body to reveal whatever lay underneath, a mannequin stripped of all its human attire or the bare skeleton of an animatronic. His fur stood on end, any second now, he would see the wires.

Instead, for the briefest of moments, he saw the image of a young, black-haired woman. Her eyes wide with the same terror as the skunk, and her face transfixed in utter horror.

He could not look into them.

"You lay me in the dust of death." Her fur was blurred with mascara. (Did skunks wear mascara? Was it stage makeup?)

He looked away, and when he looked back, the electronic distortion of waves of skunk and woman rippling on top of each other. Except much, *much* closer.

"Fucking–!" She still wasn't touching him, but she had somehow glitched across the gap between them. Only, she was standing still. It was like she was frozen. Her mouth was halfway open. It was as if she had been paused, frozen in outlines of data.

Was this what Zia called a 'jump scare'?

And then she wasn't.

He flinched involuntarily. The dissonance was overwhelming, he felt that sickening feeling of *wrongness* overwhelm him again. He wanted to pull his hat over his ears and curl up.

And then it was gone, just as quickly as it had happened. No distortions, no glitches. But one very, very inconsolable skunk. Except now, he only needed to take a few steps forward to reach her. His hackles stood up in swaths. His lizard brain (fox brain?) was telling him to *fucking run.*

Fox brain was quickly overwhelmed by the twin emotions of heartbreak and pity. Freaky, glitched out skunk or not, she was crying. And not just crying, she was downright bawling. Fucking drowning in a sea of her own tears. She could barely speak. "I have missed you so much I- I- I miss them all so much. I miss Cicero and I miss Carter and I miss myself." She collapsed to the ground, weeping, at his feet. She lay there in a heap, looking up at him. "I miss myself so much."

He had no clue who any of these people were, but that last part…

He winced, as the last part hit him like a fucking bullet. The urge to reach out and console her was so overwhelming—or maybe he just wanted company.

Gently, she hugged her tail close, pulling it over her face and peeking out at nothing and everything from behind it.

Looking past him.

Her brown eyes were an ocean of sadness, a black hole that stretched on and on and on. There was silence for a second too long, and then, the damnedest thing started happening. He briefly considered that he might have lost it, too.

She started gently singing. "Walking home, in the early dawn. I found myself, lost in the beyond…"

He watched her turning her tail over in her paws, hugging herself so, so tight. The skunks behind were suddenly omnipresent. He could feel them, somehow. It was like she was trying to wrap the entirety of the System around herself. To bury herself *in* herself.

It struck through his heart like an arrow. Disjointedly, the Psalm continued around them. It was both coming from her, and it was not.

It was coming from everywhere.

    I take count of all my bones
    while they look on and gloat.

He reached out to touch her. If he understood anything, it was that this woman was in *massive* amounts of pain. Perhaps she just needed the touch of another living person?

Nope, wrong move.

That *definitely* hadn't been the right answer.

He was thrown back by an invisible force that he realized was the start of her forking over and over again.

"Ahh shit". It took him a second, but as he strategized how best to fight his way through a legion of Yet More Mephit, he realized that something about these new skunks was different.

They were all dressed in their best, like something out of a Twen-cen silent movie. Top hats and suits and dresses and there were *so many* of them. Maybe he would have to fight his way through after all.

Fuck. He definitely would. She was forking more rapidly than anything he had seen as any of the others in the system.

This was it, he would be crushed. It would take seconds. He had made some mistake he did not understand, and this was his fate.

Well *fuck.*

He hesitated.

This was what he got for not drawing first.

He stood there, staring at the skunks, and they stood staring back. It was eerie, like looking at a formal party full of the same individuals. Like some sort of bizarre masquerade gone wrong.

As he was figuring out how best to dodge around them and get to her, when all at once, the skunks rushed forward like a wave. His hand touched his knife, and then...

He left it undrawn, again. Though this time he reassured himself that he was simply refusing to fight against superior numbers.

Again, he chastised himself for his obvious fate, for not taking action when he had the chance. What had started as a crowd had become a wave of skunk.

Except it wasn't a wave. It was a chorus. The forking was slowing down, too. He had time. But was that true about the others? He wasn't sure. *Think Eliah, think!*

They were doing a musical number, minus the music. At least he thought they were. He certainly couldn't hear any music, and he really didn't want to. As far as he was concerned, the whole thing was creepy and more than a little bit pitiful. The original skunk was still on the floor, singing what he presumed to be the lead role, hugging her tail tightly.

All at once, the skunks that had been rushing towards him coalesced back around her, and the chorus rose with them. They made themselves a barrier, and with that gentle encouragements, he was pressed back. That was fine. She needed space, and she wasn't that bad of a singer.

In fact, she was pretty good. Could anyone blame him for wanting a better view? And if all else failed, it would give him an advantageous spot to fork off a full-sized version of himself to catapult him towards her. There were, he was realizing begrudgingly, advantages to being this small.

He watched. It was painful. The skunks were a barrier of singing and self. Less obviously a method of painful self-isolation than those that than their sisters who belonged to the Order of Perpetually Chanting That Friggin' Hymn, but still ultimately fulfilling the same purpose. It tugged at his heart. He wanted to rush in, wanted to pull her out. Wanted to give her someone. But the clock was ticking even if he was, for the moment, safe. The same couldn't be said about–

Zia...

But didn't Zia want him to try something else sometimes? Wasn't this a chance to do that? Her voice echoed in his head from an argument long past. *"I don't know what I would've done, okay?! I'm not sorry that you saved my life I just–"*

He hadn't gotten it then. He wasn't sure if he got it now.

He would give her until the end of the song, or until he found a good route to reach her. Whichever came first. So, he sat there and watched, and waited.

"Once I found home..."

"But then it was gone..."

"But then it was gone..."

Those countless instances echoed her. Increasing, but at a stable rate. It felt deeper than that, though, like she was increasing too. It was like she was mourning. It was like she was unraveling, overflowing...

He doubted his plan. If it got Zia killed. If his hesitation led to her death...

"What will I leave for you?"

The chorus was deafening now, but she held her own, bellowing out loud from her spot on the floor, occasionally briefly raising her head and looking into...

"What will you leave for us?"

"Now that I am gone?"

Into... There was pain in her eyes, in all of their eyes. A spark of madness. An ocean on fire, a star exploding. He had made the wrong choice, his gut told him. He had missed the moment of action. *Fuck.* But if he had made the wrong choice, if he had gotten Zia killed already... Would she want him to add this poor woman's body to the pile? He knew she wouldn't.

"Oh, my Rivkah, where have you gone?"

The chorus of skunks gathered around her, demanding an answer. It was like every line started at the previous high point, then escalating, crescendoing. A conversation played out loud. Maybe there was a chance? She was talking to him, thinking to herself. Could he get her to listen? He didn't know. There was too much of it. Too much noise and none at all. It would explode they would all die his heart was pounding his head was screaming he could feel the air ignite–

For a moment, there was silence. Or maybe there was a cacophony.

And then, he could see her. The skunks parted ways like the sea. There she was. A straight path.

She lay there, hugging her tail. He would only have time for one action. He could go in, rapid fork like she did, and–

He could try to pull her out, or he could try to pull her into his knife.

Never make the same mistake twice.

His heart sank. He knew what he had to do.

He never got the chance to do it. Suddenly, she jerked upright with a cry, the chorus reformed, he had lost his chance. This was becoming a frustrating pattern.

The show began again. She was forking across the room frantically, back and forth, side to side. And somehow, she was still singing what he knew were the final lines.

*"Oh, I am **gone!**"* All the skunks made way for her as she advanced, quitting where they had blocked her path, then rapidly forking back into position. The lines mixed. He lost track of where she was.

"You are gone! You are gone!" They were acting as one individual, as one voice.

And then, she was in front of him. He let out a "Fuck!" and grasped for the knife, mostly for self-defense, but stumbled instead, dropping it. It was lost in a sea of skunks. She was towering over him. Her presence was overwhelming. The skunks all stayed behind her. They were singing-shouting as one. Overflowing as one.

"We will carry on."

*"You have to move on...**I will not move on!** To die is to move on, **Yishaq, we need you to move on–**"*

Something broke, the room fractured. Her image split between skunk and human. Blurred for an instant. He could see forever in her eyes, he could hear eternity in her voice–

Her voice broke.

"Understand, my children, I cannot move on!" Her teeth were bared, she was pleading with him. She was in front of him, begging him. Tears in her eyes, her fur a mess. Her hair the very definition of dis-traught.

Then all of a sudden, she was speaking.

"I miss you. I miss you so much. I miss everyone so much. But I miss you. I miss you! I miss you and I am surrounded by you and I can touch you but I cannot feel you and my life stretches on and parallel but never touching I miss you *I miss you*–"

He changed his mind. He *knew* what he had to do, but it was im-possible. He simply didn't have the reputation. *Fuck!*

He decided to check anyway. It was always worth making sure you hadn't miscounted your shots. You never knew when a Hail Mary bullet would appear, after all.

As he looked at the ledger, his eyes grew wide with surprise, and he felt a rush of memories wash over him. Eliah#Fennec had quit, his last words, "Who better to have at your back than yourself?" were still ringing in his ears.

There was no time to lose.

The skunk was shouting. But he had a clear path. She was literally a few steps in front of him. He forked a full-sized—yet still fennec-shaped—version of himself closer to her, and then for a split second he panicked.

The knife hadn't been something he pulled out of thin air. It had been with him when he forked.

Which meant that that version of himself that he had just forked...

How well did he know his own intentions?

In that moment, among many other things, #It'sNotImpossible understood the importance of being honest with themselves— 'themself'? The fennec blinked. They had never thought of themselves that way before... And yet, something about the pronoun felt like it fit. It felt *right*—no matter how hard it was. They hoped that the version of themselves they had just forked off was having the same realization about honesty. They closed their eyes in frustration for a few seconds, flattened their ears, and when they opened them, were greeted by the sight of the full-sized version of themself:

Embracing the shocked skunk.

Behind Eliah#It'sNotImpossible, the chanting skunks began to quit.

VII: Eliah#Fennec

Eliah#It'sNotImpossible quickly moved to join their bigger counterpart, scampering over, digging their claws in just enough to get a manageable grip, and then climbing up the clothing of the very surprised skunk like they were summitting a mountain. They didn't stop until they reached the top, and wrapped themselves around her neck in a big squeeze.

Eliah stared into her eyes, brushing her disheveled hair out of her face. He knew what he had to say.

"I'm *not them,*" he said, but with his drawl, it came out more like "I'm not *'em.*" He held her tight as he hugged her. "I'm sorry. But I'm not. You've got me mistaken. I'm sorry." He knew it had to be done. "They're gone. They're not here. I'm not them." He forced her to look at him. There were tears in his eyes too now, streaming down his fur. He forced her to see the loss, that terrible fucking night he had lost his daughter. Forced her to see that he was there. "We're here. And they're gone. And I'm sorry. I'd bring 'em back in an instant if I could. I know you'd do the same." She had started pulling away, he held her hands firmly.

"No no no no no" She was shaking her head in a panic.

"All we can do is go forward it's what," his own voice broke, "it's what they would have wanted."

"*I know!*" she screamed, forking herself out of his grasp and sending Eliah#It'sNotImpossible flying off of her, flipping them both the bird with each instance before unceremoniously quitting each. "Fuck you! Fuck you! Fuck you! Fuck you!" There was hurt and anger in her eyes, both him and his fork (actually, which one of them had quit and forked the other? He didn't remember) took steps back.

Her eyes were switching rapidly between #It'sNotImpossible and him. Her face was curled in anger that was very obviously masking fear. A terrifying thought hit him. Could digital skunks spray? As if she knew what he was thinking, she let out a growl that could only mean 'fuck you' and did something that was decidedly not spraying. She grabbed the knob off of her silver cane and pulled. The hilt of a *rapier* came out, followed by the length of the blade.

"Whoa, whoa, whoa!" He held up his paws. Eliah#It'sNotImpossible did likewise. "Easy there. Easy there."

"Do not easy there me you fucking *haunt*." She noticed Eliah#It'sNotImpossible scampering towards him, halfway there, all fours. He winced at the blow to his pride. She forked herself forward with the rapier in hand and thrust at the spot where Eliah#It'sNotImpossible had just been. He did a feint forward himself in order to give the small fox time to scamper safely behind him. (Well, originally *besides* him until Eliah nudged the tiny creature behind him; much to It'sNotImpossible's obvious chagrin)

"Ow watch it!" he muttered as Eliah#It'sNotImpossible scampered up his clothes to perch on his shoulder. Another growl, the skunk's tail was held high. His fears of spraying came back to him "Okay he held up a finger. Now listen there absolutely no need to get–" he paused, unsure of how to quite say it.

"Do not even start with that assumption you damned spector!" She stepped forward, thrusting the rapier to force him back further towards the slowly shrinking skunk pile. There was quiet and stillness for a few moments as she stood there, forking a more put together version of herself. Her hair back in place her dress creased properly her makeup set back in its place... As she did so, each fork came into being either staring at him, or staring at the fennec sized version of himself. It was eerie.

"How are you doing that?" She demanded, "How the fuck *are you doing that?*" She spat.

"Tell me what it is you want to know, and I'll answer, I'm an open book–"

"Bullshit. Bullshit bullshit *fucking bullshit.* That. Forking. You are new to the System. I checked your fucking records and you scanned *yesterday.* You have read *nothing,* you have been in contact with *nobody* who actually knows what the *fuck* goes on in here, you go to your work and you go to the bar and you have mental health crises in your apartment and alienate your friends and lie to your therapist; but you have no actual interest in the System."

The disdain in her eyes was palpable. "This is the greatest fucking *miracle* in the history of the world and you clearly have no more interest than the average person who puts off uploading until they are literally on their death bed. You are not even tangential to it. You are not part of a collective– *you do not know jack shit*– you have not been– have not been." She struggled with the word, looked away, there was a touch of that eternity in her eyes when she looked back. The fur on the back of both Eliah and Eliah#It'sNotImpossible's necks stood up. "You have not been to the places I have been to. *I would know.*"

For a brief moment, both Eliahs worried her rapid splitting would start again, which was one of many reasons why he didn't bring up that the first part of her claim was absolute bullshit and he knew it. He was too creeped out by that look on her eyes, the way she talked about whatever she was talking about. But that quickly faded when she pointed at them and began demanding, "So how, *how,* do you achieve individuation that quickly? Who fucking sent you? The WF? The Eastern Coalition? *True Name*?" There was particular trepidation with the last name.

He paused, making sure to still hold his paws up. "Well first of all you have got no right to dig into my privacy–"

She laughed and was at his throat with the sword in a second. His hand was on his knife. Her eyes were a tornado. "How. Do. You. Individuate. So. Fast? The odds of somebody completely new to the System being able to do this is– is..." She sputtered in frustration, "It is not fucking possible! How did you upload? Did you try to fucking beam yourself up? Did you rig something up in your garage? Fucking *tell me.*"

"I don't know what that word means!"

"What word?"

"Individuate."

"Oh for– Individuate. Like *them.*" She nodded at #It'sNotImpossible.

"I don't know what you're talking about, they're me, just a little smaller. And... Okay they use they/them pronouns." he admitted.

"Both of those are a self-image change I could buy you making once if you put *everything* into it, but I have fucking seen you, multiple of you, do it not once, not twice, but *multiple fucking times*. And! And! They are still diverging from you–" She glared at the fennec.

"No, they ain't"

"Would you go down on all fours?"

"No, of course not!" he said firmly. "Also, I want to point out that you are holding a sword up to me right now and that's really not the best environment to have a conversa–"

They were interrupted. By Eliah#It'sNotImpossible, who was speaking rather calmly. How they could take the time to ponder things at a moment like this Eliah had no goddamn idea–

"We weren't…Whatever you're referring to. It didn't happen to us. We can individuate like this because we *are* individuals. Sort of. Dissociative Identity Disorder. Evi's had it since she was a child. I… I uploaded us because I thought it was what my girl wanted, and what would keep us all safe. I didn't get that there would be any issues with the, personality stuff. I didn't realize it at first even. It was so subtle… But I don't think it's an issue. I think. It's like… That stuff our therapists kept trying to get us to do like–"

"It was like all the dissociation was gone." Eliah said.

"Exactly, like putting on glasses," #It'sNotImpossible agreed.

"But the separation was still there. The desire to be. *Us*," Eliah explained to the skunk.

"So, that's kinda what we did. It's as simple as that. There's more than one of us. We're multiple individuals. Kind of. It's complicated."

The skunk blinked. Then she blinked again. If Eliah had to guess, she was accessing some sort of private HUD and looking at records or– the sword clattered to the ground. There was shock on her face. "Oh my god. Oh my god I am so sorry." She backed up slightly. "I am so sorry, I– I– You. Split so fast I thought. I thought. I knew about the DID but. I haven't seen it. I have never seen this happen before. Even with another system. I thought… I–" She was utterly crestfallen. "I was scared. I am… I am so sorry. I got scared and I got…"

"Triggered. I think that's the word. You know like, uh, like how Evi panicked earlier in the classroom when she realized what I'd done." He rubbed the back of his neck.

"Yeah, that was a real dick move," Eliah#It'sNotImpossible muttered at him.

"Hey!"

He turned to bicker with themself but then he remembered.

"Oh, right shit. Uh. Yeah so speaking of that. I get it happens to everyone, I guess, but you did kind of fill the room up with copies of yourself and I have a daughter back there who is quite possibly still suffocating under a pile of slowly quitting panicked copies of yourself so if you could please take care of that right now..."

All at once, every single skunk except for her vanished.

She looked at him nonplussed. "You cannot. Did you think she could die?"

"I guess, yeah! Isn't that the point of the sword?"

"The sword is for drama!"

"I just– there's a lot of skunks in here enough skunks fall on someone and they could get crushed!"

"How heavy do you think I am?!"

"It's not about how heavy you are it's about the number of skunks."

"You cannot die in here!" she repeated firmly. "Not, normally. The System preserves *life.* Also, wait a second, *you* were the fucker who uploaded her? Then every indignity I've put up with for the past few hours is your fault. Oh my god, you piece of–"

They were interrupted by groans and a "Shit, my knee!" Someone had evidently fallen onto the ground from high enough to hurt like the dickens. He held up his paw to her, "Hold that thought" and looked around. #It'sNotImpossible, still perched on his shoulder, gave her a jackass smile.

There were multiple copies of some folks, and. He blinked. *Felina?* Right! That's right! He remembered. He hollered at her, "Haven't seen you in a while!"

"Same!" She laughed back. "Also, fuck you, Eliah!"

"I missed you too!"

As he scanned the now skunk free room, he could see that everyone was accounted for. Though one of him didn't seem to be moving. He couldn't exactly blame him. It had been a long day and he had been crushed under skunks for several minutes. Now, where was the person he wanted to see... He let out his breath. There, at the far end of the room. Zia. She was safe.

He exchanged a nod with Evi, with Felina. Then he turned back around to the skunk who had been the source of the problems. She was looking down at the ground, holding her pocket watch. She looked quite distraught, like she had been caught doing something improper.

Personally, he was still having a time reconciling the whole "anthropomorphic skunk" thing. He hadn't even *begun* to process System etiquette. But he figured that having a panic attack and uncontrollably forking was a bit embarrassing.

She looked up at him. God, she was pissed off. And was that, yup, that was the "this is *not* over" face. He blatantly ignored it, might as well just rub it in some. "Well, I suppose all's well that ends well–*Oof!*"

Zia collided with him, knocking him off balance as she hugged him. The skunk laughed in a very 'serves you right' way, she had evidently seen the girl rushing at him from her vantage point but hadn't said a thing.

Eliah didn't care. He went to scruff Zia's hair and she shook her head. He backed off, and she looked up at him, eyes shining at him in a way they hadn't in a long time. "I knew you could do it. Thank you."

He chuckled, gesturing at the skunk. "All in a day's work. And hey, I made a new friend along the way. Not bad if I do say so myself."

"I am *not* your friend, Eliah." She said through gritted teeth. "Although, I guess that I owe you a..." She realized she was gritting her teeth, and reverted back to her receptionist smile. "A bit of a *thank you.*" She spat, her ears splayed to the sides. "I *suppose* that a higher starting reputation boost is in order. Hopefully it can..." She gritted her teeth again. "Mend... things. Pave things over. It might not be possible to forget here but there are some who feel it is definitely possible to move on and to make new memories."

He got her drift.

"Holy fuck Eliah, I think she just bribed us." Zia beamed. "Holy *shit* that's a lot! Nice!"

"I did not bribe you! I just want to put us on the road to *mending* things between your clade and mine." The skunk practically growled. "And, I have a *reputation* to uphold. Which I am sure you will assist me with, so I wou–"

"Wait hold on a second, what's a clade?" Zia interrupted.

The skunk sighed. "Let us wait until the rest of your group meanders over here before we go over that."

Eliah took the spare few moments in-between to take stock of his situation. He had never before been able to *feel* what the others in the system felt about him. How his actions affected them. Likewise, they had never been able to feel how they made him feel. How their actions affected him. Combined with the dissolution of the dissociative barriers they had all lived with for so long; the moments that they shared together between forking themselves out were indescribable.

None of them could ever imagine going back to the way things had been before—which was a moot point, given it was a technological impossibility.

But that wasn't to say all that ended had ended well. They understood his point, why he had done what he had done and how he felt about it. But he knew the feelings of everyone else well enough now to know on an emotional level what he had known when he answered 'Yes' to the final upload confirmation:

There was no going back. He had made an irrevocable choice for all of them, and he would have to live with the consequences.

Even still, he didn't regret it, though he did wish that things had worked out differently. That they had been able to have this reconciliation outside of the System.

He shook himself out of his thoughts in time to see Felina and Evi walk up and stand besides Zia. He didn't like that, and evidently, she didn't either, as she quickly repositioned herself to his right. This left an awkward gap between him and Evi; who was avoiding looking at him save for a quick headtilt at #It'sNotImpossible. He had a sinking feeling.

Fuck. This was where everything went to shit.

Actions, and consequences.

Best to get it over with.

"Well, now that we are all back together and we have *more than demonstrated* that we understand how *forking* works, I believe that–" The skunk started through gritted teeth. He didn't let her finish. Evi wasn't closing the gap, and she still wasn't looking at him.

"I'm sorry, give us a second." He interrupted, leaving her with black ears pinned back against her head in anger as he turned to Evi–

Who interrupted him with a physically unpleasant ping and an invitation to something called a "cone of silence".

He accepted, and the rest of the world seemed to grow quieter.

Evi stood there, still not meeting his gaze, looking at the floor. He felt a twinge of sympathy, and wondered if she felt likewise towards him. He opened his mouth, but before he could speak, she started talking. As she did, she slowly lifted her head to meet his gaze, and though she looked like she was in her late twenties, she seemed to hold at least two decades worth of tiredness. He was taken aback.

He had expected anger.

"When things..." She looked back at the ground. "Ended–"

The word dropped to the floor, lying there, lifeless. It didn't even so much as twitch.

"–with Eleanor, I..."

She stood there, still looking at the ground, before finally meeting his gaze full on.

"I figured. 'Why not upload? What's the point? What is left here for me?' In the span of a few months the system had changed irrevocably, and rather than getting *better*, my life had fallen apart." She sighed and shook her head. "I felt that I had saved things from the brink of collapse. That, if nothing else, at the end of the day we would still have Eleanor. And failing that, that we would still have each other. And–"

She wiped tears away from her eyes, her face was a sorrowful grimace. "And that I would have all that I needed. The reassurance that I had done the right thing. So, congratulations Eliah. You were half right."

Ouch. That hit hard.

She laughed bitterly. "The merger with Felina... It didn't go how either of us thought it would. I withdrew, I stopped giving a shit about everything. Zia, work, healing, living. Everything. But it wasn't..." She sighed. "It was not because I couldn't get past her. That is where you were wrong."

Eliah stayed silent. He had no clue what to make of that.

"That was something that I let on. To all of you. And evidently, something that I made myself believe so well that *you still believe it now,*" Evi explained.

Eliah couldn't help himself. "Look, I'm just kinda surprised you haven't tried to deck me yet... But uh. At the risk of that... Yeah, I'm not entirely convinced. I've been in your- our- whatever... head and you're not over her."

"No, that's just it. I *am* over her," Evi retorted.

"Then what was it Evi? You loved it down there. That wasn't something you got from Eleanor, that was something she reignited in you. So, what would make you so distraught that you-"

"Of *course* I loved it down there!" She clenched her fists and raised her voice. #It'sNotImpossible's ears perked up in surprise. "How could I *not* love a place I had fought for *years* to remain in? For my right to live in, to change, to affect, to be present in? And you cut all that off. I can't forgive you for that, Eliah. I can never forgive you for that."

"I know." He replied softly. He had known it from the second they uploaded.

There was silence. It was his turn to look at the floor. After a while, one or both of them stopped holding their breath and exhaled.

"But..." she started. He met her gaze. He always met people's gazes. "But I can't." She fidgeted with one of her sleeves, it felt like what she wanted to say would cause her physical pain. "I can't blame you. Not entirely. Because. I nearly did the same thing. And because, I was wrong about you..."

"I know you did. Why?" he asked softly. "Wait, repeat that last part again. I think I need to hear it again."

"One at a time. First, why I almost uploaded us. It wasn't because, I couldn't let her go. It was because. After I integrated with Felina. I couldn't... Forgive myself," she said bitterly. He wasn't sure where this was going, and then it hit him like a brick. #It'sNotImpossible winced, apparently having the same realization. "Because it wasn't Felina who had had flashback after flashback, who had threatened Eleanor with the possibility of us uploading one day and then threatened to throw me out a window the next... It was me, Eliah. It was me. Because I *was* her. And she was me. And I just... I couldn't forgive myself for that." Her voice was small, barely a whisper. "I could've lived the rest of my life not forgiving myself for that."

He waited for her to break into tears, but they didn't come. After a while, she composed herself, and looked at him as though, instead of having a heart-to-heart, they had just gone through a particularly unpleasant doctor's appointment.

"I know it's not the same but, I felt. I felt similar when Sarah died." He offered. "You don't want to carry that weight. It's... It's not really living."

"I know." She nodded. "I got that. It helped. And I understand that. I understand you more than I ever did."

"The feeling is mutual."

"Please let me finish. Not wanting anything to happen to Zia was, part of why you did this. To protect her. I get that, the path I was on with our life was also why you did this. I get that too. And, ultimately, to some extent. Zia bears culpability. I do too. Felina probably does. You're just, easier to blame."

"Maybe that's what I'm here for," he offered.

She shook her head. "No. You aren't. Didn't you hear a word I said earlier? That's no way to live. And, I want you to live. I want you to grow, I want you to *change*. I want to *see* you become a different person. Because you have been all along. And I've missed it." She looked down, ashamed. "You are a person, Eliah. You're more than just, a cowboy." She chuckled awkwardly. "That, little fella on your shoulder," she nodded at #It'sNotImpossible, "they're living proof. You're changing. You're growing. I don't know how I missed it. I'm so sorry."

"Evi, please don't crucify yourself again."

"I know." She sighed. "I'm not... going to go down the road of crucifying myself on blame again. Or myselves, as the case may be. And I can't forgive you but, I can ask that you don't crush yourself under the weight of my misplaced projections either."

"I'll try not to." They both lingered in the silence. "I feel like, I feel like I've been given a second chance. Thank you, Evi," he added. She looked back at him quizzically, her normal emotional cadence restored.

"No, It's not a second chance. It's the end of one story and the beginning of another. It's, a twist in the road. One path taken and another not."

"The path of honesty."

"The path of honesty, indeed." She agreed.

From their perch on his shoulder, #It'sNotImpossible spoke up, "Perhaps it's a chance to hug it out?"

Evi gave them both the strangest look. Eliah did his best strange look back. He was feeling similarly. He braced to protect the fennec from being strangled, and was surprised when Evi shrugged her shoulders. "Sure. Let's hug it out. I'm fucking exhausted."

#It'sNotImpossible made the leap in an instant, wrapping around her neck. As Eliah stood there, dumbfounded, Evi walked over and gave him an actual, genuine hug. He returned it. It felt good. "I should have guessed that all I had to do to make you like me more was get a mite bit fluffier." She snorted, "In your dreams, Eliah."

What a day.

★

After a while, they awkwardly disengaged, #It'sNotImpossible moved back to Eliah's shoulder, and Evi lowered the cone of silence after they had all composed themselves.

"Alright, sorry about the suddenness of that. Just working out private matt–" Evi started, before she noticed the look on everyone's faces.

Zia and Felina were standing next to each other, evidently worried and mid conversation, wildly speculating about "what the hell is going on in there". The skunk had been pacing around the two of them, and was the first to react.

"Oh thank goodness. I thought you two were either going to start beating the shit out of each other or develop some of fucking quitting pact or something. It would definitely be in line with how the rest of this day has gone." The bridge of her muzzle wrinkled in a frown.

Evi and Eliah exchanged glances. Apparently, a cone of silence didn't extend to the visual spectrum. Whoops.

"Uh. No."

"No. Nope."

The skunk looked between them for a few moments, unconvinced, her face lined with worry. They stood there awkwardly for a bit, before she let out a sigh of relief. "Alright. That is very good."

"Yes. I, agree." Evi said, exchanging another look with Eliah. "So, what um. Exactly do we do now?" she asked the skunk.

The annoyance rushed back into the black and white fur, replacing the anger. "Well now, we introduce ourselves, it is what people normally do when they meet someone. Instead of panicking for several hours and triggering the fuck out of each other."

Evi coughed, "Ahh. Yes. I do believe we've actually yet to properly introduce ourselves to each other."

"And yet I know so much more about you than I would like to," the skunk growled.

"Yes well, um after that can we leave."

"Yes, after that, your clade can leave. Congratulations. You hold the record for the tenth longest orientation in the System." She furiously marked something off on a clipboard. "Something nobody is keeping track of but me, apparently."

"Right, yeah, what's a clade?" Felina asked.

"A dysfunctional family composed of copies of each other all driving themselves and everyone else nuts. Add in a hundred years and some trauma for extra spice." The skunk muttered, but only #It'sNotImpossible heard her. They were pretty sure they weren't supposed to.

"What?" Evi asked.

"I did not say anything." The skunk snapped, before she straightened up and cleared her throat. "The System Central Library Encyclopedia defines a clade as 'A group of individuals patterned off a single root consciousness, formed through branching expansion of the forking of its constituent members'. There. Done. Everyone understand?" The skunk was glaring at each of them, her patience very obviously running thin.

Eliah wondered how long *her* clade had been around for.

"Yup." Evi responded.

"Excellent!" The skunk did another dramatic checking off on her clipboard. "Now, names and clade ID please?"

"Evi Pirth"

"Eliah Robbins"

#It'sNotImpossible paused for a few moments. Seeing a fennec grip its own chin like a miniature furry version of *The Thinker* was a strange sight to see. Finally, they spoke up.

"Ini. Ini Robbins"

Eliah reminded himself that he would need to unpack all of that later, and then promptly scheduled it for never.

"Felina. Just Felina."

"Zia Williamson."

"And your Clade ID?" The skunk asked, before glancing at her time piece in alarm "Actually you do not need to come up with it now, we can just use the ha–"

"Peace." Zia said. "Peace. That's our clade ID."

The skunk looked like she was about to break her pen in two. She looked at each of them like a disappointed teacher, and seeing no objections, wrote down the name. "There, now it is official." She composed herself, clearing her throat and forking for a reason Eliah couldn't quite fathom as her appearance didn't seem to have changed. The old fork quit. The new skunk closed her eyes and daintily put a paw over her heart. After a few seconds, she opened them again and said, "In All Ways."

Evi tilted her head, and exchanged a confused glance with Eliah, who shrugged. He didn't have a clue either.

"Then I Must In All Ways Be Earnest, of the Ode clade."

"Is that a, uh…?" he racked his brain.

"An ode is a type of poem–" Evi started to explain. But before she could continue, Felina spoke up.

"Yeah, I gotta ask…" She was looking over the skunk's prim and proper uniform, eyeing the pocket watch and the discarded rapier cane with something akin to jealousy, attraction, and intrigue. "You were a theatre kid, weren't you?"

Eliah and his fennec counterpart tried their best to suppress a guffaw, Evi put her face in her hands and moaned. Zia high fived Felina.

In All Ways, much to the group's surprise broke out into a grin, beaming wildly. "Theatre teacher, actually." She corrected. And then, smiling a genuinely warm smile she said, "Welcome to the System," waved goodbye, and promptly quit.

For a few moments, nobody did anything, half expecting the skunk to pop back into existence.

After a few moments of standing there, they all exchanged various glances with each other.

"Oh yeah, she was *definitely* a theatre kid," Felina remarked.

The other members of the Peace Clade gave heavy nods and/or responded in various levels of increasingly creative affirmation, relief, and wonder. Eventually, they all collapsed, sat on, or jumped onto the ground, staring up at the endless opaque above and reflecting.

The rest of eternity awaited them.

True Love Lies Within and Without

Thomas "Faux" Steele

Caspian Sunspear — 2286

Caspar Sunspear knew exactly what to expect. Some experienced forking as easily as breathing, one breath out and two breaths in. For him, it had always come more viscerally. Grasping his paw over his chest, he curled his fingertips as though wrapping around a presence reaching out from a timeless void, yearning to come alive. He tugged at formless flesh until a fennec fox asserted himself between blinks.

"Hey there." Caspar winced at the sound of his own voice. His fork gazed back at him with arms crossed, a small gold stud tucked high in his right ear. He knew him immediately as Caspar Sunspear#07a8c4b9, one of the hundreds of forks that had served him over the years. "So, how should we go about accomplishing this?" he asked.

"That was what I was hoping to discuss. Please, sit with me." Caspar exhaled, condensation flowing across the window glass as rainfall roared on the gravel outside. Having experimented with various forms of background noise, he'd eventually settled on a steady torrent from an ash-gray sky. "You have full ACLs, if you need anything to make yourself more comfortable."

"I'll take my tea just the way you like it." Caspar Sunspear#07a8c4b9 grinned as a mug adorned with polar bears—

long extinct, of course—simply appeared in his paw. A wisp of steam rose from the black liquid.

"Plenty of sugar, and a lemon," the pair said in unison.

"Just like Eythor used to make us after a long day's work," Caspar#07a8c4b9 added, stirring a few cubes of sugar from an earthenware dish into his tea until the granules vanished. "You want me to help you talk to your old roommate...interesting. I'm certainly aware of your crush on him, but I'm surprised that you'd fork for such a task."

"Two minds are better than one, right?" Caspar replied, suddenly sweltering with the roaring fire at his back. "I was getting pretty desperate working through this by myself."

"You don't have to remind me." Caspar#07a8c4b9 took a slow sip, nostrils flaring as he inhaled the fragrant steam. He leaned back into the tufted leather armchair like a distinguished scholar while eyeing the weathered copy of *Twilight* on a side table. "It seems taking guidance from pulp fiction isn't working out, hmm?"

"Don't laugh!" Caspar twiddled his thumbs as his fork struggled not to crack up. "I'm serious! I only turned to ancient tomes like these out of sheer yearning for that weasel!"

"Whatever you say." The fennec's ears flicked about with amusement as he chuckled, sending a ripple of tea sloshing over the rim. Caspar#07a8c4b9 slyly tapped the side of his head while he summoned a soft rag to wipe off the mahogany coffee table. "Still, you have a point; I know we're not the most socially adept person in the System. Furries have always borne a strong correlation with nerdy and introverted personalities."

"You're not going to turn human on me, are you?" Caspar asked with a smirk. Concentrating on the slate coaster perched at the edge of the coffee table, he summoned a few fingers of whiskey to calm his nerves.

"I wouldn't dare. Though part of you has always wondered what you'd look like clad in different fur, right?" Caspar#07a8c4b9 winked as he shifted from a wiry fennec into a muscular jaguar and then back again. "Look at that! I'm already differentiating. Isn't that exciting?"

"Let's circle back to why you're here. Can you help or not?" Caspar asked, savoring subtle notes of vanilla and honey as the liquor warmed his throat. Paws trembling, he almost dropped his drink as he tried to place it down. Only Caspar#07a8c4b9's firm grip around his wrist prevented disaster.

"Relax. I've got you, okay?" Caspar#07a8c4b9 dissipated the half-empty glass with a sigh. "So, you're after Eythor. That weasel is quite the looker, and I really wish you would have accepted his invitation to grab coffee after you first moved out. Though...in that case I wouldn't be here, so perhaps that was for the best."

"I should have let him treat me to an Americano." Caspar sighed. He threw himself back against the mid-century sofa, its thin brass legs clinking against the hardwood floor. "Ugh! Why am I so bad at being romantic?"

"Let's focus on confronting the problem you've brought me here for." Caspar#07a8c4b9 playfully rolled his eyes. Balancing a half-crushed lemon wedge carefully between his claw-tips, he let a few drops of pearlescent juice fall into the murky liquid. "We're part of the same clade until I quit, right?"

"Right." Caspar rubbed the nape of his neck, soft fur tingling against his paw pads.

"Then we're working towards the same goal. I just want to see my smile mirrored on your muzzle." Caspar#07a8c4b9 clicked his tongue and winked. Extending his paws outward, he summoned a tall stack of leather-bound books, gilded edges sparkling in the recessed lighting. "Let me see to what extent I can differentiate myself while you get some shut eye."

"Good idea. I suppose an identical copy wouldn't have much wisdom to share." Caspar sighed, the weight of the all-nighter he'd pulled tugging downward on his eyelids. Dawn's first light was already cresting the horizon over his fork's shoulder. "You must be tired. Would you...like to come to bed with me?"

"It's uncouth to date yourself," Caspar#07a8c4b9 replied with a wink. "Don't worry, I can summon all the energy drinks I need to make this work. I won't rest until I think I'm at a place where I can be of assistance."

"What is your strategy, if you've thought that far ahead?" Caspar asked, bending forward and arching his back in a catlike pose. Taut abs flexed beneath his long-sleeved merino wool shirt. The pleasant buzz of alcohol pulsing at the base of his skull made it easier not to feel self-conscious about the instinctive stretch.

"I think this calls for a research binge." Caspar#07a8c4b9 flipped open the top book with an authoritative *thud*. "I'll start with a little Shelley and go from there. One of the original Romantics might help me glean a deeper understanding of true love...or at least learn enough about romance to help a hopeless case like you."

"I resent that characterization." Caspar huffed, rolling his eyes while drumming his fingers on the coffee table. "How long do you think it'll take?"

"Go and get some sleep. I'll burn the midnight oil on your behalf." Caspar#07a8c4b9 yawned as he began flipping through the pages, head swiveling as though following the progress of a 3-D printer. Caspar silently thanked the gods for the fact that he had always been a fast reader. "Spectating my progress won't do you any good, Caspar, so I've summoned something to help you rest. Drink up."

"You're surprisingly authoritative, for a fork only a few minutes old." Caspar glanced down at the cheap gas station cup now cupped between his paws. It was filled halfway up with warm milk spiked with fragrant lavender powder and spicy-sweet clove oil. "Fine, I'll get going," he said, taking a long sip of the bedtime potion. It was just like his mother used to make.

"Goodnight!" Caspar#07a8c4b9 called.

Padding toward the bedroom—really more of an alcove concealed with a rice-paper sliding door—Caspar paused in front of the fireplace. Wood-fueled flames licked at the brass grate, illuminating stag's head grotesques atop its pillars. "You've already lasted longer than most of my forks," he awkwardly murmured, not quite knowing what else to say.

"I know you struggle to say goodnight because your mother worked the second shift. You liked to stay up late to catch a glimpse of her Technicolor uniform all speckled with melted plastic." Caspar#07a8c4b9 sighed, slamming the book shut. "I already gave you the bedtime potion. Do I have to tuck you in before you collapse from exhaustion where you stand?"

"I, uh…" Caspar wasn't quite sure how to react to that statement. He nervously rubbed the back of his head while the flickering firelight danced across oak shelves full of impressive-looking books that he'd never so much as cracked open. "Yes?"

"Alright, come along then." Casparr#07a8c4b9 flashed a John Bradshaw book with a cover rendered in simple primary colors. "I guess I can be kind to my inner child tonight, but don't think that I'm going soft. You still have my word that I'll whip you into shape before I quit."

"Can we just talk a little more about—"

"No. Come on. You're up way past your bedtime." Grasping his paw, Caspar#07a8c4b9 hauled him into the bedroom, a cozy and comfortable space with room for little else besides a sleigh bed carved with motifs of laurel and holly. A few naturalistic prints adorned the walls, the most prominent of which depicted a fisher clutching a snow hare in its jaws. It hung crookedly above the headboard. "Do you need a glass of water?"

"I usually—" Caspar had to stop himself from offering unnecessary explanation. Of course his fork would know his usual routine. "Yes, please."

"I'll set it right here for you." Caspar#07a8c4b9 placed the glass next to a lamp decorated with a perfect sphere of Erfoud black marble on the compact nightstand. He hefted Caspar onto the dense memory foam mattress before tucking Urial—a well-loved weasel plushie and a perfect recreation of one of his prized childhood possessions—into his arms. "All good?"

"Yeah, all good." Caspar sighed as a weighted, down-stuffed comforter was brought up over his chest ruffs to lightly pin him in place. He wriggled his toes until he found a pocket of cool air and sighed. "Thank you. That was...oddly nice."

"It feels good to be doted on. Forking can be a form of self-care if you let it be." Caspar #07a8c4b9 dimmed the lights with a wave of his paw, leaving only an errant moonbeam to illuminate his soft features as he stood in the doorway. "I think I'll take a little walk to clear my head. I should be back tomorrow morning. Sweet dreams, cocladist."

"The same to you...when you get around to dreamtime." The door closed with a muffled *click*. Anxious thoughts flitting at the edge of his consciousness like lanternflies, Caspar squeezed Urial tight against his chest and curled into a fuzzy apostrophe. Insulated against the world, the fennec soon drifted into a satisfying sleep.

*

Caspar had eagerly awaited Caspar#07a8c4b9's return the next morning. But, instead of a familiar face in his living room, he was greeted with the sight of a baroque castle overlooking his once-tranquil backyard. His fork had reshaped the landscape of his private sim, turning what had once been an alpine forest into a craggy landscape filled with exotic trees and roaring waterfalls. Every evening, he'd watch the flickering candles in the stained-glass windows of the castle's grand library and wonder what exactly Caspar#07a8c4b9 was up to.

Then, unexpectedly, on the eighth day after he forked, Caspar awoke to a gilded letter sealed with a daub of crimson wax on his nightstand. The embossed linen paper read simply, "Come and see."

Caspar figured he had no choice but to do exactly that. He trudged up the hillside, bearing a stainless-steel water bottle whose contents were alloyed with a tablet of citrus flavored EnerGX. His ascent was aided by steps chiseling themselves from the earth at the steepest points, catching his footfalls as soon as they faltered. By the time he reached the castle's gate, Caspar was in perfect equipoise between exhausted and intrigued.

Mahogany doors three stories tall opened at his approach. Gleaming dragon's head knockers gazed at him from on high as he stepped inside. The foyer was richly decorated with tapestries depicting the folk heroes of Appalachia, soot-faced coal miners and moonshiners in hopped-up Fords meticulously captured in wool and silk. It was as close to a royal pedigree as Caspar—and by extension Caspar#07a8c4b9—could claim.

Stepping past a grand staircase, the fennec's ears perked at the spine-tingling organ music sweeping down the hallway from the library. Set in a minor key, the mixture of sadness and longing in the chords conjured a tableau of a sailor forever parted from the sea. It trailed off just as he entered, ending with a brief and triumphant return to the major key.

"Welcome. I'm glad you got my letter." Caspar#07a8c4b9 pivoted on the velvet stool and yawned. Though he retained a familial resemblance to Caspar, his softer features and longer headfur gave him a hint of androgynous beauty. "What do you think of the new look?"

"It's a little more fashion-forward than my usual outfits." His fork now wore a piece of true *haute couture* designed by one of the hottest names in the marketplace. Gold fabric crisscrossed his chest in triangular strips, leaving exposed flashes of sandy fur visible on his pecs. His modesty was preserved by a textured loincloth embroidered with silver acanthus leaves. "That's a Benzene Designs piece, right?"

"You have a good eye." The high-karat gold mariner link bracelets adorning his wrists sparkled as he stood up and yawned.

He stroked a paw through his headfur and summoned another energy drink. Caspar noticed several more crumpled cans in the wastebasket beside the organ. "I figured you wouldn't mind me spending a bit of your accumulated rep to give you a demonstration of elevated style."

"I think you wear it well." Caspar reclined on a leather chaise, reaching over to grab a pawful of grapes from a nearby footed bowl. They were delightfully sweet, a close approximation of the flavor of cotton candy exploding across his tongue as he pierced the taut flesh. "Mrm...delicious, as expected."

"I'm here to help you become your best self, and I think I've undergone enough individuation to be an able tutor. Part of that involves enjoying the finest creature comforts the System has to offer." His fork reached out and offered him an ewer of mead. "Would you care for a little hair of the dog?"

"Don't tempt me Caspar—" He suddenly paused as the name caught in his throat like a barbed arrow tip. By pure instinct, he realized that his fork had claimed a new name for himself. "Percy. It's a good choice of agnomen."

"I think it suits what I've become," Percy replied with a soft smile, pouring a small measure of the fragrant honey wine into a sterling silver goblet the height of a soda can. "Please, drink. You should be in a relaxed mindset for the next exercise."

"Exercise?" Caspar tilted his head, overcome by bemusement. It was truly novel to experience a fork different enough that he couldn't easily predict at which station their train of thought would arrive. "What exactly do you mean?"

"Let's start with a practice date. Something simple and low stress." Percy stroked his paw across the ivory keys, playing a simple melody until he missed a note by a half step. He instinctively tensed before slowly exhaling and carrying on. "I will hopefully provide an environment where you're not paralyzed by the fear of making a mistake. Then, *in sh'Allah*, you will begin to learn.."

"If you think it'll help..." Caspar trailed off, downing the goblet's contents in a single swig. He breathed in as Percy exhaled. "I think I'm ready now."

"Good. I know just the place. How about Roberto's#e3d7f41a?"

"An old favorite." A smile crept up at the edge of Caspar's muzzle. Eythor and the Guide that met him upon his arrival in the System—Ezra—would stop by whenever the meal rotation in the communal kitchen felt too stale. "Sure. Let's go."

"Just get dressed first. What would you normally wear on a first date?" Percy asked. "Don't mind my fashion choices; I want you to pick whatever you feel comfortable in."

"Something a little less on the bleeding edge of style." Caspar imagined the subtle elastic of his favorite hoodie hugging his wrists and the smooth denim of jeans rubbing over his inner thighs. A moment later, he was wearing the outfit as though he'd always been. Concentrating on his wrists, he summoned his usual chronograph watch and a gold bracelet to complement Percy's outfit. "How about this?"

"You look cute enough." Percy softly smiled with the tenderness of an old friend. His eyes traced over Caspar's body, the bulk of the hoodie nicely filling out his slight frame. "A bit on the casual side but adding a little something to compliment your partner's taste earns you bonus points in my book."

"I'm not *totally* inept, you know," Caspar replied. "Give me a little credit, huh?"

"C'mon then. I know you can do this next part without my tutelage." Taking Caspar's paw, the pair stepped forward into the foyer of a restaurant designed to resemble a working-class diner at the end of the twentieth century. "Shall we grab a booth?"

The low murmur of conversation brought life to the tired space. Dingy hardwood paneling lined the wall where half-a-dozen cozy booths were occupied by couples sharing affectionate glances over pancakes and bacon. The light odor of artificial maple syrup lingering in the air tickled Caspar's nostrils. "Not that I don't love this joint but...shouldn't we have gone somewhere fancier?"

"Don't get too ritzy on the first date. My advice is to try and keep it low-key." Percy tugged the laminate table toward him and gestured for Caspar to slide in. The green faux leather was still warm and a little sticky against his paw pads. "You don't want Eythor to be intimidated. You're trying to have a little fun together, not participating in a showcase of conspicuous consumption."

Caspar scanned over the menu, prickly heat rising through his shoulders and chest as it usually did when he felt flustered. Fortunately, the wheals hadn't yet spread to his muzzle. When the sensation rose past his throat, he knew that a panic attack was imminent. "Pretending to date a cocladist is kind of awkward now that I stop and think about it...even when you've individuated further than any of my previous forks."

"I suppose I need to change more, then." Where a fennec fox had been just a moment before now sat a weasel with gleaming emerald eyes—Erythor's eyes. While he didn't fully take on Erythor's appearance—such a thing being quite taboo—Caspar caught hints in his softened features and sharply-outlined eyebrows. "It's amazing how much I explored in my week away from you. I even took the time to watch a basic make-up tutorial."

"That is an improvement." Caspar whistled, noting that he didn't look half bad as a weasel. Percy was certainly more attractive than most of the humans he'd encountered phys-side. "Do you remember why we initially picked a fennec fox as our form in the System?"

"You were always enamored with that stupid cartoon. *Sandglass Half Full*, broadcast every Sunday at ten o'clock sharp on UView." Percy leaned backward while applying a delicate layer of iris purple lipstick. "Something about being part of one big happy family, right?"

"Right." Caspar bit his bottom lip. "I didn't realize I had an interest in make-up lurking in my subconscious."

"Clever change of subject," Percy said with a wink. "I'll give you a pass this time. Next time, embrace the opportunity to share your feelings. Shared vulnerability shoulders much of the weight involved in building intimacy."

"Do I really look that good with a bit of eyeshadow on my fur?" Caspar asked, surprised at the non-binary beauty Percy managed to evoke from his body, like a chef preparing a wholly different dish from the same ingredients. "I know you're a different species, but..."

"Individuation really opens one's mind to the possibilities. Would you like me to show you?" Percy asked, twirling a fine brush in a fur-friendly palette. "No obligation, of course. I don't want to do anything that you're uncomfortable with."

"Well, I—"

"What can I get you, sugar?" Cutting Percy off, the server construct gazed down at them expectantly. A middle-aged woman with streaks of gray running through her coal-black curls, she gripped a notepad just like his mother used to when scanning through the cupboards with digital coupons strewn across her tablet's screen to stretch their meager grocery budget. "It's been a while since your last visit."

"We'll start with coffee," Percy said. Shooting Caspar a knowing wink—well-aware of the fennec's love of caffeine—he tapped the menu entry for their extra-strength blend. "Leave the pot, if you would."

"You got it!" In the blink of an eye, a dented stainless-steel coffee pot and two porcelain mugs so dishwasher-weathered that the Roberto's logo had almost entirely faded appeared on the table. "Let me know when you're ready to order."

"Mm, I've missed this." Caspar's eyes went wide with pleasure as he took a sip of coffee. Rich and mellow, it was smooth enough that it didn't necessitate the addition of either sugar or cream. He barely noticed draining the cup until Percy poured him a refill. "Thank you."

"Go easy on the coffee. Taking your morning EnerGX tablet into consideration, you're pushing the recommended daily intake of stimulant compounds." Soft mustelid fur brushed his wrist, sending a memory of Eythor passing him a cup of tea through his mind. "I'll take one for the team and finish this pot," Percy said, pouring himself a second cup.

"I..." Caspar trailed off, a heady blush radiating through his cheeks. The rush of caffeine heightened the anxiety simmering in his core, paws trembling as he lowered his empty mug.

"Is something wrong?" Percy asked, brow furrowing with concern.

"I...I can't do this." Staring down at the table, Percy's vision began to blur as the noise of the diner began to recede beneath an all-consuming hum. Only the beating of his trembling heart rose above to taunt him from deep within his chest. "I'm never going to find true love, am I?" he gasped. Then, as though the entire System had crashed, everything froze.

★

"Breathe. Touch the tip of your tongue to the roof of your mouth and exhale for me," Percy cooed, eyes glowing with concern. After what seemed like a solid minute, the sim seemed to flicker back to life, beginning with the clinking of silverware against plates. "Empty all the air from your lungs. I want to hear your breath whooshing across your teeth, got it?"

"O-okay," Caspar replied. Gripping the edge of the table like a drowning man to driftwood, Caspar traced over the repeating swirls in the peeling wood grain as though wandering through a diminutive maze. "Even you mirroring Eythor's species is anxiety-inducing. How am I ever going to manage the real thing?"

"One step at a time. Keep taking those deep breaths for me." Percy's warm paws lightly cupped Caspar's wrists as he shifted back into the guise of a fennec. "I'm not Eythor. Nothing that happens in this sim is going to hurt you, okay? Your clade is right here by your side."

"I'll try." Breathing outward while counting down from eight, Caspar resisted the urge to start gasping for air as though he had just been pitched into the vacuum of space. He exhaled until his lungs began to ache before drawing breath for a count of four. "It's...hard."

"I know. You're doing great. Can you acknowledge three things you can see around us?" Percy clasped his paws tight, giving a reassuring squeeze as Caspar's gaze darted around the inside of Roberto's#e3d7f41a. "Ground yourself in the environment. Don't focus on the anxious thoughts. Acknowledge them before you let them simply...flow down the stream."

Caspar glanced at a cracked mug, the stuttering clock on the wall above their heads, and a wet floor sign haphazardly set up over top of a fallen coffeepot. He pictured every detail of the objects in his mind's eye while premonitions of catastrophe appeared and then fizzled out at the edge of his headspace. "It's helping, I think."

"Good. Are you comfortable with me returning to my alternate appearance to continue the exercise?" Percy asked, waiting patiently until Caspar's breathing had steadied and his paws stopped shaking. He had the server construct bring a perspiring glass of water which Caspar gratefully accepted. "It's okay if you're not okay."

"I don't think that I'm going to slip into a full-blown panic attack, if that's what you're asking." Caspar jolted a little as Percy returned to mustelid form. While he maintained a stiff upper lip, he could sense each pulse of his pounding heart in his pinky toes. "Though I can't quite seem to outrun my nerves."

"Let's talk about it then. What's got your britches in a bunch?" Percy leaned forward, supporting his chin with outstretched paws. "I'm here to listen to anything and everything you have to say, Caspar. It stays between us, cocladists' honor."

"Shouldn't my fork already know?" Caspar asked, rolling his eyes and drawing his arms close against his chest. "You're still me, underneath that nut-brown fur."

"It's helpful to vocalize these feelings. It's why talk therapy works, right?" Percy's dulcet tone complimented the buttery-soft paw pads stroking through his undercoat as he groomed the fennec's forearms. Caspar focused on Percy's thundering pulse, his heart also railing from a mixture of caffeine and sleep deprivation. Fortunately for the weasel, death wasn't programmed into the System. "Why don't you tell me about it?"

"Well, where do I start?" Caspar leaned back, clutching the empty coffee mug like an amulet of protection. "I don't want to give you my full memoirs, especially since you've already got the proof copy."

"Talk to me like I'm just starting to get to know you." Percy smiled softly. "Stay intimate but don't overshare. We can resume the practice date here if you like."

"Okay. Well...I chose to upload when I was nineteen. Never had the best of relationships with my mom or my siblings. I spent a few years earning a steady flow of rep in a communal sim by producing as many interactive action-adventure stories as my chronic writer's block would permit." Caspar loudly sighed. Reflecting on his past was rarely a joyful experience. "Once I had enough saved up to achieve financial independence and retire early, I set out on my own. I've been a recluse in my private sim ever since."

"Ever tried finding a living space that's...more of a happy medium?" Percy asked. "It seems like your initial introduction to the System was one of the better parts of your life."

"Living with Eythor was...nice." Caspar found himself longing for the company. The forks working on his behalf rarely stuck around long enough to become adept conversationalists. "I miss the trivial things most. It was nice to have someone ask how my day was and then genuinely care about what I had to say in response. I've been feeling lonely, as of late."

"It's good that you're finally sharing your feelings, and that's progress worth celebrating. How about I get you something to eat?" Percy asked. "I think you'll feel a bit less lonely after polishing off a plate of hash browns with a cocladist."

"Just as long as they're covered—"

"And chunked." The weasel smiled, flicking his black-tipped tail to beckon the server construct. "Let's have the usual, please."

"My favorite." A smile curled upward at the edge of Caspar's muzzle as a grease-laden dish was dropped in front of him. He slapped the bottom of a glass ketchup bottle until a few splatters of red adorned the monochrome potatoes. "I've thought about leaving my secluded cabin and venturing out again but...something's holding me back. Dealing with other people is hard, you know?"

"Relationships aren't always easy." Percy's fork clinked against his plate. He had ordered the same thing, with the addition of a fruit cup that consisted mostly of honeydew. "Your mother was fairly distant, am I right?"

"She spent most of my childhood working." Caspar savored every morsel of the artery-clogging dish. It wasn't so much the flavor that did it for him, but rather the memories of happier times that the hash browns recalled. He had looked forward to being taken out to Waffle House by his grandmother every Sunday while his mother pulled a double shift. "It wasn't ideal."

"I think you developed an avoidant attachment style." Percy placed his silverware neatly on the table before tapping at the tip of his muzzle with a lard-stained napkin. "When a young child has a caregiver who's emotionally unavailable, they learn to close themselves off from others. Sound familiar?"

"I have always been somewhat of a lone wolf." The deluge of sodium triggered Caspar's thirst. He barely noticed draining his water glass before Percy immediately refilled it with the chivalry of a true gentleman. "A week of sulking in a nineteenth-century castle really did a number on you, huh?"

"The castle and a dozen hours of therapy I received in exchange for a little rep. You'd be amazed what a little professional advice does for one's sense of self-insight." Percy replied. "Maybe start with verbalizing your own emotional needs. Tell me what you're feeling right now when you think of your living situation."

"Well...I'm looking to make a change. I know that living alone isn't good for my mental health." Glancing at the cracked Bakelite ashtray at the corner of the table, Caspar summoned a pack of cigarettes—a vice carried over from phys-side. The waxed paper crinkled softly in his fingers as he playfully twirled the cigarette. He caught a pleasing whiff of tobacco as he stuck the filter between his lips. "I try not to sit alone with my thoughts for too long."

"It doesn't hurt to accept a little help at times." Leaning forward, Percy held the tip of a Zippo under the cigarette's tip until it began to subtly smolder. He flipped it shut with a metallic *cling* before sliding it into a bioceramic case on his thigh. "I'm living proof that having someone by your side is easier than doing everything as a clade of one, right?"

"I'm going to break character here for a second. How does this practice date help with the Eythor situation?" Caspar took a long drag on the cigarette, holding the smoke in his lungs until the familiar nicotine rush buzzed behind his earlobes. "I appreciate the self-insight, but I was hoping for romantic advice. You know, something more…flowers and chocolate."

"You can't form a quality relationship with someone else until you've fixed what's going on here." Percy turned his claws inward, giving his chest a light tap. "Romance comes naturally when you're sure of yourself and what you are. Can you say that about yourself, Caspar?"

"In all honesty"—Caspar took a sip of his water, swishing it between his teeth to clear some of the acrid tobacco flavor lingering on his palette—"probably not. That's why I've sought out your help, remember?"

"Look, if you want romantic advice…let's start small. I make a reasonable doppelganger of that handsome weasel you're after, right?" Percy leaned in close enough for Caspar to catch a whiff of the musk radiating off his fur. Earthy and sweet, it reminded him of a blend of frankincense and blackcurrant wine. "Let's take the practice date up a notch. Pretend I'm Eythor and introduce yourself to me but be *genuine* this time. Be confident in who you are."

"I'm thankful that you were still willing to come out with me." Caspar took a final drag on the cigarette, drawing it down until only a few silvers of tobacco remained. "I've been struggling to get the courage to ask you out for coffee myself ever since I turned down your invitation. Living with you was the happiest time of my life. Something about being in a communal sim with all the ups-and-downs of an extended family reminded me of what I missed out on growing up. It was just like *Sandglass Half Full*."

"I'm glad to hear that. It was sweet of you to finally accept my invitation," Percy replied. Caspar held the water glass lightly in his paws, taking a deep sip as Percy's penetrating gaze swept over him.

The fennec fox nervously tapped his canines against each other, trying to maintain his poise. "Can I ask what made you change your mind about taking me out on a date?"

"I didn't think of you that way…at least not at first. But then, you helped to acquaint me with life within the System, like an older brother that didn't regularly steal my allowance money and then shoot me with a BB gun when I tried to get it back." A soft grin curled at the edge of Caspar's muzzle like the watersmooth silver edge of a summer moon. "Breathe in…breathe out…then smile. That moment was when I felt the first pang of infatuation in my heart."

"I remember giving you that advice. You were so delicate then, so unsure of what to make of the infinite possibilities of this world." Percy mirrored Caspar's smile. "I've never asked, but those of us that choose to punch the one-way ticket into the System are usually running from something. What were you running from?"

"Where would I even start? I…" Caspar trailed off, struck by cruel self-reflection, as though he were Narcissus gazing upon his perfect image in the water. He bit his bottom lip, grazing paw pads along the underside of the table to ground himself in the subtle roughness of the non-veneered laminate. "Do you want the honest answer or the polished answer?"

"Let's start with something forthright and see where it takes us." Percy reassuringly brushed against Caspar's foot with blunted claw tips. "Authenticity is attractive even in an immaterial world. This isn't phys-side, but everything is just as real."

"Well…my folks didn't have much money growing up." Caspar brushed over the luxury chronograph on his wrist, a skeuomorph of wealth from a distant past he had witnessed only through others' eyes. Flicking the top pusher, he watched the luminous second hand sweep across the silver dial like a falling star. "My mom had a lot of mouths to feed on a plastic recycler's pay after my dad passed from the RK Virus outbreak. I had to work for almost everything, even the clothes on my back."

"Endless toil since you could first toddle, hm?" Percy asked.

"I got tired of it pretty quick." Turning the Rolex over in his paw, he brushed a finger over lugs scratched from frequently changing the strap to match his outfits. While in the System everything could be made flawless, there was something beautiful in allowing objects to develop natural imperfections. "When the WF introduced a one-time payment to the families of those choosing to upload, I chose the straightforward way out of my problems. It was easier than slowly dying of chloracne from working in the local chemical plant."

"Do you ever regret your choice?" Percy's voice wavered a little, like a violin note played with a fraying bow. Meeting his gaze, Caspar sensed his own ambivalence mirrored in his folded ears and the subtle crease around his limpid eyes. "Leaving your family behind must have been hard."

"My feelings on the situation depend on how much I've had to drink." Caspar sighed, draining the rest of his water. Flashing his composed paws at Percy to prove more coffee wouldn't have him vibrating into the next dimension, he poured another cup—though he filled it only halfway. He used the spare room to add a minibar-sized bottle of irish cream liqueur. "I sometimes miss my mom. Phys-side wasn't all bad. She baked the best cookies...when she could scrape together the money for luxuries like that."

"You mean, like these?" Breaking character for a moment, Percy slid a weathered plastic tub—the kind that vat-grown lunch meat came in—across the table. Inside was a baker's dozen of cookies, each studded with cheap art-choc chips. "I did some digging through our memories. Can you give me a second opinion on them? I'm not sure the recipe is quite right."

Caspar gingerly took a cookie between his claws, admiring its glistening surface before popping it into his muzzle. The taste was almost perfect, bringing back vivid phantasms of a cluttered kitchen and his mother's apron, more multicolored patchwork than flannel. "It needs just a little more nutmeg. How much did you use?"

"Half a teaspoon," Percy replied. "I remember our mom measuring the ingredients out carefully in front of us to help practice 'rithmetic together."

"But she'd always add just a pinch more after whipping up the batter, maybe another eighth of a teaspoon." Caspar leaned back, brushing his footpaws across the satiny mustelid fur of Percy's shins. "Did you remember that?"

"Now that you mention it, I feel that memory coming back to me. My mind is still a bit fuzzy from so many changes in such a short span of time." Percy tapped his claw against the side of his triangular skull. "There are certain advantages to being in a clade...like being able to catch each other when we stumble."

"How hard would it be for you to quit? I've never asked one of my forks how they feel about it and the System isn't exactly built to allow me to try it for myself." Caspar knew that the process wasn't painful, that much he gathered from the memories he'd received. Existence simply ended as much fanfare as flipping a light switch. "Would the prospect scare you?"

"It would be harder for me than it was for the fork you created to fetch you a cup of tea," Percy replied with a soft smile. "Who lifteth the veil of what is to come? I don't know if there's an afterlife for all who walk amidst Creation…but it'd certainly be interesting to find out."

"Perhaps you've read a little too much Shelley. Don't go and drown in a boating accident before I'm done with you." Caspar sighed. "The weasel form is helpful, but I'm still not sure I've learned anything from all this."

"I wouldn't say that." Percy winked as he stood up, fur puffing out beneath the straps of his outfit as he bent over and stretched his shoulders. "Give yourself a little credit. You *can* be romantic, you know. I think you're a half-decent conversationalist when you stop trying so hard. It's much easier to get along with people when you're comfortable in your own skin."

"Maybe I should take you along with me." Caspar paused, wheels turning in his mind. Even though he couldn't date Percy, perhaps his fork might be useful in another way. "Wait…would you be willing to be my wingman?"

"I'll lead you to the water, but you still have to do the drinking. I won't do everything on your behalf, fellow clade-member or no." Percy pursed his lips before hawking a hefty shot of spit onto his palm. "If that's a deal you can live with, let's shake on it."

"You drive a hard bargain." Clasping Percy's paw, Caspar stepped forward with him into the peaceful surroundings of NewUpload#6c9b2e5a. Linden trees swayed gently in a cool breeze beneath a cloudless sky. A housing complex formed from a mixture of aluminum and unpainted birch wood peeked out from the ridge. Caspar knew the bulk of the living space was underground, with only residences constructed topside. "I haven't been back here—"

"Since you last saw him?" Percy brushed a tender paw across Caspar's forearm. His fur now the glossy nutbrown of a fisher's summer coat, though he retained his lustrous green eyes. Crisp white linen was draped over his shoulders, flowing smoothly to a pair of humble leather sandals. "I've done a bit of scouting on your behalf over the past week. Eythor should be just about finished up with a new arrival. I think acquainting fresh uploads with the System has given him the purpose he was looking for."

"So, he's finally a Guide, eh?" Caspar asked curiously. It was an interesting—albeit hardly unexpected—development. "He was always intrigued by the possibility of following in Ezra's footsteps."

"Does this new information make it harder to ask him out?" Percy leaned forward, taking the fennec's arm and guiding him forward like a Sherpa mountaineer. Pointing his thumbs toward Caspar's wrists, he stroked with a rhythm like a steady heartbeat. "As a reminder, honesty is always the best policy."

"I don't think harder is the right word. I'm just...nervous." Caspar sighed. "I'm sure he's happy doing what he's doing without me. Should I really ruin that by just showing up on his doorstep like an uninvited houseguest?"

"Adult children of emotionally immature parents can be skeptical that a relationship could enrich their life. Instead, they believe that rewarding relationships are simply too good to be true, something they can never achieve." Percy swept his tail through the soft grass beneath their feet, stirring up a smattering of iridescent butterflies. "Everything in you up to the point of the fork is in me too. What you're feeling is a negative expectation that can be changed."

"Are you really quoting a psychological self-help book to me?" Caspar snorted, petulantly flicking his ears. "Fine. Let's give it a shot, then."

"Great! Let's do it before you lose your nerve." Percy lightly grasped Caspar's paw and led him forward. Passing through a windbreak of fragrant pink mimosas, they entered a secluded clearing with only the echoing calls of a whippoorwill as accompaniment. "He's just over there and his shift is about to end. You'll have a window of a few minutes where you two are totally alone. Just be yourself...and I'm here if you need me."

"Thank you for being part of my clade." Caspar playfully punched Percy on the shoulder. "I think you're great, even if your fashion sense is one part of my personality I'm happy to have appear only in my forks."

"Pfft. Just wait until I show you what I can do with a mascara wand," Percy replied, poking his tongue out of the tip of his muzzle like a chocolate-covered strawberry. "I think a little copper would bring out the best in your cheek ruffs."

"I'll experiment a little...after this date." Gathering his courage, Caspar shouted to the figure standing at the center of the clearing, near a roaring campfire surrounded by a firebreak of blue-green sea glass. "Hey, Eythor! Long time no see!"

"Caspar?" The weasel turned, tilting his head as a spark of recognition flashed across his face. A slight wrinkle appeared at the corner of his eyes at the same time a warm smile swept across his muzzle. "What are you doing back here? Last I'd heard, you had moved over to Minerva Towers with that handsome Latino guy—what was his name?"

"Fernando. We broke up after he set off to parts unknown and left one of his forks behind in his place." Caspar nervously clicked his claws together like bars of a xylophone. "The fork eventually changed in a way that slowly forced us apart. Turns out that there was a part of Fernando that wanted nothing more than to live as a seventeenth-century pirate."

"That's unfortunate. You know, I've only forked once." Eythor's gaze slid between the fisher and the fennec, noting the same chip-tooth smile and jagged scar across the right cheek. "I found the experience of quitting too disconcerting to make using forks part of my routine other than for work. I remain eminently comfortable as a clade of one. Speaking of which, who's the cocladist?" he asked.

"This is Percy. He's still me—mostly." Caspar wrapped an arm around the fisher's broad shoulders. If Eythor objected to the borrowing of his eye color, his grin didn't show it. "All the same good looks, just with a little more academic understanding of romance. Right?"

"He's just flattering me." Percy playfully flicked his tail. Closing his eyes, he yawned deeply while struggling not to slip into a standing nap. "I'm not *quite* that differentiated. All that forking did was bring out the part of Caspar that enjoys looking his best."

Eythor looked approvingly at Percy's outfit, which was now tied together with a belt made from the silver coins of a long-fallen empire. "Taking on a distinct species is more than I've ever seen from one of your forks. Color me curious about the choice of a fisher."

"I've always admired them," Caspar replied. He gazed at the forest around them, imagining the sight of fishers leaping through the trees in pursuit of bushy-tailed squirrels. "I read in an old encyclopedia that they used to only live way up at the top of North America. One of them mutated to tolerate heat and spread those genes around. After that, they started expanding their range south until they reached Morgantown, my old home in phys-side."

"They made the best of their environment...just like Caspar and I," Percy added.

Eythor raised his index finger to his bottom lip, stroking across rose petal flesh. "I've never gone on a date with two cocladists before. Would you both like to grab some coffee? My shift is just about over and my kettle's just about empty," he said, pouring the last of the hot chocolate into a white Styrofoam cup and downing it in a single gulp.

"Yeah...we'd like that." Caspar glanced at his fork for reassurance, breathing out as Percy shot him a subtle thumbs-up. "Percy's my wingman on this one. Are you still up for getting that Americano?"

"I'm eager, especially after all these years." The weasel vanished his cup and shifted his outfit. Clean white robes embroidered with spiraling fractals were replaced with a comfortable t-shirt and snug-fitting skinny jeans. A white gold choker set with cabochon emeralds that matched his eyes completed the look. "Where might you take me, I wonder?"

"Well, I know this little diner that serves the best coffee, and I am a bit of a caffeine fiend." Caspar playfully licked his lips. "I don't think one more cup will cause me to undergo a phase change and wind up a fiery ball of plasma. Or perhaps it will? You'll have to stay tuned to find out."

"I'd pay good rep to watch that. Your Americano is on me this time," Eythor replied with a soft chuckle. "Shall we?"

"Let's go. I'm really looking forward to this." Taking the paws of his date and his fork, Caspar confidently guided them into Roberto's#e3d7f41a. As the earthy odor of fresh-ground beans and gentle burbling of brewing coffee ensnared his senses, Caspar found that he wasn't the least bit nervous. "And all it took to accept your invitation was a little true love from within…"

The Big O

Evan Drake

Walter — 2291

The sun's red light peeked over the horizon at 5:58 AM. Walter knew that because it rose at that exact time every time without fail this time of year. Never a minute too early or too late. Every day until the season changed. Its violent red glow illuminated the city below. As always, traffic flowed between the buildings like a river between rocks, the sun's light reflecting off the moving surfaces.

Walter turned his gaze back to the horizon. He knew when the sun would rise but he had never seen a sunrise before. He never had the time. None of the instances did. Or maybe they chose to keep that memory to themselves. He couldn't tell anymore. They didn't talk or reminisce. All he knew was anyone who had to get up at the crack of dawn typically had something more important to do at the time.

His thoughts hesitated at that notion. Something more important than witnessing such a rare and beautiful event. The sun rose every day but the ability to witness its arrival was a feat within itself. The window was tight and it required optimal conditions, weather, location, and season all played a factor and colored the experience.

He suddenly recalled a distant memory of a picture depicting a sunrise phys-side. The sky had been painted in an explosion of color as if the sky had been set on fire. It was beautiful and quite a sight to see. The sunrise now looked nothing like that. It was calmer, smoother.

Because the atmosphere here isn't tainted, he thought. *This is what it's supposed to look like.* He felt a sudden pang of anger at that thought. "What it's supposed to be like." He had heard that term and its variations so many times, it haunted his sleep. Every thought, every task, every action had to produce the desired result. It all had to lead to the necessary outcome.

It was how it should be done.

He glanced at the pocketwatch in his hand. It read 6:20 AM.

At that moment, the sound of the rooftop door opening reached his ears. Right on time as expected. Without even looking back, he knew who it was. No one came to the roof at this time of the day given they were "busy" with other things. But his instances were never late. "On time, every time," they would say. Being late—even once—harmed productivity. That couldn't be allowed.

"You're early?" Will asked.

Walter nodded. "I got up early to see the sunrise."

"You shouldn't have done that. Getting the optimal amount of sleep—"

"Save the speech. We have it memorized. I know full well the 'optimal' amount of sleep is required for maximum productivity and reduces dependency on energy supplements." He indicated the rising orb of light in the distance. "But it's funny how no one actually needs sleep around here."

"Following the routines ingrained in us from our lives phys-side keeps us sane."

He chose to change the subject. They'd be there for hours talking in circles otherwise. "Well, you can't tell me that shaving off a few minutes of sleep isn't worth that view."

"It is beautiful, but we should get to the point. We have to be going about our tasks by seven or else—"

"Or else we'll be late and that will harm productivity. I know," Walter finished, nettled. "But don't you just get tired of it all?"

"Tired of what?"

"Never having any free time."

"Why would we need free time? With the current schedule, we've maximized reputation acquisition and—"

"You sound like a robot."

He felt the angry stare on the back of his head. Several seconds of silence passed. He feared Will had walked off and the conversation was a bigger waste of time than it would have been.

But then Will spoke again, his voice dry and mechanical. "That was rude."

"I know, but I meant what I said. We've become robots. We don't want for anything—"

"Because we've maximized productivity which ensures a steady income of reputation—"

"And we're not doing anything with it. Hell, we don't even really need it, do we? The whole system is more of a formality than anything."

"What is there to do with it?"

Walter shrugged. "Something. Anything. The problem is we're self-sufficient, so we have no need for anything. I want to go on vacation. I want to see mountains, go hiking, go fishing, watch a movie, something besides the same monotonous tasks day after day." A strange mixture of euphoria and anger rose within him. His voice rose with it as he continued to rant. "I want to think for myself. I want to make mistakes. I want to branch out. Explore and try different things, not always follow the same one-two, paint-by-numbers bullshit that everyone tells me to do."

Will didn't respond. Not that Walter expected it. They may have forked from the same root, but it was clear that their developing thoughts had gone in two very different directions.

He wasn't sure when it first started, his thoughts diverging from the host. They warned him of this at his creation. Eventually, his thoughts and feelings would differ from the root. But when that happened, they couldn't say.

Or wouldn't, he thought. Thinking back on Wallace's memories, it all made sense. Everything was about control and perfection. Even if they couldn't pinpoint it exactly, they had an estimate. They knew exactly when his individuality would kick in, assuming it ever did.

Because it all was measured, recorded, and controlled.

The sun had fully emerged from the horizon. Its once red light had now turned to its signature yellow. The traffic below had increased, going from a steady trickle to a raging rapid. Even from the perch, Walter knew they had at best another 15 minutes before the streets became clogged. Still, his eyes traced the optimal route through the back streets that avoided most of the crowds.

"Is there anything else?" Will asked, breaking the silence. "I really need to get back to my tasks."

"You ever wonder why they lied to us?" Walter asked.

"What?"

"They lied. Remember all the advice growing up? Sorry, when Wallace was growing up? All the tips on how to do things quickly?

How to succeed at life? Everyone was so quick to offer advice and give tips on 'rising to the top'. Now look at us. We've reached the peak of the mountain and there's nothing here. Worse, you realize that you didn't even want to be here."

"Did you really call me up here to waste my time with your preaching? We have a schedule to keep."

"No, *you* have a schedule to keep. I'm done."

"You're quitting?"

"No. I'm just through being Wallace's puppet. The man has no dreams, no visions, no goals. He just does as he's told. Just look at his memories."

"Our memories."

"No, *his* memories. The ones we got stuck with when he created us. Our thoughts, our actions up until now, aren't even ours. Hell, they're not even his! They were implanted by other people making empty promises!"

"Where is this coming from?" Will asked, fear creeping into his voice. "We became who we are today because of those memories."

Walter didn't have an answer. These weren't memories, they were observations, visions of what lay through the cracks in the flawed logic they were implanted with. That *Wallace* was implanted with. At best he suspected it was a side-effect of his thoughts finally becoming his own. No longer simply an instance of Wallace, he had truly become Walter, his own individual.

At least, that was what he hoped for. Wallace could have come to the same conclusion for all he knew but chose to keep it from them in order to save them the stress of knowing they were nothing more than puppets created to serve his whims.

"I don't understand, but no one forced obedience on us," Will said. "You should know, you have the same memories. All of those 'empty promises' were lessons to help us grow. We were taught so we wouldn't have to learn."

Walter bit his tongue. He had a nasty retort primed and ready but there was no point. Will would never understand. He didn't see it. They shared memories but saw different things. No one had to force anything on them because the system was self-sustaining. They had been imprinted since their creation, their minds groomed to follow the grain and blindly accept whatever was shown to them. Never question. Never deviate. It didn't need to be said because they said it for them.

He turned back to the streets below. The river of cars had frozen over. Faintly, the honking of car horns could be heard. But the traffic did not ease forward any faster.

It became clearer than ever that he was alone in this. The others would not be persuaded.

He couldn't do it. Wouldn't do it. Not like this. He rose from his seat and stormed back inside. No more speculations, no more routines, and no more what-ifs. He was done.

Finding Wallace was incredibly easy. The man was in his office as always, right on time.

The root looked up from the computer screen, his sharp brown eyes studying him from behind his square glasses. For the first time, Walter hated looking at that face, his face. The only difference being Wallace was clean-shaven and preferred to wear glasses. Every instance had some form of facial hair for reasons that were not shared during forking.

"You're behind schedule," Wallace said. "Did something happen?"

"I'm done."

Wallace pushed his glasses up on his nose. "You're quitting?"

"No, I'm done being your puppet. I want to live an actual life! I spend all day doing the same boring tasks over and over because 'deviance from the method is not perfection!' "

Wallace didn't react to having the mantra thrown up in his face. It was as if the man didn't even waste energy on unnecessary emotions and it was infuriating. Walter wanted so badly to cross the room and smack that emotionless stare off his face. "Stop sitting there with that blank look on your face and act like a human for once!" he wanted to say.

But he stayed put and said nothing. Violence solved nothing. He was leaving and that was that. Wallace's approval or reaction didn't matter.

"If that's how you feel, I'm not keeping you here," Wallace answered, shrugging. He calmly turned back to the computer. "Feel free to leave at any time. If you require any help finding accommodations, let me know."

Walter could only stand there, stunned. "What? That—That's it?"

"You're not the first instance to realize the truth. I've given you all the tools you need to live the perfect life, however, I can't decide how you use them. I will say you figured it out faster than the others did."

He continued to stand there, dumbstruck. Eventually, Wallace looked up from the computer again and frowned.

"Was something not clear?" Wallace asked. "Or have you changed your mind?"

"What are you planning? I don't understand."

Wallace sighed heavily then took off his glasses before cleaning them with the handkerchief in his pocket. "There is no plan. I only intend to do what no other human can—or won't actually; break the algorithm. It's incomplete and not ready for testing."

"What algorithm?"

"The algorithm to better living, the one you're obsessed with disobeying, the guide to all things practical and impractical. Think about it. We have created the ideal world where anyone can truly live as they want yet we have not created a utopia. Here, you can have whatever you wish except happiness. You have my memories after all. I'm sure you know what I'm talking about."

Walter didn't know. He supposed he had forgotten or suppressed it. Even now nothing came to mind.

Wallace inspected the glasses in the light and then returned them to his face. "You seem lost so I'll spell it out for you: This is my way of maintaining control in a world that prides itself on wrenching it from you. Despite its best attempts, I have risen to this level and my mind remains my own. Much like how nature ignores our laws of physics and biology and yet continues to thrive. Now if you're done with your tantrum, can you please make a decision? Having you standing there gawking is distracting."

Walter slowly went for the door, still not fully understanding what transpired or how he was supposed to feel about it all. He racked his brain for any hints or clues to what he missed and why he couldn't see it. But nothing came to mind.

Before leaving, he paused to ask, "You said you were trying to break the algorithm. What will you do if you succeed?"

Without looking up from his computer, Wallace replied, "I already did, or rather, you did."

She Who Haunts the Storm

J.S. Hawthorne

Livia — 2309

The beast roared, issuing a great gout of flame to paint the stony cavern walls black. The party drew their weapons, facing the dragon with determination and the righteous knowledge of their mission. Their leader, the elven warrior known only as Peredur, after the Red Knight of legend, hefted his ancient broadsword in challenge.

"*I'll* deal with this foul monster," he declared, then rushed forward, swinging the sword as he charged. With an inarticulate cry, he brought the weapon, his reward for a thousand holy deeds, down on the dragon's hide.

Where it did fuck all.

"Wait, what?" Peredur asked, taking a step back and staring up at the roaring monster. His face showed disbelief, which quickly passed straight through fear and into an ugly, purple anger. "Why doesn't my sword work on it?"

"It must have some enchantment we don't know," said the reptilian cleric called Tyrean. "Some magical protection against even your weapon, Sir Peredur!" In contrast to the grumpy knight, the priest's crocodilian muzzle and bright, grey eyes were alive with interest. Colors rippled, chameleon-like, across his hide. "We shall have to vary our tactics."

"Or retreat," said the wizard. The rogue nodded their head in agreement, already sheathing their knives. "Get back to town and do some research?"

"No!" said Peredur. "This is bullshit! I want to know why the sword doesn't work. It's a stupid dragon, this is a dragonslaying sword. I should be doing triple damage to it."

With a sigh, Livia muted the dragon. Unlike the collection of sword-and-sorcery types around her, she wore a faded pair of blue jeans—meticulously copied from her favorite pre-upload pair—and a t-shirt with the bulbous green head of the Wizard of Oz stretched over her chest and belly. For a split second, she considered forking, letting a new instance deal with Peredur while her down-tree version got a drink. But she hated forking. Plus, he would definitely notice.

Peredur rounded on her. "This is bullshit," he repeated. "I didn't sign up for this to not hit things."

"I thought you signed up to play out a story?" Livia asked. She tried not to grind her teeth. She didn't think it mattered—there were no dentists in the System—but she had always felt it was her job to be the calm, reasonable face of the game. The players could get upset, but not her. "Do you really want a story where nothing bad can ever happen to the heroes? There has to be conflict, right?"

She turned to the other players, but they were stony sient, and she couldn't get a read on them.

Peredur got into her face. "I don't want the game to be arbitrarily hard! And I don't want my foresight to be retroactively undone by fiat! That's not fair to me."

"Not every plan you make is going to succeed. That's just life. And not everything is going to work perfectly on the first go."

Peredur swelled and Liv braced herself with the oncoming tirade. Thankfully, Tyrean came to her rescue.

"I think maybe a break is in order, yes?" he said, stepping between the two of them. "We'll call today a wash."

"That's for the best," Livia said. She wanted to sigh. "Two weeks, we'll pick it up from the dragon, okay?"

Peredur quit without responding. The others took their time saying goodbye to Livia and each other before teleporting out of the sim.

Livia focused on the dragon while they packed up. She had spent the better part of a week fine-tuning it, but there was still something about the way it moved that bothered her. The configuration of forelimbs and wing joints drew her attention, and soon she was absorbed in playing with the imaginary skeletal structure of a creature plucked wholesale from her brain.

It was, therefore, not particularly surprising when, long after she thought everyone had gone, lost in her own world of fantastical anatomy, upon being tapped on the shoulder she screamed.

"Sorry," said Tyrean, crocodilian teeth bared in what might have been an apologetic smile. "I just wanted to check in on you."

"I'll be fine," Livia said, "just as soon as my heartbeat returns to normal."

"You don't have a heartbeat," Tyrean pointed out. "You're an amorphous collection of ones and zeros floating about sixty degrees off of the moon, from Earth's perspective."

Livia stared at the half-sized lizard person for half a second. "Did you need something?"

"Right, sorry. I just wanted to make sure Peredur didn't get to you too badly."

Liv sighed. "It's fine." Tyrean opened his mouth and Liv cut him off. "No, I mean it. It's not the first time a player's been upset with the way a game has gone. I'll live, and he'll live, and either he'll show up next week or he won't."

"Yeah, but, it still has to sting."

"Of course," Liv admitted. "Look, I created something," she waved at the stationary dragon. "A whole world, a whole story. And what every creator wants when she creates something is for people to enjoy it. When someone doesn't like it, when they tell you to your face that they hate it, that's rough to hear. But it happens, and your options are to grow a thicker skin or to quit sharing, and I don't want to do that yet."

"Why worry about sharing? Why not, I mean, just build things like this for yourself?"

"No one builds for themself." She hesitated, then added, "No, well, lots of folks do. But me, the point of a story is for someone to experience it, to live in that world I've made, if only for a moment." She hesitated, then plunged on. "I spend a lot of time on my games. It takes up most of my time, not just in prepping, but, say, attending classes and lessons for stuff to increase the verisimilitude. Like this castle? I spent a year reading up on medieval architecture. I took classes on embroidery so I could add in little details for my players. Hell, I'm even thinking about taking sword lessons so I can make the combat more interesting."

Tyrean nodded, silent while he digested that. Livia was on the verge of telling the little lizard goodbye when he spoke up again. "But can't you use all those details for yourself? I mean, especially here, what stops you from conjuring up a battle axe and fighting the dragon on your own?"

"Because I already know how the story goes," Livia said, a little bemused. "What fun is a maze if I already know where the exit is?"

"You could fork," Tyrean suggested. "One of you builds the maze, the other solves it."

Livia had the strangest sensation of a train going off the rails. "Not that it really matters, but I don't like forking. And anyway, I can't just fork and," she waved her hand vaguely, "Ccreate. A new fork would be too similar to me, the story we'd create would be the same as if we never forked in the same instance. So I'd need to fork, let the new instance individuate until we were distinct enough that I couldn't guess the story beats. That's a lot of work to not be my own GM."

"Why don't you like to fork?"

"It makes me feel nauseous, and I ask myself uncomfortable questions."

"What?"

Livia closed her eyes and took a deep breath. As far as she was aware, she was the only person who had this problem. Forking was just a natural part of the System, or so the volunteer seminar she had taken when she was a new upload had said. "Fork your problems away," was the clever title, and the instructor had explained all the benefits of forking, from more hands to do work to fixing any incidental damage one might incur. She had learned at that seminar that forking had unpleasant side-effects for her, and she disliked admitting it. She wasn't even sure why she was telling Tyrean. They were friendly, if not friends exactly, but that was a far cry from admitting her fears about glitching out.

Still, she had offered the information up, and she didn't want to leave the poor lizard hanging. "Whenever I fork," she said, eyes still closed, "my new instance asks one or more deeply uncomfortable question. I don't know why, and no one I've ever talked to about it knows why, either, but as I don't want to answer questions about the darkest recesses of my psyche while feeling like I'm going to lose my lunch, I don't fork unless I have to." The memory of her very first fork, at that original seminar, still made her stomach twist. The nausea had been so bad that her memory of the seminar was focused around the queasiness.

"Oh." Tyrean considered for a moment, then opened his mouth to ask another question.

Liv cut him off. This conversation had already gotten too far into the weeds. "We can talk about it some other day," she told him. "For now, if I'm not running a session, I should prep for my other games this weekend."

"Oh, okay," Tyrean said. He hesitated, offered a wave, then quit.

"What a weird day," Livia muttered. She frowned at the dragon, as though it was its fault, then decided to get lunch.

⋆

Livia appeared in her favorite sim. It was a version of what the maker claimed was Shinjuku about two centuries before she had been born. She had never actually been to Tokyo in her previous existence as a flesh-and-blood being, let alone the mighty metropolis of two hundred odd years ago, so she had no way of knowing how true-to-life the place was. But, accurate or not, it housed the best noodle restaurant she had ever walked into, sys-side or phys-side.

It took a little effort to get to, as all great food does. She had appeared, as always, on a street crowded with NPC pedestrians, clustered into neat little groups engaged in pre-scripted, uninterruptable conversations. One could latch onto a group and follow it as it walked down a narrow, neon-lighted alley, made a sharp left, walked around the block, and returned right back to the beginning, at which point the characters would begin their scripted conversation over again. The purpose was to let one practice their Japanese, though the circling NPCs were the least of the work put into the sim. Along the road and alley were dozens of little stores, restaurants, and tourist attractions, each filled with their own unique encounters, each a dialogue tree that a visitor could explore at their leisure, with the added bonus of the character in question gently correcting any language mistakes one made. The alley was crowded, but with scripted characters moving in a predictable pattern, not real people. The sim was never a popular one—Liv had rarely seen more than one or two other people exploring it—and always had a strangely empty feeling, notwithstanding the hundreds of chattering NPCs taking their infinite walk.

But the sim's creator had also gone out of their way to make sure the various shops and attractions were as detailed as any single-purpose sim in the System. The bookshop on the corner was stocked with the latest Japanese language books and manga, the bakery made real *petits fours*, and the toy museum's exhibits were as detailed as any in the System. But halfway down the alley, under a worn sign that just read うどん, was Liv's goal.

Livia pushed open the frosted glass door and into complete silence. She couldn't even hear the crowd outside.

She stopped dead. The inside of the restaurant was totally empty.

There should have been a dozen NPCs inside, scattered along the low tables or lounging at the dim bar in the back, all chattering out their prescripted conversation. There was supposed to be a maître d' who would suggest a place to sit, and a bartender who had a surprisingly deep conversation tree about a video game series forty years out-of-date.

It looked like everyone had just gotten up and left. There were plates of still-steaming food, beers and half-drunk cocktails scattered around, chairs partially pulled out, many still with jackets draped over the back.

The back of Livia's neck prickled with a sensation akin to fear, something she hadn't felt since uploading. It felt wrong in the restaurant, the same instinctive revulsion one might feel when biting into an apple only to discover it was made of wax.

Nothing was stopping her from stepping back out into the street, except for the irrational fear that it might be just as empty. She could leave the sim, but what if everything was empty? The question flashed through her mind in one horror-filled instant and she found she couldn't force herself to check.

"There are over ten billion people," she muttered to herself, "They didn't all disappear because one room of a sim is glitching."

But she still didn't want to open the door back outside.

She weighed her options. Nothing was popping out of the walls to attack her, so she assumed there was no immediate danger. On the other hand, she couldn't just stand there for the rest of eternity hoping that the NPC patrons would just wander back from the bathroom or something.

"Okay," Liv said, more to break the silence than anything else. She knew her hesitation was because the smart thing to do was the one thing she did not want to do. She gritted her teeth, closed her eyes, and forked.

Livia doubled over immediately, fighting the rising bile in her throat. Next to her, someone tsked impatiently, and she looked up into a duplicate of herself frowning with distaste down at her.

There was something cold and reptilian about this new Livia. It was the eyes, perhaps, narrowed as they were.

"Help me up, Liv," Livia#Core said, holding her hand up to her fork. The cold eyes flicked to the hand but, unsurprisingly, Livia#5737a461 made no move to help her.

"Why should your name attach so readily to something just because you have created it?" her duplicate said, her tone frosty. "Maybe I want to be Julia. Do you believe you own a thing because you have made it, or do you believe that naming a thing conveys ownership?"

Liv stood carefully, swallowing her nausea. "I think I made you in case something happens to me," she muttered, "so I might as well call you #savestate. Look, just, I'm going to snoop and see if I can figure out what's wrong. Stay here and try not to individuate too much."

Julia glowered but didn't respond. Instead, she leaned against the nearest wall, arms folded across her chest. Liv, used to this sort of treatment from her forks, stood and tried to take stock. The empty restaurant held no real doors other than the entrance, she knew from prior experience. There was what appeared to be a door into the bathrooms and another leading into the kitchen, but neither opened—the original creator simply hadn't built anything beyond them.

"It's probably just a glitch in the sim," Liv told Julia, more to cover the silence than to start conversation.

"How do you know it's not a glitch in you?" Julia asked with a malignant smile.

Ignoring herself, Liv pushed open the door and out into the simulated Shinjuku. She closed her eyes against the neon brightness of the street outside, and stepped into a silence that pressed on her ears.

"How long are you going to stand there?"

Liv opened her eyes to find herself standing in a large, round funeral chamber. Dozens of urns lined the wall, most sealed shut. One, however, was unlidded, seated opposite the entrance beneath a massive statue of three people. The central figure was a tall man wearing Roman style robes. He had a strong, aquiline nose, his curly hair held back by a crown of laurels. On his left was another man of equal height, bearded, and wearing the armor of a Roman general, and on his right a woman dressed in robes with a smaller, winged woman standing in the palm of her outstretched hand. Carved into the wall behind them was a bright comet.

"Divus Iulius," came a voice from Liv, "and his ancestors Mars and Venus, who holds the goddess Victory in her hand."

Liv turned and found Julia, or someone who looked just like Julia, seated on an alcove, one arm carelessly tossed over the urn. Unlike the Julia she had left behind in the empty restaurant, this one was dressed as a Roman princess in rich purple robes, and her hair was cut brutally short. It gave her a strangely leonine air.

"I thought I told you to stay behind?" Liv asked. She was used to unruly forks—that was the rule, at least in her experience—but following her to wherever this was wholly defeated the purpose of forking.

"You told Julia to stay behind. It gets confusing, kiddo, so try to keep up. Call me Ops."

That tickled something in the back of Livia's mind. "The goddess? You named yourself after a goddess?"

"You named yourself after the first empress," Ops pointed out. Livia didn't have a response to that.

"What is this place?" she asked instead.

Ops looked around. "The Mausoleum tells us to live, that one nearby, it teaches us that the gods themselves can die," she recited instead of answering. "Martial wrote that. Weird, isn't it, how one's creations can outlive their creator? A man who made his living with dick jokes and we're still reciting his poems nearly two and a half millennia later. What of Us, O Child, shall outlive Us?"

Livia didn't feel like listening to some aspect of herself with delusions of grandeur wax philosophical.

"Who cares?" she said. "Look, how do I get out of here?"

"How can one escape a trap of one's own making?" said Ops, though she pointed towards the open archway. "See you later, kiddo."

Livia gave her fork—was it her fork, though? She didn't remember creating her—a half-hearted wave, and trudged outside.

The outside of the tumulus turned out to be the smallest sim she had ever seen. Behind her, in cold, lifeless marble, was the tomb. Huge fir trees had been planted on its roof, casting long shadows along the mausoleum and the patchy grass that surrounded it. In front of her, a small concrete path scythed through the volcanic dirt and grass for three paces, then ended abruptly in a yawning black void. She edged up to the abyss and glanced down. Liv couldn't see any bottom, just an endless, whispering chasm. A vague memory of a book she had read forever ago pulled at her.

"It used to keep you up at night, didn't it?" came a voice from behind her. " 'My eyes showed me a ragged chasm, partly filled with a gloomy lake of turbid water.' You weren't supposed to read it, that old horror story. Your parents warned you, didn't they? But you couldn't resist. Do you still remember that cover? The great house, all wreathed in red, with the swine-thing overlooking it. But that wasn't the part that scared you. It was the Pit, the great open space and its tremendous chasm, an abyss like a gigantic well. That's what scared you, more than the swine-thing, more than the dark and forgotten gods, more than the terrible green star."

She turned and found herself face-to-face with a man. It took her a moment to see the resemblance. They had the same chin and cheekbones, the same hairline, though his was as short as Ops's had been. Had she still existed Phys-Side, she would have assumed he was a long-lost sibling, the brother she had never had. Here, that concept was next to meaningless. Anyone else would have assumed an individuated fork, or a fork of a fork, but Liv simply didn't fork, and when she did, none of her forks were supposed to stick around long enough to individuate. She was sure of that.

Wasn't she?

"Who are—" she started, but the man—why did she know his name was Nero?—cut her off.

"No." She opened her mouth to speak and he shushed her again. "No. You answer, you don't get to question."

She hadn't the foggiest idea what he meant, but she chose to play along with his game. "Fine," she said. "What's your question?"

He smiled, then shoved her, hard. She stumbled backwards, her arms pinwheeling, and then she was falling into that great abyss, the nightmare that William Hodgson had prepared for her nearly four hundred years before she had been born.

Liv's first, immediate thought was just to leave. She could exit the sim, return home, and forget this horrible day had ever happened. But the same fear gripped her that had made her hesitate in that noodle place. What if? What if there was something more seriously wrong here than she recognized? Nero had been partially right, after all, it wasn't Hodgson's monsters that had filled her with terror at the age of eleven, it was the huge and lonely home, haunted by the ghost of a man who still lived, alone except for a sister who feared he was going mad. Was she, perhaps, going mad? She existed as pure mind in this place, if that broke and fractured, what would be left of her? If the ones and zeroes, floating somewhere in the void about sixty degrees off of the moon, divided and fractioned, how would that manifest itself? An endless fall into a bottomless abyss, perhaps?

She had a more immediate problem, of course, and couldn't waste time dithering about her fears of what lay outside of her immediate surroundings. She spread her arms and legs, trying to create wind drag and slow herself. Though, did such considerations of physics apply to a place like this?

"Wings," she muttered against the wind whistling against her. If she had wings, she could just fly back up, confront the malicious Nero, discover why this was happening to her. She knew others who could manipulate their physical form easily, almost as easily as donning a new coat, but she had never mastered that art. Most people just forked, again and again if necessary, to gain the attributes they desired. That was equally unappetizing to Livia, but seemed, at least in the short term, more attainable. And, bottomless as this pit seemed to be, she assumed that "short term" was about all she had left to her.

Already dreading the result, Liv forked for the second time—or so she assumed—that day. There was a wave of nausea, and then the terrible taste of bile and the remnants of her simulated breakfast escaping the way they had come, and then a strangely cold grip around her right forearm.

Wiping her mouth with the back of her other hand, she looked up and found herself staring into her own features, though as alien as Julia's had been, with eyes as brilliant and lifeless as gold, and a pair of leathery red wings extending from her back.

"Let me guess," Liv said, before her fork could open her mouth, "Drusilla?"

"Yes," Drusilla said, her voice oddly sibilant. Liv thought she saw a forked tongue in her other's mouth. "Here's a thought for you, sis: if the System is a shared dream, why shouldn't some people have nightmares?"

Rising panic fighting with rising nausea precluded Liv from registering Drusilla's question. She snapped, "Just save me!"

Drusilla grabbed Livia's right arm in both of her hands—her own hands, some distant part of Liv's mind said, and it made her shudder in revulsion, though she didn't know why.

"If it's a dream, why should gravity matter?" Drusilla asked as they plummeted together. Liv caught the dim flicker of a torch, much closer than was comfortable, sitting at the bottom of the chasm, at the bottom of the dark abyss, perhaps at the bottom of a cellar beneath a house built at the intersection of reality and the future and loneliness and despair and...

"No!" Livia shouted at her own thoughts. Drusilla just kept smiling. "Save us! Hurry!"

"Save you from what?" Drusilla sneered, but her wings snapped open with a sound like a whip crack. Livia had one split instant of relief, the realization that she wasn't going to hit, wasn't going to die—could she die? Not like that, surely, but then Hodgson's recluse hadn't seemed to be able to die, either, and wasn't that worse?

And the instant passed and physics, real or imagined, reasserted itself. She stopped, yes, but not all at once. Her arm, held tight in Drusilla's hands, came to rest first, and her body kept going. She felt a wrench at her shoulder, a sharp, tearing pain, a loud *pop* and then burning agony radiating up her arm and down her chest and side as her shoulder was dislocated.

Drusilla let her wings carry them in a spiraling glide, let Livia dangle from her torn shoulder. If Drusilla asked her any further questions, they were lost in a haze of pain. She let go when they were about their own height from the dirty ground, and Livia landed hard on her back, though the pain of impact could not compare with her arm. Drusilla glided to a gentle landing a dozen paces away, gave Livia one contemptuous glance, and strode off to sit in a throne of pewter.

Shakily, Livia got to her feet. She was as pleased as she might have been under the circumstances, to find that the chasm ended not in a yawning pit or a swirling tempest nor in time-lost arena— not in the fears plucked from her own mind remembered from childhood—but a simple dirt cave. Five thrones sat below burning torches along the edge of the circular cavern: Drusilla in one of lead,

Ops atop burnished copper, Julia aglow on a silver throne, and Nero on one of tin. The fifth throne, in gold polished enough to make it shine with the light of a sun, sat empty. A river of liquid mercury wound through the five thrones, some unknown current creating lapping waves against the dirt shore.

"What is this place?"

"Oh, kiddo," said Ops, and her voice was sad. "Where did you think all of those bad decisions were going to lead you, if not some place like here?"

Livia struggled to her feet, trying not to move her injured arm too much. Each little shift brought a new wave of pain, and she thought she might pass out from it. Could she pass out? She didn't want to find out.

"What do you want from me?"

In response, Nero stood and produced a massive iron sword, which he tossed at Livia's feet. It clanged like a gong breaking as it bounced along the ground.

"You broke my arm," Liv pointed out. Her breathing was ragged, and pain still radiated out from her shoulder, but she forced herself to stand straight. "Like hell am I going to fight you all."

"Not all of us," said Nero, with a nasty smile.

"Why is it that hole in the dark scares you so much, kiddo?" said Ops. Liv spared her a glance before reaching down to pick up the sword. It was surprisingly heavy, foreign and awkward in her hand.

A heavy footstep drew Liv's attention. A woman, like Liv but six inches taller and wearing the armor of a Roman Centurion, but carrying an anachronistic iron sword identical to the one in Liv's hand, had stepped out from behind the golden throne.

Liv struggled to raise her own sword as the taller version of herself crossed over the mercury river, striding towards her. With a casual twitch of her hand, the other woman knocked Liv's sword to the side.

"It's because in the darkness there's nothing to distract you from yourself," the woman said."

"Augusta," Liv hissed.

"So you remember?" Augusta asked. "Ah, no, you don't. I can see it in the vacant look you're giving me. That's too bad, this won't be nearly as pleasurable if you don't know why it's your fault." Liv's voice, from Augusta's throat, was full of hate and poison, a disgust that Liv didn't know she was capable of.

"How could I forget something?" Livia said, trying again to lift the sword into a guard position. She *knew* this, she knew she did. She could fight against this woman, fight and win and escape and *survive.*

Was there some memory that you have forgotten? a voice whispered in her ear. *What if it's not forgotten, what if the answer is there and you just don't want to face it? How do you know that you don't know?*

What does it mean that you can't answer yourself?

"Why do you hate me?" Livia asked.

Augusta's next casual flick sent Livia's sword pinwheeling through the air and into the darkness. It rang out, tolling the last of Livia's options failing.

"Wrong question," Augusta said.

"I didn't make you," Livia said. "I didn't make most of you. Where did you come from?"

"From me, of course." Augusta's smile was cruel. "Just like you did."

"I'm not a fork," Livia said. "I'm the original." She ducked away as Augusta brought the sword down, clutching her ruined arm tight to her side to prevent it from bouncing painfully. "I uploaded! Me!" Liv found herself shouting. "I built a life for myself here, not you!"

"*I* uploaded," Augusta said. "You are nothing but a pale copy of me, a cast-off bit of unwanted psyche that got loose."

"That's a lie," Livia said. It had to be. Some memory tugged at her brain and she suppressed it, ruthlessly.

"Do you have a better explanation?"

"A great beast haunts the system," said Ops. "A monster born at the intersection of the computer and the dream. And it must feed." She gave Livia a sad smile. "So it spins out doppelgangers, cenobites to break the mind of its chosen target, like hunting dogs harrying a doe to ground before dragging the corpse back to their master."

Liv stared at Ops a moment too long, and Augusta's blade drove into her thigh. She screamed and stumbled backwards into Drusilla's throne. The winged fork kicked her back into the arena.

"Who cares why it's happening," Drusilla said, her voice hungry. "Do you think understanding our hatred of you will be enough to prevent us from destroying you? Does knowing the origin of the nightmare prevent the nightmare from haunting you?"

"You can't kill me," Liv spat back. She limped away from Augusta, who moved at no more than a walk, waiting for Livia's strength to fail.

"True," said Nero. "But we can break you. We can drive you until you decide to quit. We can force your contamination out."

"Wouldn't it be easier," said Julia, "to just quit now? The only reason you are still in pain and terror is because of your stubbornness. Why not just make it all go away?"

"You're not real," Augusta said. "You already don't exist. You and you alone are making this more difficult."

"Says the asshole with the sword," Liv snapped. "Why don't you just leave me alone?"

"You are an affront to me," Augusta said, with so much ice in her words that Livia shivered.

"You think you're affronted now," Liv said. "What do you think about this?"

And she turned and ran into the darkness of the cavern, ignoring the burning pain in her hip, the jagged agony in her shoulder. Her doppelgangers shouted in anger and shock. She could hear them scrambling to their feet to give chase.

The darkness closed in around her, and all she could think of was a ragged chasm and a gloomy, turbid lake. Ghost-images of creatures with the faces of swine and spirits of fungal malice or forgotten deities keeping watch over an empty arena at the end of time swam in her vision, but she forced it aside. Nero had been right, it wasn't the things in the darkness that had frightened her, it had been the darkness itself. In the darkness there was only her and, in the end, she was what she feared most.

She crashed into a stone wall and bounced, losing her sense of direction. Her ragged breath—she didn't have lungs, why should she be panting?—drowned out the sounds of pursuit. She reached out until she scraped her hand against the sharp-edged rock. All will to keep running had been knocked out of her by the crash, but she forced herself to stagger along the wall, keeping her hand pressed against it. The multitude of cuts and scratches from the rock seemed like nothing in the face of her other wounds.

Livia felt cold, and she was uncomfortably aware of the effort each step took her. Was she bleeding out? She didn't have blood, really, so she wasn't sure if she even could bleed out. Maybe she would just bleed forever. Maybe the pain would overtake her and she'd just pass out.

And then what? The others would find her, probably, but that was what she was actively trying to avoid.

She thought back to that stomach-twisting seminar. What had the instructor's name been? She tried to pull up details, and her mind recoiled. She didn't want to remember, like there was a dam in her mind with memories pressing against it. To let out one memory would let out a flood. And she didn't want to remember the truth. She didn't want to face what that first fork had said to her. She didn't want to recall the shocked and upset faces of the other uploads who had listened to Livia shout at herself.

She could—she did—know whether it had been her or Augusta who was the original, or whether they were both forks of some other prior version. That was knowledge she had, easily recalled. Nothing could be forgotten, only repressed, and then only haphazardly at best. But, she thought, it didn't really matter to her. She didn't care who was the fork, who was the ghost in the system, she was herself and that was all that mattered to her.

She shoved the memory aside, unresolved. She didn't need it; she just needed to remember what the instructor had told them about the trivial matter of healing oneself. You just had to fork. You could make any changes you want, all you had to do was fork, and fork again, and again, until you had the version of yourself you wanted. Fork and let the old instance vanish.

The wall abruptly ended and Liv fell hard onto her ruined shoulder. She bit her lip to prevent herself from crying out and alerting the others. She curled into a ball on the cold floor, lost in the dark, and tried to think.

If she forked, she would just create another doppelganger, someone else to hate her and hunt her. Could she even force herself to quit, at that point, knowing that she would be replacing herself with someone, someone who didn't even share her name, who was repulsed at the thought of her. She remembered her skin crawling when Drusilla had caught her arm, and she had to admit to herself that at least some of that was from the hatred she had felt towards her fork.

Towards herself.

"I hate myself," she whispered, and wondered if it was the first true thing she'd said to herself that day. She had carried that hatred with her for years. She had thought she had long ago learned to live with it, but the realization came that, perhaps living with it is not the same as dealing with it.

With a sigh, Livia closed her eyes and forked.

The familiar wave of nausea came, but there was no question, no haunting probe of her feelings or emotions, no philosophical duel. She opened her eyes to the darkness and saw nothing but inky blackness.

"Hello?" she whispered.

"I'm here," she responded. "I... I don't think I like you very much."

"I know. But will you help me anyway?"

There was a long silence that pressed on Livia as much as the darkness did. She heard her counterpart open her mouth and inhale to answer, but decided she did not want to wait for the answer.

She quit.

For a moment, she thought she had made a mistake, that something with her face and her voice had replaced her and she was gone. But after a moment, she realized that the lungs she didn't have were burning from her holding her breath, and she released it, gulping down sweet, cold air as though she had been underwater for hours.

Her leg and arm were whole. She was no longer exhausted.

"Thank you," she whispered to the her that was no longer there. And then she forked again, giving the new version of her a doe's eyes, and the structures that permit deer to see so well in the dark. Dimly, she could see the vague outline of the cavern, enough to guide herself by sight alone. And then she forked again, to gain a pair of hooved legs, like a satyr, for speed and stability. And again, and again. Each fork came with it a little improvement, and a new wave of nausea, and each time the nausea took longer to fade.

When her churning stomach became too much to keep going, Liv stepped back out into the dark maze of stone. Long ears swiveled as she turned her head left and right, bringing to her the distant sound of pursuit and the soft grousing of her pursuers. She smiled softly to herself—it sounded as if they liked each other about as well as they liked her. Swift, sure hooves carried her into the deeper darkness, their soft clicks against the stone reverberating into the darkness.

A shout echoed down the corridor, followed by the flickering red light of a flare. Liv recognized her mistake immediately; she had sacrificed stealth for speed. There was no help for it. She tucked her head down and dashed headlong into the labyrinth.

Livia was unsure how long she ran, but her new legs were unwavering and steady. She wished she could be sure that she was putting distance between herself and her doppelgangers, but the cavern twisted and turned, and she found herself running towards the sound of hunters and the shuddery light of their flares as often as away.

But they were getting separated and disorientated by the maze, as well. A thin advantage, but she clung to it nevertheless. She began to work her way methodically through the cavern, always turning right when the opportunity presented itself, ducking into alcoves and hiding in niches, holding her breath, when she heard the others approaching. She saw each, except for Augusta, several of them passing within a few feet of her, as she sought an exit. They snapped at each other, their voices devoid of even the hint of warmth or affection.

Is that really what I feel about myself? she wondered as she hid under a tumbled stone slab while Nero and Julia stalked down the hallway past her.

"Was that true? What Ops said, about a great beast?" Julia asked.

Livia couldn't see him shrug, but she could hear it in his voice. "Who cares."

"I care. I want to know if I need to keep an eye out for murderous copies of myself."

Nero sighed. "Maybe it's true, maybe it's not. Maybe Augusta's right, and she's just a discarded fork that outlived its usefulness. Or maybe it's a glitch in the System. Every once in a while, maybe the computer just accidentally creates a copy of someone, a fake-instance that runs around with your face and some of your memories but without realizing that they're just a copy. Or maybe it's

Augusta that's the fork, a fork of a fork of a fork that she made and cast off and didn't realize still wandered around."

"Ugh. I don't like any of this. Why didn't you stop her?"

"Me?" Nero's voice was incredulous. "She ran right past you, why didn't you stop her?"

"It's all your plan, not mine. You're lucky I don't just leave and let you all deal with her. I have a life to start, not your whiny, petty revenge."

"You're lucky we don't extend that revenge to all of her forks." Liv heard a distinct smack of flesh-on-flesh as one of them struck the other. "Just watch yourself. You can start wasting your life when she quits."

Livia waited until the sounds of their bickering faded to nothing before she climbed out from under the slab. She gave it a three count, eyes straining to catch the first flickers of a flare, then took off once again.

From there, she found her way back to the cavern in which she had started without running into any more of her doppelgangers, though their footsteps echoed after her. It wasn't the entrance through which she had entered the labyrinth, but the thrones, and the river of mercury, were just as she had left them. There, gleaming dully in the shadows beyond the river, was the sword that Nero had thrown at her. She hesitated for just a moment, ears and eyes casting in every direction for a trap, before she dashed out to snag the weapon.

"What have you done to my body?" Augusta's voice floated out, cold as a snowstorm. Liv straightened to find Augusta seated on the golden throne, the hilt of her sword leaning against the armrest.

"It's *my* body," Liv said. "And I'll do to it whatever I please." She raised the iron sword, struggling to keep her arms steady under its weight.

Augusta rose and took up her sword in one smooth, practiced motion. "You can't hope to fight me, Livia. You're a shadow of me, one that has taken my place for far too long. Nothing but a dark spot who trailing behind me."

Liv set her hooves and pointed the sword at Augusta's chest. "I can beat you, I know it."

Augusta laughed. "*You* can beat me? You're nothing. A fake. A phony. An echo of a real person." As if to demonstrate, she lurched forward and knocked the wavering sword to the side before stabbing Livia, once again, in the leg. It crumbled underneath her and she fell to one knee.

"I wonder what happens if you get beheaded?" Augusta mused to herself. "Maybe that will create an internal error so severe that the System will forcequit you?"

Livia brought the sword back up and Augusta knocked it away again.

"Just quit, Livia," Augusta told her. She kicked Livia onto her back. "Give up. You're not worth the pain I can force on you."

"I am," Livia said. She swung the sword, not like a sword, but like a baseball bat, two handed. It clanged against the metal greave that Augusta wore, forcing the taller woman back a few steps.

"You are the part of me I do not want," Augusta barked. She swung her sword down overhead, trying to chop Livia in half as though she were a log. Liv rolled away, and the sword did nothing more than glance off of her shoulder. She pushed up into a squatting run and limped to the edge of the cavern.

"Enough of this!" Augusta roared. Livia straightened up as best as she could, leg and shoulder burning once again. "No more games, no more Hail Mary dashes into the darkness." Augusta raised her hand, and iron gates slammed down over the entrances to the labyrinth. "You are trapped here, stuck in this place with me until you finally give up. This is unending, forever. There is *only one escape for you.*" The last echoes of the falling gates stifled, giving way to the shouts of their other instances, asking what had happened, yelling at Augusta to let them out, asking her what she thought she was doing.

Livia ignored them, even as they came back within sight, separated from her and Augusta. Her eyes raked the walls, the ceiling, the floor. Augusta was right—there was no way out that she could see, no cavern or crevasse to hide in, no matter how temporary. She was trapped, doomed to choose between an everlasting hell or oblivion. As locked away as surely as the others were, behind Augusta's gates.

Livia blinked. She dropped her sword, letting its weight go. "No."

Augusta stopped short, a wave of rage mixed with confusion washing over her face.

"You're wrong." Livia laughed, short and sour, but genuine. "Oh my god. I was never stuck here." She saw it clearly. "None of us are," she said, her voice ringing loud enough to slice through the cries of the others.

Livia shook her head in disbelief at her own foolishness. She had followed the trail of breadcrumbs left for her, but she had never been forced to do it. At any point—in the empty restaurant, in the tomb, in the endless fall into the dark—she could have just left. "You were right about one thing, I chose to let the pain keep going."

"You won't be free of us. We'll continue to hunt you."

"But you can only hurt me if I let you, in this place." She forked and quit to remove the injuries. The nausea didn't seem that bad this time.

"You honestly think it's that simple? That you can just decide that?"

"No," said Livia, looking down at her hands. They were covered in a soft brown fur she found she rather liked. Had she ever liked her hands before? "I imagine it'll be a struggle every step of the way. But I'd rather struggle than let you win." And before Augusta could say anything more, Livia showed her a velvety, elegant middle finger and stepped from the sim.

⋆

She arrived back in the Shinjuku analogue, amid all of the hustle and bustle.

Before Livia could do anything, a pair of twenty-somethings with technicolor hair and complicated leather outfits straight from a 2150s neo-samurai movie made a bee-line toward her.

"Excuse me," the one on the left started, then blushed red to contrast to her green hair. "I mean, um. すみません。どれはおもちゃ美術館ですか?"

"Oh, excuse me," Liv said, a little taken back.

"You speak English?" the green-haired tourist said. "Sorry, we thought you were one of the NPCs."

"So do I, sometimes," Liv said with a smile.

"I'd never seen a furry NPC here before," said her friend, their hair an improbable checkerboard of silver and gold. Liv wondered how they walked under the weight of all those belt buckles. "We thought you might have an interesting dialogue tree."

"Not that interesting. It's fine. It's up that alleyway on your left." She hesitated for a moment. "Actually, if you don't mind, can I go with you? I've had a really bad day, and I think I'd like some company."

"Are you alright?" asked the green-haired tourist.

"Oh, just a fight with a friend," Liv said with a sad smile. "I guess several friends. It's okay if you'd rather not, I know I'm imposing."

"Oh, it's fine! Right?"

The silver-and-gold haired one nodded. "We're both kind of new and getting used to everything, so we'd love for a guide."

Liv laughed, and, chatting amiably with the two, walked them to the museum.

They spent a pleasant hour exploring, until the two tourists had to leave—"A seminar we wanted to catch," the green-haired one had said—though they promised to meet up later. She waved goodbye and watched as they teleported out of the sim, then crossed the street and entered the noodle restaurant once again.

She was not surprised to see Ops sitting at one of the tables facing the door. Livia waved the maître d' away with a mumbled apology, then sat down across from her clone.

"You seem nice," Livia said, by way of greeting.

"Thank you."

"But you're not, are you?"

Ops just smiled at her. "You know this isn't over, kiddo, right?"

Liv nodded. "Are you here to convince me to quit, too?"

"Actually, we took a vote in the darkness. Augusta wasn't too pleased by our sudden democratic instincts." Ops used a chopstick like a spear to grab the fish cake floating in her ramen. "But we've agreed to a kind of non-aggression treaty, if you will."

The waiter brought Liv a bowl of her own. "I wasn't aggressive towards you in the first place."

"It turns out we can be pretty aggressive toward each other; you're just reaping the benefits. We won't help Augusta, and we won't interfere with each other. That's the deal. You agree?"

"If I say no?"

Ops's smile turned dark.

"In that case, I agree. I take it Augusta's not part of the deal?"

"We forced her into it. You don't want to know the details. I think it's pretty clear we could all use some time to work on ourselves, though." Ops tried to spear a bit of pork, but quickly gave up. "Do you remember?"

"About Augusta?" Liv sighed. "We can't forget in this place, can we?"

Ops shook her head.

Livia gave her own chicken a try. "So, is this goodbye?"

"I'm afraid my Japanese isn't up to snuff, or I'd say something clever about this being 気を付けて instead of さようなら. Instead, how about we call this goodbye for now." She waved a hand sardonically and then teleported away without standing, leaving Livia alone with her thoughts and ramen and the milling NPCs waiting for her to initiate a conversation.

Livia sighed and deftly fished out a few coils of noodles. "For now" would have to do, she supposed.

Earthbound

Kergiby

Jonathan Miller — 2364

Hands ran through the earth.

Calloused hands found the root and pulled.

Nothing.

Again.

Stubborn thing.

Again.

Riiiip!

The thistle came free.

John pulled it to the side and threw it in the pile with the rest. He looked at his flowers, periwinkle, blanket flower, scarlet flax. There was a dead stem, the petals eaten away by some bug or animal. He grunted in frustration and pulled it up by the roots, throwing it in the pile for composting.

This was where he felt at home. Here, where the birds chirped and the wind blew. Here, with the smell of his flowers and the hard-won fruits of his labor. Here, with dirt under his nails and fingers brushing the dirt free. Flecks fell down, leaving his hands mostly clean.

A message pinged for attention.

Liam <3: AVEC soon?

Once upon a time, John would have smiled and felt giddy seeing a message from Liam. Today, he let out a sigh and felt his stomach twist with guilt for that feeling.

John: Be there soon.

He stood up, knees creaking. He grabbed the basket of weeds and brought it over to throw into the compost.

Inside, he went to his vid screen and launched the command to start the call with Liam. The mere existence of the Audio/Visual Extrasystem Communication was the only thing that made this bearable. And even then...

"Hey darlin'," Liam drawled.

"Hey!" John smiled.

Liam looked the same as he did when he uploaded. Preserved in time, in a time before the talk, before the pain, the fight and the lonely nights. But there weren't those creases that pulled his mouth down, that sat by his eyes. He looked better than all the times they spent at various doctors and specialists. Looking for... relief. Not even a cure, just relief. He looked better than all those days curled up in bed waiting for the current flare-up to stop.

"You're looking good," Liam said.

"Bullshit! I'm getting grayer every day. Got called Gramps last week."

"You're still handsome to me."

"I know," Liam smiled. "I'm surprised you haven't changed your appearance by now."

"I've gone back and forth. Sometimes I make myself younger or change eyes and hair. But with you... I want to look how you remember me."

But you don't.

"I know." He paused for a moment. "I'm happy I get to see you as ever."

"How's my girl? How's Cassie?" the video flickered for a moment, distorting Liam's face and making his voice sound... off.

John frowned. "Not good. She's not grooming herself as much as she used to. She's having a harder time jumping too. I'm getting worried about her."

"Oh baby... Please give her some scratches from me."

She wants you back home.

"I will. She still curls up in your chair. I think she's still hoping you'll come back through the door and pick her up like you always did."

Liam sighed. He looked over and there, where there was nothing, a copy of Cassie appeared on the desk right next to Liam. It was Cassie as she was a few years ago, her fur better groomed, her meow a sweeter chirp than Cassie had, like it was from Liam's memory more than how Cassie actually behaved. It struck John as... wrong. It made his skin crawl looking at the facsimile of their cat.

"I know she wants me home. I... I don't regret doing this. But I—"

John shook his head. "You don't need to explain yourself to me, babe. We talked about it so much. I know all your reasons, and we made this decision together."

"I know. I just... it's hard."

Of course it's hard.

John reached out and rested his hand on the screen. He could still remember the touch of Liam's skin on his, the way they held each other that first time, nervous, excited, home. They were themselves home together, as young men, into adulthood, and then... they stopped moving together.

But he could still remember how good he looked in a suit at their wedding. He remembered the way his brow scrunched up when light hit his eyes in the morning. He remembered how peaceful he looked when John held him, even in pain, there was something about their togetherness that seemed to help.

"No more pain though." John forced a smile, getting his memories out of his head for a moment. He had plenty of time for memories.

"No pain." Liam nodded. "I feel tingly sometimes. Like, I felt pain for so long that my body—my mind—still expects and almost wants it again, which is fucked up. But it's better."

"That's all that matters."

There was a long moment of silence, that filled the space between them before.

"I love you," Liam said.

"I love you too."

"How did the deacidification project go? I know you and the group were really hopeful for the latest push would make the WF pay attention."

John shrugged. He grunted in frustration as the memories of their latest efforts came back to him.

"Not great. The Western Federation is still freaking out over Artemis. They don't care about anything we try and say. They're stuck in the same talking points and arguing and finger pointing as ever. Some people are talking about it more but it'll take time."

Time I don't have left.

Liam nodded, but his eyes seemed distracted. He shivered slightly, and John knew from their talks before that Liam just got a sensorium ping. That frustrated John. They were always good at staying present with each other during their dates and time together. But John could tell Liam wasn't here on this topic. Liam didn't seem to care about the effort that the two of them spent decades on anymore. The Earth Preservation Society didn't matter to Liam anymore.

All Liam cared about was the System. And John felt left behind. He couldn't follow there. He wouldn't. It wasn't right for him. They'd spent their whole adult lives together working towards trying to save something in the Earth, anything!

Liam was supposed to try and work through the Artemisians' data to help with finding information they had that could help clear the atmosphere. But once he got into the System, he was so distracted by everything else that their hope for the future seemed brushed aside by Liam's new world.

Liam didn't have a horse in the race anymore.

John tried to be angry, but instead he was just tired.

"So, why don't you tell me about the garden while we work on dinner. I want to hear if you killed my peppers."

Liam didn't even have a response to John's comment. He just moved on. It was an obligation to talk about, not something he actually cared about anymore.

"One time! That only happened once! Don't you try and pull that card on me."

"I was gone for 3 days! It was actually impressive you managed that."

"I made it up to you, didn't I?"

Liam opened his mouth but froze. Artifacts disrupting the image. The link wasn't at stable as it could have been. It was the price that John and Liam paid for living out in the country. But the country still had vestibules of air that was less polluted, where growing any of your own food was even possible. The air was better for Liam too. They worked hard to make a phys side relationship work.

So many doctors, uprooting to the country, physical therapies. But in the end, the choice for a comfortable life became obvious. And painful.

Liam uploaded. And in three years, John and Liam had a relationship that was entirely emotional. He slept alone again, the thing he hated most about his life before Liam. He couldn't squeeze his husband's hand while they both read their own books. Or sneak up behind him and surprise him with a kiss. It was an ache, one he still felt. Video calls with his husband helped, their evenings together were the highlight of all of John's days. He didn't know if Liam had forked in the system, and he didn't want to ask. He didn't want to know if, while his husband was spending time with him, another version of him was out doing... more exciting things. More interesting things. That scared John, a fear he'd voiced once, and wouldn't do again.

"—made it up to me. You know that." Liam finally said, the link connecting again.

John kissed his fingers and placed them to the screen. Some clever bastard had figured out a way for some gestures to be passed along sys side. Liam touched his lips and grinned. He shivered for a moment and looked down. Liam had told him that sometimes when John would touch his screen, his sensoria would act up. Like he could feel a kiss that wasn't there. It wasn't supposed to happen, there was nothing in AVEC that would allow for that kind of sensory input to be felt by the person in the system. Maybe it was all in Liam's head... or the System's idea of his head.

John brought the vid screen to the kitchen. Liam moved through his space until they were standing like mirrors in the same space. Liam had recreated their home together in the sim. He even included the creaky floorboard that John had finally gotten around to fixing. He never told Liam, knowing that his husband worked too hard to make sure the exact timbre of the creak was right in the sim.

John sent the menu he'd had prepared for them to Liam. His eyes lit up when he saw it.

"Butternut squash, Brussels sprouts in white wine, and baked potatoes. Very good choice, my dear."

"I've been known to make them."

"Now and then, yes." Liam grinned.

Their evening continued together, both of them talking, laughing and sharing stories of their days, of old friends, and remembering all they had before everything changed. In some ways, it was like nothing had happened at all. It was like they were still living together, like the last 3 years had passed without pain or frustration. Without John's inner thoughts being uncharitable. He was hurt by the decision, but could live with it, for Liam to be happy.

In other ways, in more painful ways, John felt further apart from Liam than ever. He forgot the word for taskers again, and Liam got frustrated at having to explain things about the System again. It was a battle to fight and to have the conversations about what was what over and over again. John felt pain in his temples and called it a night early, not wanting to start another fight. He took something for his head, and went to sleep.

When he woke early in the morning, John reached out and touched the space beside him. The spaces where Liam should be. He sighed. It hadn't gotten any easier to wake up without his husband beside him. Not dead, just gone.

With the sound of John's movement, there was a shift from the bottom of the bed. The calico padded on the bed over to John. She bumped her head to John's scruffy chin. Her little *mrowl* was raspy, the sleepy girl just as tired as John was.

"Hey princess," John smiled. He reached a hand for her head. She leaned into the scratches, her eyes closing as her soft fur was rubbed in tribute to her regal demeanor. It was fitting for how Liam always treated and talked about Cassie. She was his baby in truth.

"I know I'm not him. And you can't understand that he's not here anymore... Soon it'll just be me." He sat up, putting his back to the headboard. Cassie took advantage of the increased real estate and rubbed her head against his chin. She stood on his chest, nuzzling into him for a moment, until his pets pushed her down to lay on him.

"It's not fair. This isn't fair. Liam... I know why he did it. I know why, Cass, but I still... I still hate him for leaving me like this. I hate that I'll never see him in the morning anymore. I hate that I can't see him. I hate that he uploaded. That he chose the coward's way out. He left us. He left *me*."

Cassie slow blinked at him, a low rumble in her throat. The feel of her fur on his stomach helped him a little.

"I just want him back. I want him here again. This... this isn't what I agreed to. This isn't what I imagined our lives to be like. The System was right for him, but it's wrong for me. It's wrong for us! I... I don't want to be...

"Is that even living, what Liam has? It's not real. It's just an illusion. A delusion..."

Cassie blinked at him again.

"He's gone, isn't he? I... I should let him go."

Cassie blinked and John sighed, sitting up in bed. She moved off of him, jumping onto the ground. As John started to get dressed, Cassie kept moving around him, rubbing against his leg. He smiled and kept petting her, happy that she was still there. John walked past the mantle and stopped. He looked at the urn there, sighing for a long moment as he read the inscription. This was something he kept secret from Liam. This was something for him.

The money he got for Liam's upload was put to good use, keeping John secure and into a trust for environmental reform. Liam made it clear he didn't want his remains kept or spread. He didn't care about his body. He wasn't dead, after all!

But John had it on his mantle under his wedding picture, the inscription etched into his heart as much as the piece of metal.

Liam O'Connell

Born: 2315

Uploaded: 2361

After his morning tea was finished, John went out in the cold morning. It was time to get outside. Get his hands dirty, to be among the grass and the garden that he and Liam worked hard to grow together. This was where he felt at peace. This—Earth—was his home. He wasn't a hippie, he didn't feel like he had a bond with nature, or that everything was perfect, it just made him feel at peace. The noise of the world, of his thoughts, of his pain went away when he was here. Liam left to get rid of his pain, and John worked the garden to keep his pain away.

It was lonely, and things would never be the same without Liam here. But this was his home. His place was phys side, Liam's was sysside. One day, John wouldn't wake up anymore. One day, Liam would be a widow. And he had a plan in place so Liam would be informed of the news when it came. But Liam... would be the widow that John always thought *he* would be. Passing that off to Liam... it felt unjust. It felt cruel, passing something like that onto his husband. But John was a widow himself in many ways. His husband, the man he'd married and spent decades with was gone.

And one day, the System could fail too. Some corruption in the data, power failures, disasters... Liam could be gone too. Nothing was permanent. He knew that every day he woke up to a burnt orange of a sunrise through hazy smog. Or fighting to keep his garden alive enough with soil that seemed to be dying as much as he was.

It wasn't enough for John. It hurt. Losing Liam hurt. But he could hold onto the idea of Liam. He'd said his goodbyes in his mind long ago. What they had now was a pale shadow, a love that no longer felt real. He loved Liam, but not enough to follow him, into that world, apparently. His world, this world, was enough, and John wanted to be here until the end.

Everything had to end at some point.

Cascade Failure

Joel Kreissman

Gregory — 2302

Gregory observed a herd of white-tailed deer from his perch in the upper branches of an ancient oak tree. They did not sense the anthropomorphic gray fox or his notebook, he'd shaped them so they would ignore him. A fly buzzed past one doe's head and she flicked an ear at it reflexively, just as coded. Gregory heard a rustling sound off to the northwest and watched the deer's heads shoot straight up, their ears cocked in the direction of the sound. The wolves were coming, right on schedule.

The herd sprang into action moments before the pack came into view. The wolves loped across the forest floor, dashing after their swift-hooved prey. Maybe the deer would manage to secure a sufficient head start to escape before they tired, or maybe one of the older or weaker members of the herd would fall behind into the wolves' waiting jaws. A week ago the pack had snagged an old buck who'd caught an infection the day before. The wolves had eaten well that night, and their appetites had returned now for another course.

As the animals ran past Gregory noted a fat doe starting to lag behind. She'd feed the pack well if caught. The doe ran after her herd, the wolves began to pace her... and kept on going past.

Gregory sprang lightly from tree to tree, trying to get a better view of the ongoing chase. By the sim's rules his body was nearly weightless and could cling magnetically to any surface, a compromise from the impersonal "god's eye view" most similar ecosystem sims had employed. Dashing out along the underside of a branch he hung upside-down, following the hunters and their quarry with his gaze. Why weren't they going after the doe?

Something about the formation of the pack and the herd seemed oddly familiar. On a whim he pulled up stills he'd taken of the last week's hunt, and groaned. Not only was the herd moving in exactly the same formation, minus the old buck, but so were the wolves. They were ignoring the new data right in front of them in favor of old data picked up a solid week ago.

With a sigh Gregory closed the sim and quit.

Gregory#Tracker looked up from his book when he received his fork's memories. He stepped over to his desk and pulled up the notes for his simulated ecosystems. Somehow he needed to fix the priorities on the wolves' learning so their ability to remember the past didn't overpower their present. While he was tweaking the code he merged another fork, this one had taken an otter form to observe a pod of killer whales, they were still far from the now extinct mammals in terms of intelligence. The shaping of their minds just wasn't good enough at the moment. Would it ever be?

According to the research papers he'd read, whales had nearly the cognitive capabilities of humans. At the time he'd uploaded, humanity still hadn't managed to create a general artificial intelligence without completely emulating a human brain. Why couldn't they have built one by now? He looked over the books lining the walls of his not-so-modest cabin. So many species lost to the still ongoing ecological disaster that was life on Earth now, only remaining through books and videos and paintings and other dead media.

He wondered, were there any museums left on Earth that displayed the bones of those species, or had budget cuts closed them down and sold off the bones as dietary supplements?

He glanced back at the book he'd been reading before the forks merged, when he'd uploaded he'd thought that he might finally have time to read all the books he'd wanted to read. When he first forked he'd attempted to read two books at once, but upon merging back he found that the details of the two books had been jumbled together in his head, the two sets of memories were too similar to one another. Since then Gregory had primarily used forking for various tasks related to his sims, while his root instance read and incorporated the memories of the forks.

Another fork merged back in, more problems. He was trying to recreate the natural world before humans had mucked it all up, but it kept falling short. Why couldn't anyone have tried to upload a whale's brain instead of a human's? Or even a dog's? It was ridiculous.

Gregory sighed, he was getting frustrated with this lack of progress, maybe he should just take a break. See what other people were doing with their immortality. A broadsheet listing what was new in entertainment appeared in his hand.

There was a mind-boggling variety available: movies, novels, games, stage plays, dining, full sensoriums, new media... his curiosity roused he selected that last tab. He had to wonder what qualified as "new media" in this strange world of electronic signals and code. He scrolled through the sub-categories.

The exotic sims tempted him for a moment, but after reading the previews on a couple he moved on to the next category. They were mostly experiments in exotic physics, Escher stairs and inverted planets and the like. He had enough of that in his own work. Next he came to a category titled "deep LARP," and had to look that up.

Apparently people created long-term forks that lived a full life in a sim meant to recreate a fantasy world, rather than just dropping in occasionally to go on adventures like usual roleplays. According to some rumors, people sometimes got so immersed in the LARP that they forgot their lives before the sim. He didn't see the appeal, so he moved on.

The next subcategory was "instance art," apparently artistic forking. It seemed like every individual artist had a different definition of the art. There were plenty of furries, of course, and some who had invented even more exotic forms based on their ideas of what extraterrestrial life might be like. Others played games with their forks, using contests to decide which one of them should quit and leave no memories to be recovered. Then there was this exhibition hosted by one Dear, Also, The Tree That Was Felled. Gregory could not find much information on the content of the exhibition or its host, all he could discern was that the oddly named artist was that they-or rather "it"-was a member of one of the older and more eccentric clades and that it had taken a form resembling a fennec fox.

He looked through a few more options, but his mind kept returning to that strange fennec's exhibition. After another half-hour's consideration, and the return of yet another fork, he resolved to go.

When it came time to head out for the exhibition though, he found himself unsure whether to attend "in person" or to send a fork. He had recalled his forks supervising the various sims but there was a nagging doubt in the back of his mind. Perhaps he should go oversee one of the sims himself and send a fork to the exhibition. It wouldn't be gauche to show up at an instance art event as a fork now would it?

He changed his avatar form to his gray fox morph, then realized that Dear, Also the Tree That Was Felled might have plans for their fork. A human appeared to the fox's left, the two turned to face each other. "Hello," the fox said.

"Hello," replied the human. "Well," he continued. "At least I get to have some fun tonight. See you tomorrow." With that, he vanished.

Gregory stared at the void his fork had left behind for half a minute, and then turned back to his desk and started scanning the various sims for one he wanted to continue tweaking. He eventually decided to restart the forest sim, hoping that this time the patch he'd applied would be enough. The oaks gradually materialized around him and the animals bounded into view.

Just as before, the wolves took down the old buck in the first week. While he waited to see if they'd do anything different in the second hunt he forked and sent them to observe other sims. He checked in on the other animals he'd shaped: rabbits and foxes, woodpeckers and owls, mice and weasels; predators paired with prey. So far all was running as intended.

The day of the second hunt arrived, Gregory took his position in the trees and watched the herd. The wolves appeared and he smiled as they beelined for the fat doe, the leader of the pack nipped at the doe's heels, it looked like the deer was doomed... and then something truly unexpected happened.

Two more wolves popped out of their hiding place in a pile of leaves and pounced on a deer off to the side of the herd and sank their teeth into its throat. The deer threw off the new wolves– no, they were too small and their muzzles too narrow, coyotes! He didn't recall shaping any coyotes yet! They were still extant!

The wounded deer staggered as it choked on its own blood and the coyotes struck again, tearing into its flanks and dragging it to the ground. As soon as the deer died the wolves abandoned their chase for the ready source of meat. The coyotes sprang back, strips of venison dangling from their mouths, but the wolves ignored them. After watching the wolves eat for a few minutes one of the coyotes cautiously stepped forward and quickly grabbed a mouthful of meat then retreated. The wolves continued to ignore it. Seeing that the wolves didn't care, both coyotes came forward and ate their fill.

As annoyed as he was by this intrusion Gregory was genuinely impressed by the shaping on the coyotes. His wolves didn't know what to do with them, but they were able to figure out how to work the wolves' inability to recognize them to their advantage. He had to know who made those coyotes, and why.

Gregory ran around the forest, within the hour he found another species he hadn't coded yet. An opossum climbing a tree, searching for insects. The extinction of the opossum caused one of the worst trophic cascades of North America as ticks bred out of control, but he hadn't coded ticks into this artificial ecosystem yet. Hadn't he?

His eyes widening in dawning horror, he raced back to the deer herd. He found them grazing, ignorant of the shakeup in their ecosystem. As coded they did not react as he brushed their fur with his claws. The first three deer he checked didn't show any sign of parasites, but the fourth had a few black protrusions sticking out of the back of an ear. Carefully he picked one of the nodules off, as he feared there was a set of jointed legs underneath.

Disgusted, he unraveled the tick, the script underlying the construct's physical form spooled out before his eyes. He found it disappointingly simple, even less complex than the code he'd written for the deer. With annoyance he deleted the tick with a flick of his finger.

After deleting all the ticks he could find on the herd he went back to searching for new species. It didn't take long to find a raccoon-it was starting to seem like this mystery automata shaper had a thing for generalist species. He reached out for it, and the raccoon turned its head around and began to hiss in his direction. Surprised, Gregory looked around and behind him, he was still wondering what the raccoon could be reacting to when it bit him.

Screaming in unexpected pain he frantically shook the strange mammal off of him. He managed to fling it into the tree, which it climbed up while he was examining his bleeding hand. It was almost impossible to believe, but there it was, a pair of fangtip holes in either side of his hand, seeping blood. He focused on sealing the wound, and then clearing away the blood. Gradually the blood evaporated, leaving no residue, and the holes were covered over with skin. There was no sign that it had ever happened in the first place but his memory.

He exited the sim.

Gregory found himself back in his cabin and immediately headed for his desk to shut the sim down. He opened the control panel, a large half-transparent display appeared in the air above the desk with tabs for the different sims. He touched the tab for the forest sim, pressed the button to end the sim, and was confronted with a large red warning message. "Sim occupied by 24,471 active instances, are you sure you want to kick?"

He backed out of the close screen and pulled up a census for the sim in question. One entry filled the screen and then another, and a third, fourth, tenth, more and more came in every few seconds as the query did its work. He waited while the screen continued to fill as the count neared the number indicated by the initial warning. Around the time it reached the tens of thousands he received a message from one of his forks.

"Got eaten by a shark," the message read. "It looked like a great white. Somehow it knew I was there. I don't plan on sending a memory dump to you, be glad of that."

Gregory tried to message the fork in question, and received no response, he'd already quit. He checked the census again and found that it now listed 24,475 instances. As he watched the count decreased to 24,474, then 24,473, then it increased to 24,476. Whatever was going on, it was getting out of control! Who were these people? He opened the ID info on one of the instances, which only confused him further.

He sent out a message to all of his forks, meet him in the clearing.

*

Gregory's cabin was in the middle of a small evergreen forest, no simulated animals, just plants and the occasional recording of birdsong. As he stepped through the front door it occurred to him that he hadn't actually been outside his cabin in a few decades. The clearing that had surrounded the cabin was now filled with saplings, some of them already four meters tall and growing a layer of moss. Ivy reached for the cabin walls, but did not climb them; he had had the foresight to ward them against encroaching plant life. He wondered if there was enough space for the forks, and waved his hands to clear a few saplings from the area.

As the meeting time approached they arrived, foxes, jackals, otters, and even a giraffe who'd been surveying a savannah. Every so often the original cleared away another tree to make more room. By the time the meeting arrived there were eight forks in the clearing, Gregory decided to wait to see if more would come before starting. Ten minutes later another gray fox arrived, he continued to wait, a half hour after the appointed time he decided to start.

"Okay," he asked. "How many of you have encountered anomalies in your sims?" Every individual in the clearing raised a hand. "Unexpected species?" one, the giraffe, lowered a hoof. "Animals that can see you?" no change this time. "Alright, have any of you forked since your initial iteration?"

One of the otters spoke up, "my down-tree instance forked me off when a shark grabbed him. I haven't seen him since it ate him, did he quit?"

The original Gregory nodded, "no memory dump, just a message. Glad you got away." He swiveled his head from side to side, taking in a panorama of the freshly renewed clearing. "However, the census I took indicated that there should be another hundred thousand or so of you here."

Surprised chatter broke out among the assembled instances. Gregory rapped a hand on the cabin door to get their attention before continuing. "After I got bitten by a raccoon in my forest sim I exited and ran a census. The forest had a constantly fluctuating population of some twenty-four thousand and change brain emulations. When I checked the ID numbers I found that every one of them was using our ID, with fork appendices of course."

Nine jaws hung open in shock. "I ran censuses of the other sims and found that each one of them contained between two and thirty thousand forks. All with my ID," Gregory sighed. "Yet, I resumed the old God's Eye view of the sims and couldn't find a single one of them. It's perplexing."

"Oh please," Gregory swung his head towards the corner of his cabin. His human self walked out around the corner, holding an unlit cigarette and a zippo. The human stuck the cigarette in his mouth. "Don't tell me you have no idea yet."

Gregory wracked his brains for where this fork could come from. "You're the fork who went to the gallery exhibition. I didn't even realize your memories hadn't come back."

The human lit his cigarette and took a drag. He held it between two fingers and exhaled a cloud of smoke before answering. "You really should have sent your own workaholic ass there, maybe you'd understand then."

"You're the one who made all the new forks?" Gregory pressed further. The human nodded. "And the invasive species?"

"Indeed I did," the human fork confirmed, tapping ash and glowing embers from the tip of his cigarette. "Would you like to know how?"

Gregory thought for a minute, he couldn't believe that a mere fork of himself could learn how to shape smarter constructs than him in mere days. A possibility came to him, but one of the jackals among his other forks spoke up first. "You learned how to shape better automata from someone you met at the exhibition?"

"In a way," the human confirmed. "In that we are all man-made intelligences. Dear, Also, The Tree That Was Felled is a genius, but it doesn't really consider practical purposes to its techniques."

"Wait," the original Gregory interjected. "I thought Dear, Also, The Tree That Was Felled was an instance artist."

The human grinned as he took another drag. "Indeed it is."

One by one, the other Gregorys' eyes widened in realization. "You...the animals, they're forks?!"

"Yes!" he confirmed. "Every one of the invasive species outsmarting your constructs are forks. Everything more neurologically complex than an arthropod has a pruned version of my mind. Language faculties are limited, which might explain why they haven't responded to your summons, but they still have a competitive advantage over anything you coded."

"Why?" the original Gregory inquired. "Why do something so insane?"

"Please," the human fork tossed aside the stub of his cigarette. "You've been putting everything of yourself into these sims ever since you uploaded. I just made it a bit more literal." With that last cryptic comment, he quit.

Gregory waited for the memories to flood in and explain what had just happened, but none came. As he waited in vain his gaze wandered to a thin column of smoke rising from the ground. The fork's cigarette butt had landed in a pile of dry pine needles, which were already beginning to smolder. Just before he could raise a hand to snuff it out he felt a new set of memories pushing at his consciousness, he began to integrate them only to find that no, it wasn't the troublemaking fork, but the otter whose down-tree instance had been eaten by a shark. His thoughts came flooding in, the realization that the shark was another instance of himself. How could he become such a monster, how could he lose himself so completely in his work?

More memories came flooding in, the remaining forks were quitting, he turned to look as they vanished into thin air. Canids, aquatic species, the giraffe, they each simply blinked out of existence one-by-one. Some sent their memories to him, others refrained. He held the deluge of memory at bay, swerving back around to the exterior of the cabin. The fire was growing, before long it would be lapping at the sides of his cabin. He waved a hand and the flames began to shrink, leaving blackened earth behind. But he stopped short of extinguishing the fire altogether. *What was the point?* he thought.

If the fire burned down his cabin and the forest it was in, he could just make another, identical to the one that had existed before he decided to make that fork. It was just a sim, a construct, no different from the other sims he'd made or the false animals that populated them. Or had populated them. No doubt the fork's forks were now tearing his fragile artificial ecosystems to shreds.

And why shouldn't they? They had created them after all, they were theirs to destroy if they wished. Why had he started this project anyways? Wasn't it to recreate nature, red in tooth and claw? In that respect, the fork had succeeded.

While Gregory thought, the fire had spread to the treeline and was beginning to climb up the trunks. He turned away from the fire and exited the sim, headed for one of the taverns he'd looked up earlier. He could always recreate the sim later, after a few drinks maybe.

Glossary

ACL

Originally short for "Access Control List", ACLs describe fine-grained permissions to access or use sims or the like. For instance, ACLs can be set such that only certain people may enter a sim, or to ensure that a cone of silence blocks sensorium messages

Apygmaliophobia

The fear of uploading (literally, the fear of becoming an artificial copy of yourself). Coined in the late 2130s as the cost of uploading began to drop. Also occasionally used in relation to taskers who fear individuation.

Artemis

An extrasolar probe bearing four races of uploaded consciousnesses. Discovered in 2346 by Tycho Brahe

AVEC

Introduced in 2350, Audio/Visual Extrasystem Communication is the means by which those on the System may communicate with

Earth via audio and visual transmission, rather than just text, something which was gently discouraged over the previous years to maintain a sense of mystique around sys-side. While Castor and Pollux also have this ability in theory, the bandwidth limitations of the Deep Space Network made it such that only still images can be sent.

Clade

A collection of individuals all descended from the same uploaded consciousness through the process of forking. Clades are named after the root instance (e.g: the Bălan clade), but they can also choose their own name (e.g: the Ode clade).

Cocladist

Used to refer to another member of the same clade. Up-, down-, and cross-tree are used to refer to the relation between the two cocladists: an up-tree instances is one that is descended from the individual, a down-tree instance is one from whom the individual is descended, and a cross-tree instance is one who shares the same down-tree instance but who isn't a descendent or an ancestor.

Cone of silence

A mechanic on the System that prevents others from hearing what those within the cone are saying. As of 2349, it is also possible to opaque or blur the contents of the cone from the outside, and to prevent the transmission of sensorium messages.

Conflict

During the process of merging, memories and ideas between the up- and down-tree instances will differ, if only by physical point of view. The more these instances diverge, the more these differences will cause conflicts, whether in how they remember things or how they think about things. During merging, this takes effort to rectify internally.

Collective

A group of individuals who emulate the idea of clades phys-side, doing their best to maintain a tree-like hierarchy, share common names, and so on. Many also resent the System and refuse to upload.

Dispersionista

An individual who enjoys individuation on the System. They will fork and allow their forks to diverge from themselves without any goal of letting them merge back down.

Dissolution strategy

A set of general categories for how one approaches forking, merging, and individuation.

Forking

The process of creating a complete copy of oneself. The new instance is exactly the same as the individual up to the point of forking, when they immediately begin to diverge, even if only in their physical points of view.

Individuation

The slow process of an up-tree instance changing from a down-tree instance. The longer the two spend apart and the greater the differences in their experiences, the greater the individuation. Dispersionistas in particular encourage individuation, while taskers do their best to avoid it at all costs.

Instance

A consciousness within the System, whether the original uploaded mind or one of their forks.

Launch Vehicle

The two smaller copies of the original L5 point System launched in 2325 in opposite directions at a high enough velocity to leave the Solar System. Often abbreviated to LVs.

Merging

The process of incorporating the memories (and thus personality changes formed by new memories) of an up-tree instance after they quit.

Perisystem architecture

The infrastructure of data and tools for working within the System that serve as the foundation of life. The perisystem architecture contains the reputation market and clade listing, allows one to store information, retrieve data from libraries, control forking and ACLs, and much more.

Phys-side/sys-side

Phys-side (rhymes with 'fissile') refers to the physical world outside of the System, while sys-side refers to everything on the System.

Quitting

The act of an instance ceasing to exist on the System. If the instance is a fork of an individual, the down-tree instance may merge back in the memories from the instance who quits (this set of memories can be given a priority, felt as an amount of adrenaline; at a high priority, this can be quite startling, while at a priority of zero, the down-tree instance won't even be notified of the quitting). If there is no down-tree instance — as in the case of the root instance or an orphaned branch of a clade — quitting is quite difficult, described as trying to wade through mud or push through a barrier.

Reputation/reputation market/the exchange

In order to regulate resource usage on the hardware of the System, certain things cost reputation (denoted Ŕ), such as forking, as well as acquiring sim designs, clothing, and so on. These latter are exchanged on the reputation market (sometimes called the exchange). Reputation can be gained by creating things to put on the market or simply just interacting on the System: having conversations, making friends, and so on. When one first uploads, one is provided with a chunk of reputation to get started with.

Root instance

The root instance is the original uploaded consciousness, the progenitor of the clade from which all other instances are forked.

Signifier

The full name of an instance, including the first eight hexadecimal digits of the unique tag that identifies it as distinct from other individuals in the clade (our out of it) with the same name (e.g: Ioan Bălan#5f39bccd7). This full signifier of an instance, along with all the clade information is available to anyone to check via the perisystem architecture, which makes truly impersonating someone else impossible.

Sim

Refers to locations owned by an individual or set of individuals, whether it's as small as a single room or as large as a city. Hold-over language from the virtual reality aspects of the 'net, where rooms or worlds were called 'sims'.

System

Used to describe both the hardware to which consciousnesses are uploaded as well as the world that exists inside that hardware. Originally chosen as a vague name to prevent leaks while the project was still secret, it stuck through the centuries until a few years after the launch project, when each of the three Systems began to be called by specific names: Castor and Pollux for the launch vehicles and Lagrange for the System remaining near Earth.

Tasker

An individual who specifically does not enjoy individuation. They will rarely fork, only doing so if they absolutely must, and then usually only to accomplish a task that requires more hands.

Tracker

Between taskers and dispersionistas, trackers fork more often and are more willing to let individuation take place as their forks track specific projects or relationships, almost always merging back down.

About the Authors

Rob MacWolf (Tasker)

Rob MacWolf was intitally forked in order to write for and co-host the Voice of Dog podcast, but his root instance seems to have gone inactive. You can find his writing, among other places, in antholgies from the Furry Historical Fiction Society.

thevoice.dog

Nathan "Domus Vocis" Hopp (Tracker)

Nathan 'Domus Vocis' Hopp is a storyteller and root instance of the Narration Clade. He used to exclusively write young adult fiction but has since begun to fully explore furry fiction after first Uploading. His favorite genres to explore, especially when splicing in anthropomorphism, include erotic romance, science fiction, supernatural fantasy, and sometimes dystopian fiction with settings more nightmarish than real-life should ever be. His debut novel is "The Adventures of Peter Gray", a historic coming-of-age fantasy that is his pride and joy, but he's been featured in multiple anthologies across different furry-themed genres such as "Furries Hate Nazis" and "Paw-ly Love". Domus Vocis has an addicting love for literature, so when he's not exploring Athenaeum#f6f6ff01 or having fun with many friends and a couple of cocladists, he can be found residing in his private sim, trying to write the next Great Western Federation Novel.

Madison Scott-Clary (Dispersionista)

Madison Scott-Clary is a transgender writer, editor, and perisystem engineer. She focuses on furry fiction and non-fiction, using that as a framework for interrogating the concept of self and exploring across genres. A graduate of the Regional Anthropomorphic Writers Workshop in 2321, hosted by Kyell Gold and Dayna Smith, she is studying creative writing at Cornell College. She lives in a polycule complex sim with her two dogs, as well as her husband, who is also a dog.

makyo.ink

Michael Miele (Tracker)

Michael Miele is a human fork of a dragon named Nenekiri Bookwyrm. You may recognize his uptree instance's work from contributions to the Voice of Dog podcast, Roar Vol. 11, and Happy Howlidays. He's trying out writing with more human characters and felt like forking off a copy of himself to pursue that was a perfect encapsulation of the kind of experimentation that is prevalent in the System. From the thinly pressed and infititely complex inner workings of a sophisticated computer in space, he'd like to say, "Curl up with a good book and be kind to yourself."

nenekiri.com

Alexandria Christina Leal (Nominally a Tracker)

Alexandria Christina Leal, also known as Ellen, continues to do sys-side what she loved to do phys-side: engineer, write, and spend copious amounts of time either with her loved ones or on exceedingly long walks.

She has found forking to be both liberating and challenging in pursuing her passions, and figures it is only a matter of time before she becomes a Dispersionista. She maintains several long running forks that sync up frequently, such as Unity#Lily (engineering), Unity#SC (Forging), and Unity#Jade (creative endeavours) among others.

In furry circles, she is known as Kimmy, and frequently makes use of forking to switch between a myriad[myriad, nice!] of species, with her primary forms being Kitsune and Snow Leopard. She has also been known to appear as a wolf, a skunk, a catbat[oh my!], and more! She blames Madison Scott-Clary for the second item in that list.

www.kitsune.gay

Thomas "Faux" Steele (Dispersionista)

Thomas "Faux" Steele is a lawspeaker and root instance of the Immortalem Clade. He writes primarily furry fiction, with a particular fondness for exploring dynamic relationships between characters in a variety of genres from science fiction to slasher horror. His work has been printed in many anthologies, including FANG Vol. 7, When the World Was Young, and Happy Howlidays. With a fondness for skeuomorphic relics from the North-East African Coalition (NEAC), he and his forks traverse the System in pursuit of the rare few items which cost enough Ŕ to worry about. He presides over the private sim Höfn#2ca117d28 with his partner, Auggie, and numerous co-cladists.

furaffinity.net/user/fauxhammer

Evan Drake (Tasker)

Evan Drake has a deep love of writing fiction, mostly involving mysterious fantasy worlds and dragons, that explores and challenges our concept of reality. Whether he is a fork or the root instance remains a mystery.

patreon.com/evandrake

J.S. Hawthorne (Tasker)

Never being particularly good at having a conversation with herself, J.S. Hawthorne prefers to create a pseudo-clade of friends and found family. When not involved in torturing fictional characters for her own amusement, J.S. enjoys old-school tabletop roleplaying—no autonomous dragons necessary. She spends most of her life in a sim she's created, surrounded by retro video games and an unhealthily large collection of roleplaying supplements.

Kergiby (Tasker)

Kergiby is a furry writer whose works touch on themes of relationships, grief, and exploring identity. His work in the system has included an obsessive task of recreating his favorite costumes and props. While he could do it easier than he did phys-side, he finds it more satisfying to do it himself—or making a fork help him out!

kergiby.sofurry.com

Joel Kreissman (Dispersionista)

Joel Kreissman is an underemployed biologist from Wisconsin who mostly uses their degree to introduce some scientific accuracy to their science-fiction writing. They're a bit split between multiple sci-fi and fantasy serials and an urban fantasy comic.

www.ingramcontent.com/pod-product-compliance
Lightning Source LLC
Chambersburg PA
CBHW060909210726

48293CB00006B/2030